Joss Stirling

OXFORD

UNIVERSITY PRESS

OXFORD
UNIVERSITY PRESS

Great Clarendon Street, Oxford OX2 6DP

Oxford University Press is a department of the University of Oxford.
It furthers the University's objective of excellence in research,scholarship,
and education by publishing worldwide. Oxford is a registered trade mark of
Oxford University Press in the UK and in certain other countries

British Library Cataloguing in Publication Data

Data available

ISBN: 978-0-19-273739-7

1 3 5 7 9 10 8 6 4 2

Printed in Great Britain

Paper used in the production of this book is a natural,
recyclable product made from wood grown in sustainable forests.
The manufacturing process conforms to the environmental
regulations of the country of origin.

For Samantha Golding

Chapter 1

Kate Pearl stood on the green wheelie-bin in the alley that ran along the back of her mother's house and watched her half-sister play in the sandpit. Sitting in a pool of summer sunshine, the little girl's platinum blonde hair glowed white hot—Kate's own colouring, though hers was hidden under a baseball cap. Frustratingly, Kate couldn't see if the child shared her hazel eyes. She didn't need a mirror to notice the differences between them: the toddler had the plump, pink complexion of a happy three-year-old, nothing like the skinny, tanned older sister. The little girl was having great fun burying her doll in the sand and conducting some kind of funeral with a boy doll officiating in a Hawaiian shirt. Despite her grim situation, Kate had to smile. It looked like her sister was quite a character already.

'Sally?'

Kate moved further into the shadow of the bitter-smelling evergreen hedge that grew on the boundary. Cut back too radically some time ago, it wore a brown scar of the exposed inner branches, never regrown. Kate hadn't seen her mother for four years so her sister had not seemed real until now. What on earth was she doing coming here, Kate asked herself, invading their nice ordinary lives?

Still, there's Sally. I have a sister called Sally. Touching a hand to her heart, she held the thought like a fragile pressed flower.

'Mummy, Barbie is dead.' The little girl patted the top of

1

the grave with a plastic spade.

'How lovely, darling.' Their mother, Maya, clearly wasn't listening. A slim, dark-blonde woman in her early thirties, she had the toned muscles of a regular yoga practitioner, as hinted at by her exercise mat spread out on the lawn. 'I brought you some biscuits and milk, then it's time for your nap.' She scooped the toddler out of the sandbox and brushed her down. 'My goodness, look at you! You *are* in a state!'

Sally was still staring at the sandpit. 'She's dead—like your other little girl.'

Kate almost fell off the top of the bin to hear herself mentioned. Her mother had told her sister that she had died?

The toddler patted Maya's cheek. 'So now I'm sad like you.'

Maya swallowed, then buried her head in the crook of her baby's neck. She cleared her throat. 'I can see you are sad, sweetness. Let's find Barbie and everything will be all right. Where is she?'

'Ken buried her.' The little girl pointed at the boy doll lying on his back staring wide-eyed at the sky.

Maya put Sally down on the grass and rooted around in the pit. She pulled out Barbie, who was dressed for her funeral in a glittery blue ball gown. With a jolt of recognition, Kate realized it was the same dress she had treasured for her doll when she was Sally's age. Her mother must have kept it. Kate had a vivid recollection of the pink plastic toy box—something she hadn't thought about for years. She had covered it in sparkling fairy stickers: was that somewhere in Maya's house too? Kate hadn't thought Maya cared enough to give houseroom to something of hers, seeing how their last meeting had ended so badly.

'See, Barbie's fine,' said Maya, her voice quavering. 'Just shake her off and she's as good as new.'

Holding Barbie upside down, death forgotten, Sally ran up

the garden to the table in the tiny conservatory on the back of the pebble-dashed house. She dropped Barbie, picked up a two-handled cup, and grabbed a biscuit. Sally then disappeared inside, some other idea for play having taken root in her quick mind. Maya stayed where she was, hands on hips, head bowed.

Kate's throat went dry. Could she risk speaking? Her mum had remarried four years ago on a beach in the Caribbean, no family invited—that had been the catalyst of their final horrible row. Both had said stupid, *stupid* things to each other like a pair of screaming gulls scraping over the same bit of bread. Maya may not like the existence of her older child but even she had to admit she had given Kate the dubious gift of her temper. And, of course, Kate hadn't been able to resist rubbing salt into the wound by looking up the pictures on Facebook: the sun-kissed couple in white swimsuits and flower garlands, the new husband a handsome computer programmer who worked for the university, dark hair, white even teeth shown by his proud smile. Kate had hated him on principle.

She sighed. Recent events had made her wiser, that row so trivial. Maya's new life had no place for the awkward fact of a teenage daughter, Kate understood that now. Maya had had Kate when she was still at school and it had taken her years to get back on track after that early setback. And now the couple had a sweet little girl—a reward for finally doing everything right.

Had she ever been as cute as Sally? Kate felt so tired of herself, she couldn't imagine anything nice, even in her early years. Her mum hadn't wanted to keep her so she guessed not.

Kate picked a leaf out of her hair and let it fall, still debating whether or not to make herself known to her mother. Kate hadn't lived with Maya since she was five—that was when her grandparents on her father's side took over so the young mother could go back to college. Mother and daughter had kept in touch, Kate coming to stay for holidays with a young woman who increasingly felt more like an older sister or cousin, but then Kate had had to ask for more and Maya had dropped her bombshell about getting married and moving on in her life. Kate still remembered the gutting pain of knowing she was unwanted. So, after that, Kate had protected her heart and stopped hoping Maya would play a bigger role in her upbringing; Gran had done a grand job of filling in for the absent mother. Even so, it came as a shock to hear that Maya had decided to say Kate was dead.

There were days when Kate felt she might as well be.

She looked over her shoulder at the quiet alleyway. She was being hunted. The last thing she wanted was to bring trouble on her family but she couldn't go without saying something, not after having taken the risk and come all this way. 'I'm sorry' probably about covered it.

'Mum?' Her voice came out rough, barely above a whisper.

Maya lifted her head, disturbed but not certain she had heard a voice. Her cheeks were wet.

'I'm . . .'

A crash from the house, followed by a wail, cut off Kate's words.

'Sally?' Maya spun round and ran towards the house. 'Sally? Are you OK?'

From the loud sobs coming from inside Kate guessed Sally was fine. Silence was always more ominous. Kate closed her eyes and squeezed the frond of evergreen, releasing more of the tart resin smell. Sally had saved her from making a bad mistake. It hurt that her mother treated her as dead but that was safest for the little family. What Maya didn't know about her older daughter couldn't hurt her. Better to remain a ghost.

Kate jumped off the bin, picked up the rucksack that lay

propped against the fence and shouldered everything she had in the world. Family didn't fit inside that.

Chapter 2

Nathan Hunter entered the briefing room on the top floor of the Young Detective Agency to find he was the last to arrive.

'Hey, guys. Am I late?' He checked his watch. Four o'clock. 'If so, please accept my humble and most abject apologies.' He made a bow worthy of a musketeer.

'You're right on time,' said the agency's founder and leader, Isaac, or Colonel Hampton as those outside the YDA knew him. He gestured to Nathan to take the last free chair as he set up the computer projection. Isaac's personal assistant, Tamsin MacDonald, was helping him sort out a problem with one of the leads. They made an interesting pair: Isaac, cropped fair hair, blue eyes, coiled strength of an ex-serviceman, dressed in dangerous black, being fussed over by Mrs MacDonald in her sensible shoes, beige business suit and flowered blouse. She had been with Isaac since the founding of the agency and was the only one who could get away with treating him like her son. Popular with the students, she always had an open tin of biscuits for them while they waited to see her boss.

Circling the table, Nathan bumped knuckles with his best mate, Damien.

'Glad you could finally make it,' Damien drawled, grey-blue eyes cynical, arms and legs sprawled in his usual confident slouch. Give him a heads-up that danger approached and he'd change to alert in a split second. 'Where were you, you slacker?'

'Gym. Not slacking; physical training: you should try it some time.' Nathan had been practising some agility skills taught him by a circus performer who had been brought in to train and entertain the students last year. 'Hi, Raven.' Nathan carried on round the table to kiss the newest recruit to the YDA. A gorgeous American girl with spiralling black hair, she still bubbled with enthusiasm for her new life in the agency, not having been there long enough to take things as routinely as the three boys did. Her partner, Kieran, was totally devoted to her; quite a turn-around for a guy who had, in the era known as BR (Before Raven), lived only for obscure knowledge and logical puzzles.

'How's your day so far?' asked Raven.

'Good. You?'

'Great.' Raven nudged Kieran who was head down over their briefing papers, lost in his own thoughts. 'Action stations, Ace.'

'Hmm?' Kieran lifted his intense green eyes to his girl-friend. She nodded at Nathan. 'Did I forget again?'

'Uh-huh. You can't only think hello and move on, you have to go ahead and say it.' Raven had taken Kieran in hand and was trying to steer him into being more sociable. Nathan enjoyed watching the tussle.

'Hello, Nathan.' Kieran's eyes travelled over his friend, not missing anything. 'How was the BLT you had for lunch?'

Nathan was used to his friend's deductive powers. 'Too much mayonnaise.' He suspected he had a minuscule smear somewhere on his clothing that Kieran had spotted.

'I see you trained on the parallel bars in the gym, swam in the pool, then chatted to Miranda Yang afterwards—that was why you were on time rather than early as is usually your choice.'

Raven groaned. 'You are supposed to ask the guy what he's been doing rather than tell him, sweet-cheeks.'

7

Kieran made one of his puzzled I-really-want-to-please-Raven expressions. 'Oh yes.' He searched the list of acceptable remarks Raven had suggested in previous socialization sessions. 'So, how is Miranda?'

Nathan chuckled. 'Good, thanks. And you knew I talked to her because . . . ?'

'Perfume. She wears DKNY Red. Coming straight out of the girls' changing rooms, her newly applied perfume was still strong enough to transfer to you.' Kieran's eyes were twinkling with some knowledge he was too discreet to share.

Nathan sniffed his T-shirt. It was true, he had a slight scent on his chest from where he and Miranda had, er, *chatted* in the corridor. They had gone out with each other briefly and now had a jokey/flirty thing between them, neither taking it seriously—a stolen kiss or two. In truth, he had several jokey/flirty things going with female students—something that they seemed to expect as he cultivated what Raven teasingly called his loveable rogue image. But, hey, he liked to be liked—and no one got hurt—so he saw nothing wrong in that. (That was the point in his self-justification when Raven usually batted him around the head for his attitude.) 'Not cool. I'll have to change.' Nathan sat down next to Damien, facing Raven. He winked. 'But he's making progress. Well done, Saint Raven, miracle worker.'

'Baby steps,' she said with a huge smile at Kieran. Everyone knew she really liked Kieran's awkward ways: after all, they had fallen for each other on a mission at Raven's school when Kieran was even more social inept than he was now.

'Thanks, Tamsin: that's working now.' Isaac passed the PA the old lead to throw away. 'I don't know what I'd do without you.'

'Perish miserably from running out of biscuits,' suggested Mrs MacDonald.

8

Isaac's smile acknowledged the truth of that. 'Can you tell Jan to come in?'

Mrs MacDonald nodded and headed to the door.

'OK, team, time to start.' Isaac clicked on the first slide. 'Kate Pearl.'

Routine went out of the window. Nathan looked up at the screen, his good mood draining away. There was Kate's familiar face as she had appeared on her last YDA identity card: blonde, beautiful, his once perfect girl.

'Nothing but trouble,' muttered Mrs MacDonald. She shook her head reprovingly and exited the room.

Damien swore under his breath. He knew everything. 'You OK, Nat?'

'Fine.' Nathan swallowed. He wasn't fine; he was gutted.

'The boys will remember her, but for Raven's benefit I'll just run over the background,' continued Isaac. 'Kate was one of our top students, placed in C stream, or Cats, for her ability to blend in and move freely among all kinds of people. Highly rated both by myself and Mrs Hardy, we picked her for a difficult mission to Indonesia, to accompany fellow student Agustina Meosido and penetrate a new human trafficking ring in Jakarta run by a nascent gang called the Scorpions. The mission was supposed to be a joint operation with the Indonesian intelligence service. It was a daring idea—considering the age of those concerned—but Agustina was over eighteen and Kate seemed mature enough for the task, so we took the risk.'

The next slide came up. Agustina, the shy little Indonesian student who had been Kate's best friend at YDA. The vibrant butterfly Kate and the mouse-like Tina—they had both been very good at infiltrating in their different ways: one because she was so confident none thought to question her right to be somewhere, the other because no one noticed her.

Unfortunately Tina had been far better at infiltrating than anyone had realized.

'That mission went badly wrong as it turned out Agustina had been sent by the Scorpions to destroy the credibility of the YDA. Kate walked into a trap masterminded by Agustina's older brother, Gani Meosido. Not that any of us knew he was Tina's brother until too late.'

Isaac put up a slide of a good-looking Indonesian guy of about twenty: black hair, square jaw, charming smile, total snake. Nathan stabbed his pad with his pencil, breaking the point.

'He persuaded Kate that he was in love with her and needed saving from the traffickers. Kate fell for him big time. He presented himself as a minor operative who had seen the error of his ways, when in truth he was close to the leaders. We've since learned that his cousins run the Scorpions: Alfin and Yandi Gatra.' Isaac put up two more pictures of men in their late twenties: one an overweight guy with small eyes and a chunky gold necklace; the other more like Meosido, good-looking and sophisticated, slicked-back hair and a disarmingly pleasant smile.

'Kate went against mission protocol and tried to smuggle Meosido out of the reach of the gang through the confidential chain of agents we'd planted in the Scorpions' network. These were brave people willing to save the young women and children that the gang were trafficking into the Middle East and the West. Of course, once she did that, Meosido told his cousins and they took out all of our agents. One woman was murdered; two people were hospitalized; the rest fled when they saw what was happening. A carefully constructed operation was thus dismantled in a couple of days. The YDA itself almost got shut down as the catastrophe raised questions over our suitability to do such difficult work. We were allowed to stay open by the skin of our teeth but as you'll all know rules have changed. No relationships with outsiders while on missions.'

Raven and Kieran exchanged a wry look. They had broken the rules and barely been forgiven by Isaac, but no one was stupid enough to remind him while the Pearl fiasco was the subject of the briefing.

'Then we failed Kate badly. I had sent a team to extract her, but we didn't move quickly enough. Kate disappeared. At first we thought the worst had happened and she had been killed, but then Agustina emailed us, telling us that Kate had been dev-astated by what she had done but escaped—at least she had the decency to let us know Kate was alive. As one of our best Cats, Kate proved impossible to trace. I had to call off the search when months passed and the trail had gone cold.' Isaac returned to the photo of Kate. 'She has weighed on my conscience ever since. She was dropped into the middle of a scorpions' nest and got badly stung, with no backup to help her as her partner was a fraud. I've been looking for any sign of her since but nothing's come up on the radar—at least, not until today.'

The door opened and Jan Hardy, mentor for C stream, entered. A small woman, formerly a Metropolitan Police com-mander, with iron-grey hair and a steely air of determination, she nodded to the company and took her seat next to Isaac. Isaac paused to let her settle. Nathan turned his gaze from the screen to look out of the window at the view of the Thames and St Paul's cathedral on the opposite bank. Rain splattered on the window, blurring the buildings. The weather matched his mood. Everyone in the YDA had liked unconventional Kate and her disaster had hit them hard.

'That is the past.' Isaac moved on to the next slide. 'There are more details in your briefing papers. Jan, perhaps you would like to explain what happened next in Jakarta?'

Mrs Hardy picked up the laser pointer. The screen showed a room with a bed, overturned chairs and two people sprawled on the floor. 'The body nearest the camera is Gani Meosido. I'm sorry to say the one on the far side is Agustina. Both were found shot in the head eight months ago. Kate's DNA was all over the place—hair on a brush and traces on make-up, so she had definitely been there—but no weapon was found. We think it is where the Scorpions kept her for a while. The Indonesian authorities have put another spin on the evidence and are seeking her in connection with the murders. She is their chief suspect.'

'What?' Nathan threw down his pencil. It overshot the table and clattered to the floor. 'They have to be mad! That couldn't be Kate!'

'I agree with you, Nathan, but that's not how it looks. You have to remember we know her and the Indonesians don't: to them she is just the girl who was to blame for destroying their network of agents. They think she stayed on in Jakarta and took her revenge on Gani.'

'Bollocks—it's a set-up,' muttered Damien, saying what Nathan was thinking.

Mrs Hardy let the crude language pass. 'Very likely—but why?'

'So you want us to find that out? Are you sending us to Jakarta?' asked Nathan.

Isaac shared a knowing glance with Mrs Hardy and shook his head. 'Forget Indonesia. They won't let a YDA operative in again no matter what the reason. No, your job is here. Since the Meosido siblings were murdered, the criminal underground has been working overtime to find Kate Pearl. She is Alfin and Yandi Gatra's Most Wanted. The whisperings are all pointing to this country; the Scorpions and their allies are turning up here with one objective in mind: finding Kate Pearl. So we think she is finally back in the UK, almost a year since we last heard from her. Your task is to find her first and bring her in. Whatever she has done, she is safest here rather than in an Indonesian jail or in the hands of the Scorpions. The YDA cannot fail Kate again.'

'So where is she?' Nathan turned to the back of his briefing papers. Leafing through, he saw that the sightings were extremely sketchy: a possible on a cross-Channel ferry, a more recent report from a neighbour near her mother's house, nothing definite.

'That's what I want you to find out. Nathan, as a Wolf, I'm putting you in charge of the manhunt.'

'Girlhunt,' muttered Kieran.

Isaac scowled at him. '*Kieran* and Raven will back you up, helping you get information out of witnesses and putting the pieces together. Damien will go along in case you meet any of the Scorpions, or if Kate resists capture.'

'From what I remember of her,' said Damien, 'I'd predict that Kate won't come in quietly. She has huge determination and she has to be running scared.'

Mrs Hardy smiled without humour. 'Then you have to use your legendary Cobra ruthless charm to persuade her that it is in her best interests, Damien.'

'Nat would have more luck at that than me. She told me she thought I was too smooth, like an oil slick.'

Isaac rubbed his chin. 'I'd forgotten. She did have a great line in put-downs, didn't she, Jan?'

'She liked Joe Masters most of all of us. Is he fit for duty yet?' asked Nathan. They all missed Joe, the fifth in their friendship group, but he had come out bruised from the operation that had brought Raven and Kieran together.

Mrs Hardy shook her head. 'I've signed him off for another month. He's with his parents in the States on vacation so I'd prefer not to call him in.'

'OK. We'll see what we can do,' said Damien, casting a worried glance at Nathan. 'You cool with this?'

'Fine,' Nathan said tersely.

'Is there something I don't know here?' asked Isaac, eyebrow arched.

Nathan decided it was better to lay his cards on the table. 'Damien is just anxious because I used to have a crush on Kate. I'm well over it. She'll be just another mission.'

Isaac held his gaze for a moment then nodded, satisfied by what he read in Nathan's expression.

Maybe he was better at hiding his feelings these days, thought Nathan, if he could fool Isaac?

'Not just another mission, Nathan.' Mrs Hardy tapped her copy of the briefing papers. 'She was one of us. We don't know exactly what she's been through but none of it will have been pretty.'

But Kate had also abandoned her loyalties to the YDA— Nathan had never forgiven her that. If she'd managed to escape from the Scorpions, why hadn't she come back to the YDA? He had felt the betrayal like a personal insult. He couldn't imagine running out on the YDA like that, with no explanation or attempt to make up for a mistake. It wasn't the poor judgement over Gani Meosido—he understood how that could happen—it was how she handled the fallout that had been wrong.

Nathan doodled a sketch of Kate's profile in the corner of his notepad while Mrs Hardy ran through the material they had gathered on their missing girl. Nathan wanted to make up for her lack of duty by bringing her in—irrational, he knew that, but it was as if he was somehow responsible for her and could repair the harm she had done to the YDA. *Where had that stupid impulse come from*? As the YDA's longest serving and most faithful recruit, Nathan knew he was fiercely protective of the organization that had raised him—maybe too protective if his friends were to be believed. Still, he lived by the motto that without loyalty, you were nothing. Painful though it was to admit it, Kate had chosen to become zero.

'OK, guys.' Isaac checked his watch. 'I want regular reports. Get yourself down to the last credible sighting near Kate's mother's house. Do not approach Maya Hubble directly.'

'Hubble?' asked Kieran. 'New surname?'

'Maya Pearl married a couple of years back and has a little kid. There was a falling out before Kate joined the YDA. Mrs Hubble hasn't seen or communicated with her older daughter. When I contacted her yesterday, she was understandably upset and refused to speculate where her daughter might be. She says Kate has to be dead to have stayed away so long from her grandparents.' Isaac's frown deepened. 'She's rather bitter and doesn't want to talk to us.'

No surprise there. 'Kate lived with them out of term time, didn't she?' said Nathan. There was no need to phrase it as a question: he knew the answer. Everything about Kate had stayed with him.

Isaac nodded. 'But there appears to have been some communication between Maya and the grandparents about Kate before the Indonesian mission. Maya has heard nothing for a year from any of them.'

Nathan put checking on the grandparents high on his to-do list. 'Did you tell her she was wrong about Kate being dead?'

'Yes, but Mrs Hubble refused to believe me.'

Frowning, Raven tapped her pencil on her notebook. 'Do you know what Kate is doing back here? If I were on the run, I'd make a new life in another country where there was no chance of being traced.'

'Unfortunately, I don't know what her intentions are,' Isaac admitted. 'Her training as a Cat would lead me to anticipate her doing something of that nature, Raven. She should be hiding out in another English-speaking country: the US or Australia maybe. But she's returned to her roots, bringing trouble trailing after her.'

'I see.' Raven rubbed her cheek with the pencil end. 'I don't know her like you guys but that suggests she's hurt in some way, coming back to lick wounds.'

'Very possibly,' agreed Isaac. He highlighted the little village of Castle Combe near Bath.

'Or to take revenge,' suggested Damien. 'In her shoes, I would feel angry with the YDA for dumping me in the situation. And from the sounds of it, her family have cut her off too or she doesn't feel able to approach them. She's on her own, nothing to lose now. Maybe she has a score to settle? She and her mother had argued, you said?'

From the twitch of the muscle in his jaw, Nathan could see that Isaac didn't like that idea, though he now would have to consider it.

'She didn't contact her mother and there was no indication that she was there to harm anyone,' said Isaac.

'She's not like that, Damien,' said Nathan. 'Not vindictive.'

'But we don't know her—not any more,' countered Damien.

Isaac looked to Mrs Hardy who nodded reluctantly. 'I'll put the local police on alert,' said Isaac. 'I'll ask them to keep an eye on the Hubbles. If other people are trailing Kate, it would be a wise precaution. OK, guys, I'll leave you to draw up a plan of action. Bring it to me this evening and, when I approve it, you can get moving on this tomorrow morning.'

Isaac picked up his briefcase and chucked Nathan the clicker for the computer display. 'Nathan, the mission is now yours.'

Chapter 3

It was the leather jacket that proved her downfall. A dark-haired girl slid into the coffee shop booth opposite her and unzipped the tan jacket with a satisfying zurring sound, like a cat's purr. Kate couldn't help looking up with a smile. She never normally made eye contact.

'Nice jacket.' She could almost feel what the buttery soft leather would be like to wear.

'Thanks. It was a present from my boyfriend. I take it this seat is free?' The girl finished a text with a quick tap for send. An American. Most likely here in Bath with her school for the Jane Austen tour, escaping her party for a latte.

Kate pushed her empty cup aside. 'The table's all yours. I was just going.'

Tucking the phone away, the girl grimaced in disappointment. 'Don't rush off because of me.' Glancing towards the door, she gestured to where the street fair was visible outside on the market place. 'Are those stalls always here?' The Georgian colonnade of sandstone pillars that ran through the plaza was giving shelter this weekend to a mixed collection of stalls selling artisan bread, stacks of cheeses, piles of olives, glittery crafts, doughnuts, candy-floss, and pot plants and flowers. Buskers had set up at intervals, one playing a flute, another further off singing Mozart. A man in long striped trousers walked by on stilts, juggling flaming torches. Twilight was closing in and the stalls were looking pretty, decked out with fairy lights.

'No. Just this weekend.' Kate pushed her novel into the side pocket of her backpack. 'You've picked a good time to visit.'

'Perfect. It's such a beautiful city—unreal, you know? Any advice what to see?'

Kate couldn't afford to continue the conversation. Her survival depended on not being remembered. She got up and zipped up her puffa jacket. 'Just walk around. Bath is like one big museum. Have fun.'

'Can I buy you another drink?' The girl seemed strangely keen to prolong the conversation—clingy. Maybe she was just lonely or eager to talk to a native, but an alarm bell went off in Kate's mind all the same.

'No time, but thanks for the offer.' She slid out of the booth.

The girl made to follow her, ignoring the fact she hadn't started her drink. 'OK, but could you point me towards the Assembly Rooms, then?'

'I . . . er . . . don't know the city that well myself. Sorry.' Kate took a step towards the front door but stopped abruptly when she saw two boys coming towards her. She knew them instantly: Damien and Kieran. The Yodas—operatives of the YDA—had found her. Spinning round, she headed for the side entrance. She never went anywhere without scoping another way out.

'Please, wait.' The girl tried to block her path—another Yoda, Kate now guessed. Kate slid over the table, sending sugar bowl, pepper and salt to the floor.

'Oy!' protested the cafe owner as the escape became a chase. Kate sped through the shop and burst out of the side exit only to collide with a fourth Yoda waiting outside. She should have guessed it would be a trap. He made a grab for her.

18

She had a second to register a vague familiarity as she bumped against him, but couldn't place him. A quick twist and knee to groin incapacitated him, but he still had hold of her backpack. Slipping free of the straps, she ran.

'Kate!' The boy shouted hoarsely as she plunged into the crowds visiting the fair. 'Stop! We're here to help you.'

Yeah, right. Glancing behind, Kate put on an extra burst of speed. They were all running after her, even the boy she had thought she had put out of action. Knee must have missed its target. Noticing a well-placed bin by the back wall of a bike shop, she jumped on top and leapt onto the brick ledge. Quickly scoping out her route, she saw she could escape over the connected roofs of a row of two-storey buildings. She pulled herself up by the guttering, scrambled up the tiles, and slid over the apex of the extension at the rear, out of sight of her pursuers. She was grateful to her puffa jacket for preserving the skin on her elbows as she grappled for a firm hold—and slid.

The slates were wet. Not good.

Refusing to scream and give her position away, she carried on skimming down, taking part of the guttering off before she went over the edge. Luck was with her as she landed on the roof of a van parked outside the back of the shop. Mentally sending her apologies to the owner for leaving a dent in the top, she jumped down, lost for a moment as she had no idea which direction would serve her best.

Looking up, she could make out the silhouette of one of her pursuers running along the roof ridge like a circus performer on a high wire. Crap. She set off along the alley heading for the busy shopping street.

'Kate!' From the rattling sound overhead of falling slates, he was sliding down the same path, confirmed by the thump of a body hitting the van roof. Kate didn't look behind, using the cover of the parked vehicles to hide her flight. Reaching the main road, she darted through the stream of traffic and headed for a large open-air car park on the edge of the shopping centre. Risking a look behind, she saw that she was still being chased.

Had to be one of the Wolves. Those guys never gave up.

Don't panic. Get to the bus station. She couldn't get caught. Swerving to her left, she reached the far side of the car park and saw a fence prevented an easy exit. She should have recce-ed her route better—a stupid beginner's mistake. Buses growled past on the far side. Keep calm. All she had to do was get over this, then she could slip on board a coach as it left. Still running along the boundary, she looked for something to use as a springboard to get past the barrier. No one had parked this far from the entrance so there was no handily positioned car. If she wasn't careful, she was going to get cornered.

'Kate, just stop for a second!' The boy was catching up.

Kate swung round and held up her hands in front of her. 'Stay where you are!'

The boy slowed, chest heaving after all that running. It was the one she had kneed. Dark hair, dark eyes, fit. Long and lean like the wolf his type were named after. 'Look, I'll stay where I am if you just listen for a moment.' He took another step forward.

'No! Don't move!' Kate glanced around, anticipating another trap. Were his friends circling her? 'You've got your pack after me.'

'They're not here yet, I promise. And I'm not going to bite.' He gave a self-deprecating shrug, hands spread to show they were empty. 'See: harmless.' He took another step.

Shaking with a poisonous mixture of exhaustion and fear, Kate retreated twice the distance he had moved, edging along the fence. 'I'm not stupid. You're not harmless.'

'OK: *less harmful*, then, than the other guys after you. Isaac sent my team to bring you in.'

Isaac. She had failed their leader so badly. 'He did?' Her voice caught in her throat.

'He's been trying to find you.'

Kate knew she should recognize the boy but couldn't place him. 'Who are you?'

'Nathan Hunter. Don't you remember me?' He seemed strangely deflated by her reaction, like she had insulted him by forgetting.

'Nathan? What happened to you? You look really different.' Few things surprised her any more but his appearance did. She remembered Nathan as a skinny boy in her year, a charming joker and clown, not this broad-chested athlete of a guy who was at least eight inches or so taller than her.

Nathan smiled sourly. 'I grew. Late and in a hurry, but I got there.'

'We teased you about that. I'm sorry.' Kate registered a silver four-wheel-drive entering the car park. Excellent: nice and tall. She willed it to come to the far end so she could use it to get over the fence.

Alerted by Kate's interest, Nathan glanced over at the car. 'Look, that's Raven with our ride.' He took a step closer. She would let him make that gain but no further. 'We just want you to get in and we'll take you to Isaac. He'll sort everything out.'

'I don't think even Isaac can do that.' Kate flattened herself against the fence, baiting the driver to bring the car right up to her.

Nathan's hands curled into fists at his side. 'Were you involved in the murders then?'

'What?' Kate momentarily forgot her escape plan. 'What murders?'

21

'We didn't think so.' Nathan looked pleased by her reaction. 'The Meosidos are dead—both of them.'

'Oh God, no.' Kate clutched at the fence, knees going weak. She had received so much bad news recently that she shouldn't be shocked.

With a muttered oath, Nathan made towards her.

'No! Stay back!'

He halted, like in some bizarre game of What's the Time, Mr Wolf. 'I'm sorry, Kate. I didn't think: they were your friends.'

She shook her head. Neither had been her friend. She had been their tool. 'How? When?'

'Isaac will tell you when you see him.' Nathan beckoned the car over.

Kate's resolve hardened. If the Scorpions had started killing their own, there was no hope they would spare her. She wouldn't be safe even with Isaac. The influence of the traffickers stretched far and wide, into the police and government. Isaac played by the rules; she couldn't afford to if she wanted to live.

First she had to lay a false scent to confuse the Wolf. 'Where's my bag?'

'It's in the car.'

It was a wrench to leave her bag but she couldn't think of a way of extracting it and still get away. She eyed the buses. The one heading for Heathrow was about to depart.

'I'd like it back.'

'No problem. We've not touched your things. Just get in the car.' He looked over to the vehicle.

The girl at the wheel shifted it closer when Kate showed no sign of moving. Just another metre should do it.

'Come on, Kate. It's time you came home.' Nathan opened the rear door, ready to usher her inside.

Kate sprang onto the bonnet and up to the roof. Jumping

off, she vaulted the fence and landed heavily on the far side. A shaft of pain shot up her leg. Ignoring that, she dodged into the crowd and bolted for the Heathrow bus. She scrambled in just as the door was closing.

'Sorry,' she gasped to the driver. 'Late for my flight.' She thrust money for the fare into his hand, grateful that she had enough in her pocket. She could hear shouting behind her. *Ignore it, everyone.*

'No luggage?'

'My friends put it on already.' Kate took her ticket and waved to a couple close to her age further down the bus who were so absorbed in each other they didn't see. 'Thanks for waiting.'

Muttering about schedules, the driver put the bus in reverse and backed out of the parking bay. Walking down the bus to take a seat behind the couple, Kate looked over at the spot where she had left Nathan. He was gone but she saw the car speeding to the exit. They would have to circle the one way system to catch up with the bus and they could hardly do anything as dramatic as pull it over. They weren't the police. Isaac wouldn't want the local constabulary involved in her recapture. Let the Yodas think they would corner her at the airport.

Chapter 4

Nathan watched as Raven got off the empty coach at the Heathrow central bus station. She grimaced at him then went to exchange a few words with the driver, who was checking the luggage hold was empty before he closed the doors and headed off on his break. The team already knew that Kate had evaded them when she had failed to emerge at any of the airport stops. They had followed the bus all the way from Bath when they caught up with it on the other side of the one-way system. They had spent the journey planning how to catch her at Heathrow, but she had been too wily for them.

Raven joined Kieran and Nathan by the ticket office. Damien had taken over driving and was circling the airport, as there was nowhere for ordinary cars to pull over at the bus station.

'Where did she get off?' Nathan asked.

'Almost immediately back in Bath. She scrambled on as we saw then claimed she had forgotten her passport. The driver took pity and let her off by the railway station while we were still making our way round the one-way system.'

'Of course she did. It was the most logical step,' said Kieran, admiringly.

Nathan ran his hands through his hair, exasperated with himself. 'And doesn't that make us look like prize idiots. I don't know why I was so stupid as to fall for the Heathrow trick.'

'She anticipated that we would imagine she would want to leave the country once spotted. An airport was too tempting,' said Kieran reasonably.

'I should know her better than that. Why did I think a fox would sit and wait for the hunting pack to catch up?'

Damien drew up alongside and tooted the horn. They quickly got in the car, Nathan up front with Damien, Raven and Kieran in the back.

'Don't tell me: she's vanished again?' Damien pulled away from the curb.

'She didn't even leave Bath,' said Nathan glumly. He texted a quick report to Isaac.

'So I take it we're going back?'

'Yep.' Nathan winced as he read Isaac's response. He should have left one of his team behind - a sweeper to pick up any loose ends. *Yeah, thanks for stating the obvious, Isaac.*

'It's not all bad news,' said Kieran. 'Tell him we have her bag. We might be able to work out where she'll go from that.'

Nathan nodded and passed on that information to Isaac. The bag was resting by his feet. They'd taken a brief look through it but Nathan had suggested as a sign of good faith they should leave Kate's belongings private. Now good faith was no longer an issue, he gave himself permission to make a proper search.

'OK, what have we got here?' He unzipped the main section. 'Towel. Clothes. Not many.' He noticed the silky scrap of a bra. OK, perhaps he had best not go there. 'Raven, would you?'

'You're such a gentleman, Nathan.' Raven took the bag from him and unpacked the contents. 'Two changes of clothes, all clean. Wash bag with the usual stuff. No make-up. Pack-a-Mac. Sandals. Front pocket. Passport.' She handed it over to Nathan. He flicked to the photo page.

'Catherine Jones. How original.' He wrinkled his nose at

the picture. Kate looked miserable in it, but didn't everyone in their passport? 'Fairly good fake.' Raven passed him a purse. He looked inside and found fifty Euros and about the same in pounds. No credit or debit cards. 'Anything else?'

'A man's watch—broken—and a battered copy of *The Quiet American*, Graham Greene.'

Nathan's misgivings intensified. 'Can I have the book, please?' Raven passed it forward. He checked through the pages, noting that it had been bought in the UK as he had expected.

'Problem?' asked Damien, signalling to join the motorway carriageway.

'Do you remember this book?' Nathan asked. He held it forward over the dashboard so Damien could see it.

'No. Something special about it?'

'We got it for her to read on the flight out to Jakarta, a kind of good luck present.' In fact, Nathan had bought it and handed it over in the guise of a gift from everyone.

'She's kept it for a year? Must be a slow reader.'

Nathan didn't appreciate Damien's flippant comment. 'It's been read—many times.' He could see her underlinings.

'So?' Damien frowned as he eased into the middle lane to overtake a lorry.

Kieran cleared his throat. 'What Nathan has deduced is that these aren't just Kate's possessions, they are her *only* possessions. You don't carry round a book you've read many times, a broken watch, or your passport, if you have somewhere else to leave them.'

'And we've taken them from her.' Nathan passed the purse, passport, and book back to Raven. 'I doubt she has anything but the clothes she's wearing and maybe a little cash.'

'That's good,' said Damien.

'How can that be good?' asked Nathan. 'We've even got the girl's toothbrush.'

'No passport, little money: she won't be able to run far.'

'Yes, but she will also have to sleep rough.' Kate wasn't safe and Nathan knew that he was partly to blame.

'She'll be fine. She's a Cat. They always fall on their feet.' Damien pressed down on the accelerator.

'Are you sure you were ever her friend, Damien?' Raven asked dryly.

'Have to admit, we never got on, not since she almost got me benched after a mission in London.'

Raven was intrigued. 'How?'

Nathan had heard the story several times before. 'Damien says she pulled him off the job right in front of their target— aborted the mission because she thought he wasn't handling it right. But, Damien, I don't think Isaac saw it quite like that.'

Damien shrugged. 'So he took her side—he always was blind about her. But I was still willing to be Kate's friend right until she betrayed us by running a year ago. Takes two to make a friendship.' ·

Nathan told himself that Damien had a point. They had given Kate a chance to come in peacefully. Next time the gloves would be off. She had to be caught, and better by them than anyone else. 'OK, for Kate's sake as well as ours, we have to do this. We've found her once; we'll just do it again.'

Raven groaned. 'Not more coffee? We must have searched every cafe in Bath until we found her.'

'She needs somewhere she can hide. She looks too young to pass unchallenged in pubs and clubs for any length of time so her only options are shops, cafes and places like libraries.' Nathan had figured that out before they began their search of the city. 'Only problem now is to anticipate where she will go next. She won't have stayed in Bath.'

'So why are we heading back there?' asked Raven.

'To pick up her trail,' explained Kieran. 'We have to start somewhere.'

Nathan's phone vibrated. He glanced down at the message. 'Good. Isaac's sending someone to help us.'

'Who?' asked Damien.

'Sergeant Rivers.'

The occupants of the car groaned.

'He's not that bad when you get to know him.' In truth, Nathan deeply loved and admired his mentor in the Wolves but it would be uncool to admit that. The man was, after all, his adopted father.

'He may love you, Nat, but I can tell you he doesn't see the rest of us in the same light,' said Damien. 'He thinks the only good Yoda is a Wolf. That man only likes his own team.'

'Hey, I don't think he likes me much as other Wolves,' said Raven, who was also in D stream.

'You he only tolerates because you have shown bad judgement in partnering with an Owl,' conceded Damien. 'Kieran he treats like an alien and me he just plain hates as he doesn't trust any Cobras.'

Nathan scowled. 'He does not hate you.' Well, maybe he did, Nathan had to admit privately.

'He certainly acts that way around me.'

Kieran grinned, pulling Raven to his side and dropping a kiss on top of her head. He had never been that fussed by Sergeant Rivers's disapproval. 'So am I to understand that the next few days are going to be interesting?'

'Yeah, in the Chinese-curse-on-your-enemies sense,' replied Nathan.

Full darkness had arrived as Kate waited in the lay-by for her cousin to show up with his doughnut van. Len wasn't really her cousin, more a relation by marriage to her father's best friend, but in the travelling community of the fairground folk that counted as a cousin. It made life simpler to have three groups: close family, cousins and strangers. Len would be closing up now after a busy weekend of trading and ready to move on. The offer of a lift had been instant—all she had had to do was ask. She could have picked any of the fairground folk—they all knew she was Mary and Steve's grandchild—but Len was the only one going in the right direction.

Kate hugged her arms to her side. She had hiked up here after getting the promise of a ride in case the Yodas had left a sweeper behind when they tore off in pursuit of the Heathrow bus. She was now cold and hungry. Fortunately the lay-by included a bus shelter with seats so her presence here wasn't so glaring. A couple of local buses had pulled up but she had just shaken her head and they had gone on without her. Hopefully, none of the drivers would remember her. The lay-by was an attractive spot in the daytime with views back down to the city of Bath, popular for those wanting a photograph. She recalled it from the journey here: how from this lookout point the city appeared to nestle in the valley, looking naturally grown, like a wood in a glen. In the dark, however, the same view point became a creepy spot. The city lights felt very far away, the bin was overflowing and smelt of fast food and beer cans. Imagination was running away with her, replaying all the sickening scenes from horror movies of girls alone in isolated spots. Len couldn't arrive soon enough for her.

A bright pink and yellow van pulled up and tooted its horn merrily.

'All right, love? Sorry to keep you waiting.' Len, a plump middle-aged man with receding black hair and a friendly smile, opened the passenger door for her. He had a pale complexion that made him look a little vampirish—an appearance completely at odds with his sweet nature.

Kate breathed a sigh of relief. 'Thanks, Len. Good day?'

'Yes, indeed. Think I made about five hundred.' He patted his chest pocket.

'Cool.' The van smelt permanently of the oil in which the doughnuts were deep fried, overlaid with the scent of sugar. 'Don't suppose you have anything left over? I'm starved.'

'Help yourself. One thing I'm not short of is food.'

Kate reached behind her seat and grabbed a carton of juice and a ring doughnut covered with sugar strands. Not the healthiest diet but hunger had to be satisfied.

Changing gear, Len watched out of the corner of his eye as she consumed the doughnut. 'I hope you don't mind me asking, Kate, but just what kind of trouble are you in?'

She shrugged. 'The serious sort.'

Len frowned. Kate could see he was guessing that the police were involved. They were in a way: the Indonesian police.

'Anything I can do?' he asked.

'You're doing it by giving me a lift.'

'And where am I taking you exactly?'

Kate licked the sugar off her lips. 'I thought I'd go and see Gran.'

Len looked relieved. 'That's a good idea. She'll sort it out.'

So he didn't know then.

'I'm sorry to hear about Steve. Your granddad was a good man—a legend.'

Kate's mouth wobbled. No crying. No weakness. 'Yes, he was.'

'And his passing—was it peaceful?'

She didn't know: she hadn't been there. 'It was quick. Heart attack.' Other fairground folk had told her that he had had a seizure after receiving bad family news. She feared that had been word of her disaster in Jakarta. They must have thought the gang had killed her.

'How is your gran taking it?'

'Oh, you know.' She left that hanging. There was no point telling him the truth: he might try to get involved. Everything was so horrible: it was far too difficult for anyone to sort out. Even thinking about the mess exhausted her. She yawned. 'Do you mind if I sleep? I'm shattered.'

'Go ahead. We'll be in Birmingham in a couple of hours. I'll park up on the outskirts and catch forty winks myself. You can call on her in the morning then, rather than in the middle of the night.'

'Good plan.' Kate curled up on the seat.

'Here.' Len passed her a rug.

'Thanks.'

'No problem, love. You look as though you could do with a little pampering. Mary will be just the ticket.'

As promised, Len woke her at dawn. He had the ruffled appearance of a man who had slept uncomfortably, rubbing his neck with his soft white baker's hands. Realization came late that she had prevented him stretching out on the front seats as he usually would.

'Sorry. I should have let you sleep properly.'

Len chuckled, spirits not dented by discomfort. 'One night won't do me any harm. Where can I drop you?'

'Edgbaston.'

'Righto. Do you think Mary will feel up to giving me a cup of tea? It would be nice to catch up.' And put heads together to help her. Kate guessed his intention.

'She's moved into a home. I'm not sure what the rules are on visitors,' Kate explained, not even having to lie.

'A home, eh? Is her health failing?'

'She's . . . she's not too bad.'

'Perhaps I'd better not spring a visit on her then. Tell her I'll call in after the fair in Lichfield. I should be up there a week.'

'Will do.' Not that it would be any good.

Kate got out on the road in front of The Willows Residential Home and waved goodbye to Len. Watching him drive away, she then set off into the gardens. An old manor house converted for multiple occupancy, The Willows maintained an air of genteel grandeur. She had no intention of going up to the door until she was certain no one had followed her here, or come on ahead and laid a trap. Being almost captured by the YDA once was enough and the Scorpions had been snapping at her heels all the way across Europe. She hoped that her gran's state of health would put anyone off considering her as a target but Kate had been around the gangs in Indonesia long enough to know that nothing was sacred, not even frail old ladies.

The back door to the house was open. A member of the kitchen staff was taking out the recycling. As soon as the woman lifted the big lid of the bin, masking her view of the door, Kate slipped inside. Luck was with her: the cook had her back to Kate and was singing along to Radio Two. Leaving the kitchen, Kate found herself in a service corridor. The staff toilets were across the way so she went in, planning on tidying herself before finding her gran. The view in the mirror was not encouraging: she looked like a pale-faced street urchin, dirt smeared on her cheek, her hands a disgrace of grubby broken nails. No wonder Len had been worried. Kate finger-combed her straight blonde hair. It could do with a cut: it now reached to her shoulder blades and looked messy. Taking a band from her wrist, she plaited it. Gran had always liked her hair this way. It did make her look younger as the hair pulled back from her face. The style accentuated her cheekbones and hazel eyes.

When did I start looking permanently scared? Kate asked her reflection. Once she had been confident, almost a little brazen; now she had the expression of a hunted creature. *I've become prey.*

Pressure grew in her chest. *No tears. Don't you dare cry. You must plan.* Kate wasn't sure why she had come here, other than she couldn't bear the thought of never seeing Gran again. She had lost her chance to say goodbye to Granddad. This was her last piece of unfinished family business. She had checked on her mother and everything was OK there. If she was reassured that Gran was in a good place for her condition, Kate could disappear finally with no regrets. She had weighed up that need against the knowledge that her presence put at risk those she loved. But she would be quick, she promised her reflection. Stay just long enough to know.

The door opened and a woman came in, motherly type, a little plump. She had a dark complexion and neat black hair tied up in a bun, a scarlet bindi on her forehead, and was dressed in a nursing uniform of blue tunic and loose trousers. 'Oh. I don't think you are supposed to be in here.'

'I'm not? I'm sorry. I was just checking I looked neat before visiting my gran. She notices things like that.'

The nurse smiled. 'It's a little early for a visit. Not many of our residents are out of bed yet. Who is she?'

'Mary Featherstone.'

The woman's smile broadened. 'Fairground Mary? Oh I'm so pleased someone has finally come to see her.' Kate felt a familiar pang of guilt. 'She's been here almost six months and no one from the family has visited, only friends from the travelling people she knew. Give me a second and I'll take you up.'

Kate waited by the sinks for the nurse to finish in the cubicle and then wash her hands. She used the time to clean her face and pick out the grime from under her nails. That would have to do.

'So tell me: how are you related to Mary?' the nurse asked, tugging out a hand towel from the dispenser.

'I'm her son's child.'

'She has a son?'

'Had. My dad was killed in a motorbike accident when he was eighteen.'

'I'm sorry. How tragic!'

'I never knew him.'

The nurse patted Kate's arm. Kate told herself not to flinch. She didn't like people touching her. 'Mary will be so pleased to see you. You must feel free to come as often as you can even if you don't think your visits do much good. You never know what people with her condition take in.' The nurse guided Kate up to the second floor and knocked on a door. 'Mary sweetheart, I've brought you a special visitor.'

Kate's heart was thumping as she stepped in the room. Her gran was sitting by the window in her dressing gown. She looked round, her white hair forming a halo around her beautiful wrinkled face.

'Gran?'

'Katie Girl?' Gran frowned, as if wondering what part of her mind that name had sprung from.

A tear escaped the corner of Kate's eye, emotion threatening to choke her. 'How are you, Gran?'

'Go right in. I'll see if I can rustle up some breakfast for you both up here.' The nurse laughed and put her hand to her forehead. 'I'm forgetting our rules. What's your full name, my dear, and how old are you?'

'Kate Mary Pearl. I'm seventeen.' She saw no point in lying.

'And where do you live?'

Now she had to invent a plausible background. 'I'm in sixth-form college, living in student accommodation down in Somerset. Taunton. That's why I haven't visited before.'

The nurse nodded, satisfied. 'I'll sign you in downstairs. Tea and toast?'

'Thanks.'

Gran was still smiling at them, just waiting for the conversation she didn't quite follow to end. Kate moved to crouch beside her and take Gran's blue-veined hand in hers. It was odd to see the indomitable Mary Featherstone so meek and mild.

'Katie Girl,' Mary repeated.

'Hello, Gran.'

'You aren't eating properly.'

Trust Gran to notice. 'Not really.'

'How about I make you one of my special stews? I'll ask Steve to pick up a nice bit of beef when he goes to the market.' She looked around the room, getting confused again. 'Where is he? I haven't seen him for a while. Has he got lost?'

Fresh tears brimmed. Gran had forgotten that her husband was dead.

'He's . . . gone away for a bit.'

'I see.' Gran stroked her soft blue dressing gown with her free hand. What had happened to her cat? Kate wondered. 'How's school, darling?'

'I've left school, Gran.'

Sharp eyes turned back to her. 'You get yourself right back there, Katie Girl. I won't have you neglecting your education. You can't spend your life on the fair circuit like your granddad and I. You're going to be a . . . ' Her voice faded into confusion. 'What was it you want to be?'

Those dreams were dust now. 'I wanted to be detective and join the Metropolitan Police.'

Gran nodded firmly. 'Exactly. You can't do that without qualifications. Go put your uniform on and make sure you catch the bus. Your granddad isn't here to drive you to school.'

'I will in a minute,' agreed Kate, realizing the conversation would go more smoothly if she appeared to be complying with her gran's wishes.

'You always were a clever little thing. So smart! Just like Michael. Where is Michael?'

Gran had forgotten her son was dead too. 'He's off somewhere with Granddad.'

'My Granddad? No, that's wrong—he's long gone. Died in the war.' Mary looked down at their joined hands. 'Who are you again, dear?'

The conversation circled. Kate told herself it was good that her gran didn't recall her more recent losses or her granddaughter's problems. She was in no fit state to help. If this morning was typical then, fortunately, her dementia had left her not distressed that she was moving in a fog of half memories and collapsed timelines. She was better when she talked about the past. Giving up on the present, Kate listened contentedly to rambling stories about fairgrounds of long ago and the characters who had run the rides and food concessions. She sat on a footstool by Gran's knee, letting Gran stroke her hair. This one was a rogue, always in trouble with the husbands; that one a Flash Harry, up to his neck in dodgy dealings. Gran's memory world was a colourful place to retreat to from the grim reality that awaited Kate.

Reminded of her situation, Kate checked the bedside clock. She had stayed over an hour, tea and toast all finished. She had learned never to remain in one place for long.

'I'd better get going, Gran.'

'Come again, dear. It's so lovely to see you.'

Kate straightened the picture of herself and Granddad that sat on the table by Gran's armchair. 'I'll try. You are happy here, aren't you?'

Gran nodded. 'Such lovely people. Where are we?'

'The Willows Residential Home.'

Gran chuckled. 'Sounds very posh. Fancy Fairground Mary living here!' She leant closer and dropped her voice. 'Can I afford it?'

'Of course. Granddad made sure of that. He sold the ghost train to Neil Bishop, remember? Got a good price. You retired on the proceeds of fear, he said.' Kate kissed her gran's cheek, which smelt of lavender talc. When she was little, she had faithfully bought her gran a bottle each Christmas and birthday which Mary must have stockpiled, as no one could get through so much in a year. Every time Mary had acted surprised when she opened the present.

'So I'm here to stay, am I?' Mary's forehead creased in confusion.

'Yes, Gran.' Kate gulped against the lump in her throat.

'Off to school, are you?'

'Something like that. Love you.' Kate wanted to cling but she had to make herself leave.

'Love you too, Katie Girl.'

Chapter 5

With a melancholy premonition that she would not see Gran again, Kate closed the door. *Come on, man up, Kate.* The ridiculous phrase, another favourite of her granddad's, usually lifted her spirits and worked a little now. She hurried downstairs, passing an old lady making elegant progress seated on a stair lift. She was attended by the nurse Kate had met earlier.

'Everything all right with your gran?' the nurse asked.

'All good, thanks. She seems to like it here.'

'She's settled down well. You should see her when we get a DJ visiting. Life and soul, she is.'

'Who are you talking about?' bellowed the lady on the stair lift.

'Fairground Mary, Beth,' shouted the nurse. 'This is her granddaughter.'

'Oh, Mary! Yes, she loves to sing.'

'That's great.' Kate smiled at Beth.

'Come again soon,' added the nurse.

Kate zipped up her jacket. 'Thanks for looking after her.'

'It's no trouble.'

Kate would have preferred to find the back exit but with the two women watching she felt she had to go out the front. She pushed the heavy door and let it thump closed behind her. So final. Kate stood for a moment on the driveway, head hung. All her responsibilities fulfilled, all she had to do now was keep herself alive.

A car came out of nowhere and accelerated. Only the speed bump by the entrance saved her. Going too fast, the car scraped the exhaust and had to slow. Reflexes kicking in, Kate threw herself sideways into the prickly planting under the dining room window. The vehicle overshot but braked hard with a crunch of tyres on gravel. Kate didn't wait to see who got out: she was off running across the garden.

How had they found her?

She vaulted the fence of an old paddock, through the field and then climbed the railings into an allotment. Taking a hazard on heading sharp left, she made a circuit to emerge in a housing development made up of big houses and tiny gardens. Her aim was to get behind her pursuers so they became the ones followed. She had to know who they were and lead them away from Gran. She vowed she would somehow make them regret it if they entered The Willows.

But who were they? It couldn't be the YDA: they wouldn't try to run her down.

Know your enemy. Not Granddad this time but advice from her former mentor, Jan Hardy, at the YDA.

The best place to view The Willows was from the church-yard opposite. Kate darted across the main road and through the lychgate. Crouching behind a mossy tombstone, she risked a look. The car was still parked haphazardly in the drive, a member of staff shouting at the driver to move.

Don't do that. Kate tried to send a mental warning to the irate home manager. Guys like that driver would think nothing of putting a bullet in anyone they found annoying. Fortunately, he leant against the bonnet ignoring the woman, a lit cigarette in his hand, sunglasses on even though it was a cloudy day. Young, wiry, and dark, he had an Indonesian look to him. Kate guessed if she got close enough she would find a little scorpion tattooed on his wrist, a match to the one on hers.

A second man, white, probably a British associate, came limping back from the garden and shook his head. He checked his phone, holding it out as if trying to find good reception. She could have told him that this end of the village was a mobile phone black spot, reception intermittent. Then a police car roared by, sirens blaring, spooking the men. The driver threw his cigarette away and the pair quickly got back in the car.

Kate let out a relieved breath. They weren't going after Gran. She wouldn't have to show herself. Slumping down on the fallen leaves that covered the tomb, Kate let the shakes she had been repressing take over. Another close shave. Two in eighteen hours. Her year of luck making her way back across the world from Indonesia had run out. She rubbed the back of her neck wearily. There was a sore spot there - a mosquito bite that had gone bad - a small pain to add to the much more serious ones. It was a miracle she had not ended up dead.

She felt a twinge of pity for Tina. She had only been in the game because her brother and cousins had twisted her arm. Another victim. It was hard to feel sorry for Gani. He had 'short life expectancy' written all over him once Kate realized he was ambitious to be a big league player in the trafficking ring. He must have crossed the wrong person. His cousins wouldn't have let family ties stop them killing him.

Kate shuddered. She didn't want to think about Gani— did not want not remember what she had done. The flash of the scorpion reminded her every time she looked at her arm, the memory stinging.

But none of that explained why the Scorpions were after her. The YDA's motives in pursuing her were, by contrast, straightforward; her ex-colleagues thought she was mixed up in murder. The gang's motives were obscure. This wasn't the

40

first time she had found the Scorpions right behind her—she'd barely got out of Austria alive and there had been a couple of sticky moments in the Netherlands as she made her way to the ferry port. She had expected them to give up once she had left Asia but they had persisted; if anything, they had become more intense in their search. What was the point? Her only value to them now was as merchandise, because she had no secrets left to betray; surely that wasn't worth chasing her halfway round the globe? The world offered huge numbers of easier victims to exploit. She had to be missing something— some clue to explain their pursuit.

Waiting for the coast to clear, Kate sat with her back against the cold stone. She had often been uncomfortable in the last few months and become hardened to it. She totted up the large number of cold benches she had sat on and awkward spots she had hidden in over recent days. The journey home had been long and complicated. Her fake passport had got her on a couple of flights until she reached Turkey. The gang would have caught her long ago if it hadn't been for the European network of fairground folk. The links were more tenuous the further she was from England, but there was always someone who knew someone. Talk to one of the travelling people long enough and a link that confirmed her story that she was one of them would emerge. She had met Ghost Train Neil's brother-in-law in Vienna and learnt of her granddad's death. Asking further questions had brought up the news of her gran's rapid-onset dementia. That had decided her. Coming back, she had imagined she would slip into England with no one noticing, check on her family and leave. However, the nearer she came to home, the hotter the hunt had become. She didn't understand it.

What did you tell them, Gani? Kate wondered as she crumpled a wilted purple chrysanthemum between her fingers. She didn't know anything so could pose no threat to the gang's operation. Perhaps Gani had lied and said that she knew more than she did in a last ditch attempt to save his own life—she could imagine him doing that.

What he had done or not done was no longer important. All the evidence pointed to the gang being deadly serious about silencing her. She had to run again.

But to do that, she needed money. She would have to risk a visit to her banker.

'Nathan! Over here.' His dad and mentor of the Wolves was standing by his car, coffee balanced on the bonnet. Sergeant Jim Rivers had arranged to meet Nathan and his team at the motorway service station near Cheltenham, fifty or so miles north of Bath. A large man who was born to bellow orders on a parade ground, he had never mastered the art of talking in a low voice.

With an embarrassed look at the others, Nathan crossed the car park and walked into the bear-hug that was waiting for him. He and his adopted father were about the same height these days, but that didn't prevent Jim Rivers from crushing his boy each time they met.

'How's things?' Jim asked, ruffling Nathan's hair.

'We've finally made progress.' Nathan pushed away, tempted to ruffle Jim's brush-cut, but as they were on official business decided not to risk it. The line between official and family behaviour was blurred enough. 'We've discovered that Kate Pearl got a lift north last night from one of the fast food vans leaving the street fair.'

'That's a good catch.'

'A bus driver noticed her on his trip out of town and happened to be passing as she accepted the ride. I think he was worried about her, so remembered her immediately we asked. He thought he was helping us find Damien's runaway sister, so was very open.'

42

Jim finished his coffee and crumpled the cardboard cup in his fist. 'Was she hitchhiking?' He lobbed it into the bin.

'I don't think so. It looked like she had been waiting for the van. Pink and yellow doughnut seller—shouldn't be hard to track. Kieran's theory is that Kate knows the people who travel between the fairs. Her grandparents were in that business according to the file.'

His bulldog face settling in a frown, Jim shot a look at chestnut-haired Kieran, who was hanging back with Raven and Damien. 'I see.'

'His instincts are good, Dad.'

'So you always tell me. Report, Storm.'

Kieran approached, Raven and Damien a step behind. Jim nodded curtly to the boys but managed a smile for Raven.

'They treating you well?' Jim asked her.

'Yes, sir.' She answered soberly, but grinned at Kieran when Jim's gaze moved away.

'Good to hear.' Jim jabbed his index finger at Kieran. 'Now your theory, Storm: explain.'

'Kate's grandparents, sir, used to own a number of fairground rides. They retired a few years ago but she would have travelled with them before she joined the YDA.'

'I remember her talking about it,' added Nathan. 'It sounded the perfect childhood: free rides whenever she wished. It had been part of Kate's confidence that she had come from a long line of showmen.'

'And you think she still has friends in that world and is moving about thanks to the fairground community?' Jim scowled at Kieran as if he were personally to blame. 'It's a big theory to build on one lift in a van.'

Kieran shrugged. In response to Jim's military demeanour, Kieran always got more aloof and intellectual—he couldn't help himself. 'It explains why she was still in Bath after visiting her mother's home when we would have expected her to leave the area. She was waiting for the street fair to end.'

'All right: I'll buy the theory. Where does it lead us?'

Nathan had been giving this much thought. 'I think she might be going home.'

'Isn't that rather obvious—too obvious?'

'So you would think, but I'm not sure we yet understand her motives. She went to look in on her mother but didn't make contact. Maybe she wants to do the same for her grandparents?'

'Just her grandmother,' Kieran corrected. 'Steve Featherstone died ten months ago.'

Did she know? Nathan had a flash of Kate turning up on her doorstep only to find her grandfather was in the cemetery.

'What address do we have for the grandmother?' asked Jim.

'The house is in Edgbaston. That's where we are heading now.'

'Right. Your orders then?'

The question took Nathan by surprise. 'I'm still in charge?'

Jim folded his arms. 'Naturally. This is your mission. I'm only here to observe and support. Isaac's feeling is that you might run into some difficulties. He didn't want you on your own. Until that point though, this is your lead.'

'OK.' *I better not muck this up.* 'We'll go in the two cars to Edgbaston, park up a street away to observe the property. If it looks OK, we'll approach and see if we can make contact with Mrs Featherstone.'

'Let's go then. You'll come with me?' Jim gestured to the front seat.

'Thanks. Follow us, guys?'

The other three nodded and walked back to their car. They tried for Nathan's sake not to look too relieved.

'Are you sure you are working all right with that lot?' Jim

asked dubiously. His eyes settled with particular distrust on Damien. Charming when he chose, and as smooth a mover as the cobra his sort was named after, Damien had never impressed the sergeant even though he was Nathan's best friend.

'They're good at what they do, Dad.'

'A hunt should be Wolf business.' Jim got in and started the engine. 'Raven shows promise but I don't want Storm hampering her development.'

Nathan was used to his dad's grumbles about the other types Isaac insisted on recruiting. 'She's doing well—almost got Kate at the first attempt.'

'I expect it was one of the others who messed that up for you.'

'No, it was me.'

Jim shook his head. 'Not possible. You're the best.'

'You overestimate my abilities, Dad. Kate is better. You've never seen anyone think so fast and she can move like an alley cat through cities. Plus her self-defence tactics are pretty slick.' The knee to the groin still lingered as a horrid reminder that he wasn't quick enough. He should have taken stronger hold but he hadn't wanted to hurt her—idiotic when he was facing a highly trained operative.

'We'll catch her yet.' Jim glanced in the mirror to check the other car was following. 'Enough about the mission, tell me how you've been. Your mother's been bending my ear about you. You've not called.'

Nathan chuckled and settled back in his seat to fill Jim in on recent events. The day Jim and Maisie Rivers had welcomed him into their home was the day he had first known what it was to be treated like a son, with people who fretted about him and worried that he was looking after himself. Fostering had eventually turned into adoption. Ten by the time that happened, he had kept his original surname but added Jim and Maisie's in the middle: Nathan Rivers Hunter. He never let himself forget how fortunate he was that the adoption had also brought him into the wider family of the YDA.

Nathan's news at an end and a few miles of silence passed, Jim returned to the subject of the mission.

'Am I right in thinking you were close to Kate Pearl at one time? I remember you talking about her.'

Nathan smiled sourly at the blue sign marking the first junction for Birmingham. 'You've got it a little mixed up. I wanted to be close to her but she didn't even know I existed.' As proved yesterday when she didn't recognize him.

'Like that, was it?' Jim took the exit. 'Just as well, seeing how she turned out.'

'How do you think she's turned out?' Nathan drummed on his knee. It was OK for him to criticize her, but hearing others do so was still hard to bear.

'Obviously she's gone bad. Someone with nothing to hide would've turned herself in long ago.'

'You don't think she's a victim then?'

'The victims are the ones who ended up dead because of her.' Jim had always been harsh in his judgments and everyone knew it. Isaac said it was important to have someone hard-nosed among the mentors in case they got too soft—Jim Rivers was his go-to tough guy.

'But she didn't intend that to happen.'

'Never trust a Cat—they become what they want you to think they are. Kate Pearl appeared a hero to you a year ago because that's what she wanted you all to believe. Now it will suit her to appear a damsel in distress to gain your pity. I hope you're too sensible to fall for it?' Jim glanced sideways at his son, probably willing him to be more of a tough nut, but that was one lesson that had never quite stuck.

'Of course I won't. She wasted her chance to come in the easy way; we won't let her get past us again.' Nathan tried to delete from his memory how exhausted and sad she had looked when they cornered her. He had never seen anyone more alone. Was Jim right: this was a disguise like the many she adopted as part of her Cat training?

'Make sure you remember Cats always have claws. You can't afford to let her sink them into you or anyone else on your team.'

Pretending to have a parcel to deliver, Nathan found out from a neighbour that Mary Featherstone had moved into a retirement home. Parked outside The Willows, the team studied their target.

'Shall I go this time?' asked Damien.

Nathan shook his head, not wanting to surrender the task. 'I'll go. You keep watch in case Kate is here and bolts.' Giving them a moment to find their positions around The Willows so all entrances could be monitored, Nathan went to the front door. He didn't bother with the parcel this time; it would just be taken in and, as it was empty, that would achieve precisely nothing. He decided that the truth—or part of it—would serve him best.

'Yes, can I help you?' The lady who answered the buzzer looked far from welcoming, a suspicious gaze, spiked brown hair, and metallic reading glasses swinging from a chain around her neck.

He tried for charm. 'Hello, I wonder if you could help me? I'm a friend of Mrs Featherstone's granddaughter.'

He got no further. To his surprise, the woman clutched her specs to her chest. 'Is she all right? Such a terrible to-do this morning!'

'This morning? What happened to Kate this morning?' Dread filled him.

'You don't know? Such a close thing! She was just leaving and this car practically ran her down—' her hand gestures replayed the scene of the speeding car and the small person leaping out of the way '—it's all on the CCTV, but the police say they won't do anything as no one was harmed, and she didn't stay to file a complaint. Just think if it had been one of our residents: they couldn't get out of the way like she did!'

'She got away?'

'Ran like the wind. Don't blame her: the driver was completely unrepentant. Stood there,' the lady pointed to the gravel just behind Nathan, 'and took no notice when I said I was calling the police. So rude! I don't know if he even spoke English. He drove off before the police arrived. Response time round here is shocking.'

The manager was clearly worried about Kate—something Nathan could use to his advantage.

'I'm here with Kate's old teacher. She's been missing for a few days and we're looking for her. Any leads would be helpful. Would you mind if he saw the CCTV footage?'

'You mean she's run away?'

'We're not sure what's she's doing. We're all really worried about her.'

'We did wonder. Kaasni thought she looked stressed so tried to feed her up, but what with Mary in the state she is in, we weren't sure what we could do.'

'So I can call my teacher in?'

'I don't see why not. He has identification, I assume?'

'Absolutely. He is a member of staff at our school—teaches PE.' Among other things. Finding he had a fluctuating signal on his phone, Nathan went outside to summon Jim, the lady accompanying him. 'And would it possible for me to see Kate's gran to find out if she knows where she is?'

'You can try. You do know about her, I suppose?' Evidently

the manager was expecting Nathan to have more knowledge than he did. It would undermine his claim to be a friend if he admitted his ignorance.

'Absolutely.'

'She's sitting in the day room. I'll take you.'

Nathan would not have been able to pick out Kate's grandmother from the ten or so elderly women sitting in the large room in their upright armchairs if the home manager had not been with him. Several were slumped like puppets with strings cut, sleeping. Luckily, Mary Featherstone was awake. Her eyes were on the bird feeder on the terrace outside, a magazine resting unread on her lap. Six sparrows hung from the wire mesh, chipping away at the peanuts.

'Mary, a friend of your granddaughter has come to visit,' the lady said loudly.

Mary turned round. Bright eyes, their shape so like Kate's, smiled up at him. 'Well, what a lovely young man you are. I'm so pleased you are Katie's friend.'

This was going to be easier than he had anticipated. Kate's grandmother already liked him. Nathan sat down on a footstool in front of her.

'Hello, Mrs Featherstone. I was told Kate came to visit you this morning?'

The lady smiled serenely. 'She did?'

Ah. Houston, we have a problem. 'Yes. Do you know where she went after that?'

'You have a lovely square jaw and cheekbones, young man, quite like a young Clark Gable. Do you know Clark Gable?'

'No, I'm sorry, I don't.'

'Don't you go to the pictures? He is all the rage, you know.'

'I'm sure he is. Mrs Featherstone, about Kate . . . '

'Katie Girl—such a sweet child. She's at school, you know, doing awfully well.'

'You saw her this morning and she left . . .?'

'Yes, to catch her bus. She mustn't be late. I don't know what I've done with her uniform.' Mary began to search the room. 'Where's the ironing board? I didn't press it and she'll get in trouble. What place is this?'

'The Willows.' Nathan worried he was upsetting her. 'You live here.'

'And Katie?'

'She's . . . ' running for her life '. . . fine. I promise you I'll look after her.'

'Such a handsome young man.' Mary patted his hand. 'Do you know Clark Gable?'

Extricating himself from the conversation before they did another loop, Nathan said goodbye to Mary, agreed he would take Kate to the pictures to see Clark Gable's latest, and returned to the front office. The manager was with Jim studying the footage from the drive CCTV camera.

'May I take a copy of this?' Jim was asking.

'Please do. Anything to help find the poor girl. I didn't realize she had no other relatives.'

'But she has friends,' said Jim with a hard smile. 'Even if she doesn't know it.'

'Did Mary tell you anything helpful?' the lady asked.

'Do I look like Clark Gable to you?' Nathan spread his hands.

'She was in one of those moods, was she? Every man is some Hollywood star or other from the past. I'm sorry she couldn't help.'

'Who is your contact for matters concerning Mary?' asked Jim.

'There's no one listed. No family. Social Services sorted out the placement and the family solicitor has power of attorney over her bank account. I think her husband noticed she was falling ill before his own sudden death and set things up, just in case.'

'Would you mind giving us the solicitor's name?'

'I can't see why not. It is hardly a secret. Brian Hampstead. I believe he handled all their finances after they sold on their business.'

'And Kate's?' asked Nathan. She had to be getting money from somewhere if she wasn't stealing it.

The lady frowned. 'I really don't know. He never said. But then, he wouldn't, would he? That's covered by client confidentiality.'

A little bit of after hours breaking and entering into the solicitor's office should sort that out, decided Nathan; Damien would enjoy exercising his talents.

Chapter 6

Kate helped the young mother settle her children either side of her in the little car that would take them into the Ghost Train.

'Are you sure about this?' the mum asked her eager daughters. 'I said just two rides and you might not like this—it might be too scary.'

'It's supposed to be scary, Mum. That's the point,' said the one with a short bob of brown hair. Eight or thereabouts, Kate guessed.

'We'll look after you,' promised the other with a ponytail held up by a butterfly band. A more serious ten.

The woman rolled her eyes at Kate. 'Do you sense "famous last words" too?'

Kate smiled. 'You'll be fine. Just stay in the car and . . . ' She lowered her voice to a throaty rasp, '*Scream!*' With a push, she sent the wagon through the swing doors. The family entered in gales of laughter.

This early in the day the queue for the Ghost Train was short. The quaint Suffolk town of Southwold on the east coast of England was heading out of season and there were few families around to visit the funfair that had set up by the pier for the summer. Kate settled a young couple in a wagon, then some daring pensioners who were giggling like schoolgirls. A healthy number of real shrieks could be heard over the soundtrack of booming laughter and manic screams. The grim reaper puppet dipped his scythe over the heads of the last customers as their car rumbled inside. Beyond the temporary fence enclosing the fair, over the roofs of the brightly coloured beach huts, the sea rippled more brown than blue. Clouds gathered in iron-grey dollops on the horizon. Kate put on her puffa jacket, anticipating rain.

'Everything OK?' asked Neil, coming back with coffee and sandwiches for them both from his mate at the concession three rows along. A slight man, he was nicknamed the Obama of the British seaside, thanks to his resemblance to the president.

'Yes. You've got eight punters inside.'

'Thanks for minding the shop.' He handed her a cappuccino and a goat's cheese on wholemeal. Fairground food had had a makeover since she travelled with her grandparents. Back then it would have more likely been strong tea and a bacon bap.

'Like old times - not,' Kate said archly.

Neil grinned. 'I'm off chips. On a health jag for a marathon I'm running next year.'

Kate studied the Ghost Train, feeling absurdly fond of its over-the-top Halloween approach to fear. She would take that any day over the real terrors that followed her. The train had been her granddad's pride and joy, the jewel in his crown of funfair rides. Neil was maintaining it well, keeping the paint-work bloody and the mechanical parts oiled.

'So how was Mary?' Neil asked, unwrapping his sandwich.

Kate perched on the rail by the cars and sipped her coffee.

'I see.' Neil frowned. 'Do you want me to go and visit her? There are other homes she could afford.'

Kate shook her head. 'No, she's fine where she is. It seems a nice place. She's just away with the fairies most of the time.'

'That must be hard to see.'

'I'm telling myself it's best for her. She doesn't remember anyone dying and she thinks I'm still at school, so that's good.'

Ever tactful, Neil had been holding back the question since her arrival that morning. 'And what *are* you doing now, Katie Girl?'

She was saved from answering by the car exiting the ride. Two giggling, white-faced girls clutched their mum's arms.

'Enjoyed your ride, ladies?' asked Neil, lifting up the bar to let them out.

'That was so cool! I almost screamed when that skeleton fell across the car,' said the one with the ponytail.

'You did—like this!' said her sister, screeching with great vigour.

'So did you.'

'Not as loud as you!'

The mother grinned at Kate. 'You'd think kids would be too sophisticated these days for old rides like this, but that really terrified them—and me.'

'Not old, madam—classic,' said Neil with a wink.

After the last pensioner was released from his car, there was a lull in business. Kate knew Neil would circle round to his question again and prepared her answer. She didn't want to lie to him; he would be very hurt if he found out that she had not told the truth. He thought himself a kind of uncle to her and would never betray a confidence.

'OK, Katie, spill the beans.' He demolished the last of his sandwich, throwing the crust to a gull which took it with princely disdain.

'I made a really bad mistake in Indonesia and it's still haunting me,' she admitted. 'I came back to check Gran was all right but I think it's best if I disappear for a while.' *For years*, she added silently.

He nodded soberly. 'And I take it that you can't explain

54

what kind of mistake this is? Last I heard you were out there with some friend from school?' He was fishing.

'You are truly better off not knowing.'

He reluctantly gave up on that tack. 'So you need to draw on your college fund?'

'Yes.' Kate studied at her hands with their bitten nails. She couldn't remember when she had started gnawing at them—a couple of months ago maybe.

'Your granddad meant the money to remain invested in the business until you needed it. He thought you might go to police training college or university.'

Granddad had always misjudged her, thinking her a genius because she was good at passing exams.

'I think those plans are on hold until I get myself out of this.'

Neil puffed out a breath. 'How much do you need? He had made it sound like you would ask for small regular payments—a kind of grant—not a lump sum. I don't have large amounts of cash knocking around.'

'I know. Would . . . would a thousand pounds be possible? And if I draw on other fairground people elsewhere and leave them an IOU, would you honour it for me?' That way she need never register on any banking database.

'How much are you talking about?' The businessman peeked out from behind the trusting eyes of her friend.

'I'll draw no more than ten thousand over the year, I promise.'

He smiled. 'Katie Girl, I've got twice that amount invested for you.'

'Really?' Kate mentally blessed her granddad for his fore-sight. 'Good to know. I won't run through it all.'

'I know you won't. You're a sensible girl.'

Hardly. 'Can you get it for me today?' Her skin was

prickling, feet itching to get on the move again. She scanned the milling crowds, not spotting anyone out of place but yet she felt she had stayed still for too long.

'The thousand? No problem.' Neil stood up and checked the customers ambling about the fairground. 'I'll head over to the bank. Watch the ride for me. It gets busy at about three-thirty when the schools are out.'

Kate enjoyed doing something as familiar as taking money for the Ghost Train and seeing punters in and out of their seats. The fair had its own special sound landscape—the shrieks of teenagers on the whirligig ride that turned them upside down, the rattle of pellets in the shooting gallery, the amplified music, blending in with the sirens, screams, and cackle of the Ghost Train. It took her back to the years of travelling with her grandparents, years she could honestly say were the happiest ones she had known. She had never really felt she fitted in with the normal students who had enrolled at the YDA, the majority coming from vanilla middle-class backgrounds and decent schools. Hers had been a tutti-frutti upbringing, but she was now plunged into a tub of rocky road. In the agency, she had hidden her uncertainty behind overconfidence and everyone had bought the act. It would have been nice to be able to blame them for that and what happened afterwards, but she had brought all that on herself, like a kid lying under a table and tugging the cloth onto her head, complete with full dinner service. She had wanted that mission so badly to prove she was good enough. Instead it had just proved how useless she was.

When Kate next looked towards the fairground entrance, she noticed two men approaching. White, heavy build, early thirties. Kate's warning instincts flared. Neither looked like they were on holiday: their expression all business. They had the bashed-about faces of ex-boxers or bouncers. Not wanting to serve them, she glanced up the road to see if Neil was returning. No joy.

She moved to the far side of the row of wagons as they reached the steps. 'You want a go?' she asked, her voice husky with fear. Hang it all: she was supposed to be selling terror, not feeling it herself.

They ignored her question, making straight for her.

Run! Kate dived through the swing doors into the pitch black interior of the Ghost Train and headed for the first floor level. Moving swiftly, she used her fingers to guide herself along the wall. They were following: she could hear their curses and tripping behind her intermingled with the screeching audio.

Turning the bend, she pressed the hidden release to make the skeleton pop out of his coffin, partially blocking the way. With any luck, they'd stumble straight into it. The slope was steep to the upper floor but having used the Ghost Train as her playground, she knew it well, not having to think where to find footholds on the slippery surface. Once at the top, she ignored the usual track of the cars and took a shortcut to a glassless window. The grim reaper's black cloak wafted before it: her escape route. It was a tight squeeze but she managed to get her hips through.

'Kate, what the heck are you doing?'

Neil was back and he had given away her position. No time to explain, Kate swung down the robe just as the swing doors on the lower floor burst open and the two men dashed out. They shoved Neil off the platform and dived for her. She used the swing of the robe to kick one in the head, knocking him into his partner, then dropped down to the ground before they recovered. She set off like a gazelle, jumping on the generator parked behind the train, and over the fence that ringed the fair. Taking the steep ramp to the beach, she dashed along the shore, heading towards the pier. She had to know if she was being followed. Risking a glance over her shoulder she saw that they were after her, pushing prams and pensioners out of their path.

The tide was in, washing at the seaweed draped pillars that held up the pier. If she got under the structure there was another way off the beach on the far side. She could then run into town and hide among the houses; the shore was too exposed.

Decision made, she plunged waist-deep into the water, gasping at the shock. A wave almost took her off her feet but she ploughed on, heading for the lifeboat ramp on the far side. The rain she had been expecting arrived, falling in torrents accompanied by a sudden gust of wind. Scrambling up the concrete ramp, wet shoes sliding on the layer of sand, she was instantly soaked on top as well as bottom. Lightning flickered over the white space-age dome of the Dungeness nuclear power station away to the south. Beach-goers were rapidly packing up buckets and spades and making for shelter, giving Kate a crowd in which to mingle. The problem was that no one was heading up the road to the town centre as that was now ankle-deep in rain runoff. She followed the majority into the gift shop at the entrance to the pier.

No, it couldn't be! She had just spotted the YDA team heading towards her from the direction of the fair. How had everyone found her? She was caught between two sets of hunters.

Maybe that would be her way out: let them hunt each other?

Frantic for a bolt-hole, Kate remembered the amusement arcade inside the pier pavilion from her childhood and hoped it had not been given a makeover. She had enjoyed the coin waterfalls, finding the fragile lip of ten-pence pieces trembling on the edge of tumbling too tempting to resist. Mary hadn't liked her wasting her time in such places and so Kate had learned the art of hiding here. Would that still work or was she too big?

No time like the present to find out. Taking off her soaked puffa jacket, she slung it behind one of the slot machines, hoping she would get a chance to retrieve it as it was one of the things she had kept with her from her old life. Worming her way through the crowds, she headed for the Grand Prix driving game at the far end. It looked like the game had been upgraded but the machine was approximately the same size. There was a pillar running down the wall at the back that prevented it being pushed flush with the skirting board. When she thought no one was watching, Kate squeezed into the gap.

Ow. Slim as she was, her hips and chest had grown since she was ten. Parts of her were being compressed in a very uncomfortable way.

Suck it up, Pearl. Ha! Suck it in, more like. Crouching down, she peered through the gap between Grand Prix and its neighbour—a fighter pilot game. The two scary guys—not the same as the ones from The Willows—were first to make it into the arcade, looking far from pleased that they were wet to the skin. One had a phone-sized device in his hand.

Her heart plummeted. *They've got a tracker.* That's how they had found her each time. But she had checked her belongings—she didn't have a phone—barely had anything with her that had come from Indonesia, so how could one be planted on her? Terrified that she was still wearing the bug, Kate sincerely regretted backing herself into a corner. There would be no getting away if they found her. Just now the YDA team looked a much better option. Where were they? She thought they had seen her but maybe that was only her panicked thinking.

The two men muscled their way through the crowd and went right up to the slot machine behind which she had thrown her jacket. Manhandling it forward, the one with the tracker scooped up her coat and threw it down with disgust. He rounded on a large woman in an *I* ♥ *Southwold* T-shirt who was playing the machine next to it, interrogating her brusquely. Kate held her breath. The woman shrugged, not pleased to be interrupted. Finally, when he didn't give up, she pointed to the entrance.

With a jerk of his head, the man indicated to his partner that they should continue the search outside. As they walked away, the woman's eyes flicked to Kate and she smiled. She had been more observant than Kate had thought. Thank God they had been rude, as otherwise the gambler might not have been so ready to protect her.

Kate slumped sideways—the only way she could fit. She ignored the pins and needles spiking up her calves; pain was not a priority; survival was.

The jacket. She had flown out to Indonesia in the autumn a year ago so her grandmother had insisted she wore something warm to the airport. She had never put it on again in the tropical climate of Jakarta. It had hung in her wardrobe and she only snatched it as she fled because it had zip-up pockets. Well-padded, it had been her comforter during many long nights and she had not suspected it had also been her betrayer. She knew a little about surveillance from her training. Tracking devices needed a battery so had to be fairly large—about the size of a credit card—but they could also be very light, hardly noticeable in a heavy jacket. The bug wasn't in any of the pockets so it must be sewn into the lining—Tina could have done that easily enough by going through her things when Kate was out: another little betrayal to add to the much bigger ones. The device's effectiveness usually depended on being able to transmit to a phone signal. In many of the out-of-the-way places Kate had been, that would not have been available, or only intermittently. That and the fact that she had stayed constantly on the move had probably saved her so far.

Kate swallowed against the bile that had risen in her throat. She had been betrayed in so many ways. At least she now knew: that had to be better.

She waited about an hour in her hiding place, feeling safer there than anywhere else for the moment. Her jacket was still lying on the floor. It had been trodden on several times and kicked aside. Fortunately nobody had checked the pockets - all the money she had left was in the one on the breast. Kate kept her nerve by planning her next move. When she judged it time, she would slip out and rip the device from the lining. Now she knew it was there, she shouldn't take too long to find it. The exit from the pier was bound to be watched so she would make her way further up the pier until she found a group of people her age with whom she could mingle. As the night lights came on, it would be easier to leave with them without attracting attention.

'You all right, dear?' The slot machine woman came over to her. 'You've been there an awfully long time. Those men are gone. Are you stuck?'

That was her cue. With a groan, Kate squeezed out, cramped muscles screaming. 'I'm fine, thanks. Just didn't want them to find me.'

'Don't blame you. You can always tell mean ones—men or dogs—by their eyes.'

'Good tip.' Kate shook out her limbs. The woman had a huge squashy handbag with her, now heavy with coin winnings. 'You don't by any chance have nail scissors with you?' She picked up her coat, probing the puffed lining.

'No, but I do have clippers. They any good to you?'

Her fingers found something down by the manufacturer's label. 'Thanks, they'll do nicely.'

Ten minutes later, after a trip to the Ladies to cut out and dispose of the crushed transmitter in the bin, Kate was ready to leave. Her clothes were still damp, underwear clinging to her and jeans cold. She had wrung out the jacket but it would need to be hung up to dry overnight before it would be wearable. If she was going to mix with other people, she had to look unremarkable. Shivering in a T-shirt was not the way to go. That meant buying something from the gift shop where the choice was very limited. Deciding on a navy hoodie with an anchor on the front, she fished in her pocket. The wad of cash was stuck together but she peeled off two notes for the assistant who took them gingerly, jaw revolving as she chewed her gum.

'Sorry—got completely soaked in that rain.'

'So I see.' The girl handed her a few pence change.

The gift shop was right by the entrance to the pier but Kate knew that was the most likely spot to be watched. So tempting though. Neil with her thousand pounds was only a short walk away.

But they'd found her there once.

OK, up the pier it was.

Kate took a circuitous route, looking out for pursuit. The wind on the right side of the pier blew fiercely, on the left the buildings offered shelter, so that was where people congregated. Hoping to find a group her age, Kate made her way up the planks, pretending to take an interest in the old guys and young boys crab fishing. It slowly dawned on her that she had miscalculated. Since she had last gone along the pier it had had a face lift. Posh seafood restaurants and bistros had replaced the chip shops and tacky souvenirs. The tourists who came here in the evening were couples on midweek breaks, parents and children, and pensioners. People her age had obviously decided they would only go as far as the amusements and no further. Plan thwarted, she carried on walking, deciding her best bet would be to attach herself to a large family and hopefully pass as their daughter to any casual observer. Steering round a water sculpture of cogs and little buckets that sprayed half the planks on the windward side, she thought she spotted exactly the right group up at the telescopes: parents and three children who looked like they were packing up from their fishing expedition. She'd stick close to them.

As she passed the last pavilion on the pier, someone stepped out and took her wrist.

'Kate.' The softly spoken name was accompanied by the snick of a handcuff. Taking a panicked look down, she saw the other end was around Nathan's wrist. Not stopping to think, she pulled away bringing their arms up between them. He closed the gap and hugged her, squeezing her against the rail. Bending down to her ear, he whispered, 'Don't.'

'Let me go!' Her voice came out in a hot hiss of fury. 'I'll scream!'

'You don't want to draw attention to yourself. The rest of the team are tailing those men who were following you earlier, but there may be others we don't know about.'

Kate understood. Nathan had stayed behind as a sweeper. She had been an idiot, forgetting the basic procedure she herself had been taught at the YDA. She had been so intent on the threat from the thugs that she had forgotten the more subtle arts of Isaac's trainees. But she couldn't bear to be chained like this: it brought back the worst kind of memories.

'Undo the handcuff.'

'No.'

'Please.'

'Still no.' He reached in his pocket to pull out his phone to report his success. Quick as a snake, Kate knocked the handset from his fingers and had some satisfaction to see it sail over the rail and drop into the water below. Shocked out of his triumph, he glared at her.

Note to self: don't anger the guy you are handcuffed to.

'You little . . . !' He raised his fist. Kate flinched, expecting a blow. His face registered his shock at her reaction. He eased back from her. 'What's wrong with you? I'm not going to hit you! Thump myself, yes, for letting you do that. Thump you? Never.'

Pressed against the fence, she had a cold back and a warm front. It felt too intimate to be squashed up against him like this. *Concentrate on what you have to do to escape.* Kate bit her lip and stared at his dark grey coat. Waterproof mountaineering quality, zips and velcro, pockets galore. She had scant hope of finding the key to the cuffs on first attempt.

'Let me go.' That was all she was going to say, like name, rank, and number for a captured prisoner-of-war.

'And I said no. It's the only way I can restrain you without running the risk of hurting you. Jeez, Kate, you look as though a puff of wind would blow you over.' His free hand tentatively rested on her shoulder. 'What happened to you?'

Being on the run does that to a girl. 'Let me go.'

'This is getting kinda repetitive and I'm not one for listening to repeats. I like to shuffle the playlist.' He waited a beat but she didn't respond. 'OK, this is what we're going to do, Kate. Now that you've stopped me calling for the car to come and fetch us, we'll have to walk to a pay phone, if such analogue technology exists still.' He rolled his shoulders to relieve tension. 'I'll step back from you; you'll join hands with me so no one notices the cuff and we will walk off the pier calmly, drawing no attention to ourselves. Got it?'

'Let me go.'

'Not in this lifetime. Right, I'll assume you still have a brain cell's worth of common sense in your head. Follow me.'

Kate regretted the warmth of his embrace the moment he released her. He filled the silence with a little running commentary of what they were doing.

'Let's imagine we are boyfriend and girlfriend cutely holding hands as we make our way through the crowd. I look happy but you look pissed off, so I guess we must have had a lovers' tiff. Yeah, that's it. What did we argue about? Let me see: your complete pig-headedness about not letting anyone help you. Sound familiar? Now we are going to bypass the amusement arcade and take this route off the pier. Can't see any bad guys hanging about, but that doesn't mean they aren't there so let's put up our hoods. Tricky when handcuffed - should've anticipated. Now we've reached the car park. No pay phone. Damn. I'm going to have to ask someone. Don't look towards the fair: your mate isn't there. Those guys broke his ankle when they pushed him off the ride.'

Neil! 'Is he all right?'

'So she does speak. Yeah, he's in A&E with Raven. She's the girl you met in the cafe in Bath. Last update *before* you nixed my phone was that he was doing OK.'

The short walk handcuffed to Nathan had increased her desperation. She hated his chipper, let's-be-reasonable tone. He had no idea what she was facing. He was escorting her to her death if she let him take her in. Isaac wouldn't harm her but once handed over to the authorities she would be dead within days. The Scorpion connections went to remand centres and police stations. There was nowhere in the world safe from their sting: that was their boast and she knew it was true. The Yodas weren't strong enough to protect her.

She blocked out Nathan's commentary. *Use your brain, Kate. If you aren't going to let yourself be taken in you have two choices: get the key or take Nathan with you.* He wasn't going to make finding the key easy, so just for now it was choice number two.

She assessed him quickly. Far too big for her to take down and she couldn't carry a guy of his height and weight—nearly six feet and built. That still felt so wrong after she had last seen him a fraction of the size. Boys' development was more a series of sprints than the girls' long distance run through puberty. No chance of defeating him, it would have to be persuasion. Feeling desperately short of charm, she searched for what she knew about him. All she could recall was that he had followed her about the YDA a year ago, playing the clown, trying to amuse her. He had been quite sweet then, not this cool operator who was treating her like a joke.

He had a crush on you. The memory returned, pushed aside by so many other things. In her desperate striving to impress her mentors at the YDA she hadn't really paid attention to the affect she had had on other students. She was never cruel, but she could have been kinder. Was there any residual feeling left over for her to use?

'Nathan, look, I'm sorry but can we just stop a moment? I'm exhausted and I need some water—or even better a hot drink.' That at least was true.

'Stop? Don't you get that you're not safe until we've got you under wraps?' Again, the exasperated you-are-your-own-worst-enemy tone.

She wouldn't be safe even then. 'Please. I won't try to run or make a fuss. Just a drink and . . . and a chat. Tell me what's happening.'

'I have to report in.' Was that a hint of a concession?

'I know, but imagine I hid for twenty minutes longer and you found me then. That won't make a difference to your team. Once you report, you'll have new orders and there will be no chance to pause.'

Nathan rubbed the back of his neck then looked down at her. She hoped her face looked innocent and appealing, but maybe she had lost her Cat acting skills? His brown eyes were suspicious, searching her for the catch.

Ramp it up a bit, Kate. She swayed, letting her body feel some of the exhaustion she was keeping at bay by gritted teeth.

Anxiety now joined the other emotions in Nathan's eyes. 'OK. One drink, then I'll phone in. Promise?'

She nodded.

'Your word on that.'

She was going to have to lie: she hated that. 'OK, I promise.'

Chapter 7

Nathan wondered if he was being taken for a ride as he bought Kate a hot chocolate at the cafe on the pier. She needed the sugar boost. A bright place, echoing the beach huts outside, the interior of the cafe was painted primary blue, seagull white, sand yellow. The thick china crockery had happy looking mermaids cavorting with dolphins. Pictures of lighthouses framed with old rope decorated the walls. As it was nearly closing time, they were the last customers. If the owner thought it odd that they didn't let go of each other's hands even to carry their drinks to the table, he didn't say.

Taking a seat, they watched the night approach from the east, stars emerging as the clouds hurried away westwards after the setting sun. It was a bleak view: the darkening North Sea with only a few pinpricks of lights on the horizon: distant container ships heading to Felixstowe. Nathan's mood took a matching dip into gloomy thoughts, like the cold tide eating up the sunny beach. Being near Kate caused it; she seemed to carry her own little atmosphere of quiet desperation that spread to him. Kate had so nearly been killed two days ago. Tina really was dead. He had liked the Indonesian student, or at least the person she had presented herself to be. Death was where they were all heading. The indifferent sea would continue long after they and this pier were gone.

What had got into him? He was supposed to be the happy-go-lucky comedian. *Come on, Nat, now isn't a time for philosophy*. He needed to encourage Kate, make her ready for what came next.

'Looks like the storm has passed,' Nathan said, a feeble attempt to lighten the mood.

Kate began to laugh. Her shoulders heaved, but the sound was the saddest he had ever heard. It morphed into gulping sobs.

'Kate, don't.' Tender feelings were breaking out, as unwelcome as a rash.

She mopped her face with the serviette. 'You're sweet, you know? You always were.'

Careful, Nathan's inner voice warned him—it sounded a lot like Jim. *She wants something. This isn't just about being tired*. 'What went wrong, Kate? Why did you run?'

She spooned cream off the top of the hot chocolate and licked at it—absurdly catlike. She was too thin at the moment but still the prettiest girl he had ever met: flaxen hair, huge hazel eyes, pixie face. He had always thought her like some otherworldly creature, made of finer stuff than everyone else. Much of her distinct sparkle had dimmed but he caught glimpses of it from time to time. Something about her made him want to look after her, gather her to his side, and promise everything would be all right. Damn: he was softening. *Remember that she didn't take the chances she was given. She's not trustworthy. She brought this on herself.*

'Isaac sent a team to extract you. He's been worried about you all year. He would have done anything to help. All it would have taken on your side was one phone call and he would have come and got you.'

Kate tasted her chocolate, using the time to frame her answer. 'I'm grateful he cared enough to do that and I'm sorry I messed up the mission.'

Good: she was sounding more cooperative, even if stiff. The YDA was the best thing in his life and he was sure it would help her. 'It's not too late, you know? When I take you in, Isaac'll give you a chance to give your side of things. He'll sort out the problem with the Indonesians. No one in the British government will want to send you back there.' He squeezed her hand in reassurance. Looking down he saw how small hers appeared engulfed in his. The cuff on her right wrist had had to be closed very tight not to slip off. She had always seemed fragile to him: the ballerina's stature of wiry strength but somehow breakable. She was dancing on that edge, not something he could bear to witness. 'We're your best bet. You must realize that you can't survive out there alone.'

She pinched the bridge of her nose, exhaustion obvious. 'That's the only way I'll survive, Nathan. Why else do you think I've been running?'

He shrugged. 'Maybe you didn't want to face the ones you let down?'

Her expression turned bleak, thoughts somewhere ugly. 'I can see how you might think that but, to be honest, that doesn't matter very much to me. I know my mistake and I have to live with the consequences. I do have a conscience, though you might not believe me.'

'I never said you didn't.'

'No, but you were thinking it. I get why the YDA wants me back: so I can be officially booted out and face some kind of punishment.'

'That's not what this is about.'

'Isn't it? So Isaac is preparing a marching band welcome, is he?'

Nathan shifted uneasily in his seat. What was the plan for Kate? Isaac hadn't said. 'I think he means to sort out the charges against you, make it possible for you continue your life without fear of being accused of a murder you didn't commit. The mistakes you made in Indonesia weren't criminal, were they?'

'No, they were stupid—I fell for the wrong guy.' She shuddered.

'Then there is nothing to hold against you. Isaac blames himself rather than you for what went down there.'

'It wasn't his fault; it was mine.'

'You were used.'

'Exactly. I should've known better than to allow that.'

Nathan swirled the dregs of his black coffee. 'Damien thought you might be back to take revenge.'

Kate's face creased in puzzlement. 'What?'

Clearly Damien had been way off target with that suspicion. It said more about his Cobra friend than it did about Kate, that he could have thought it. 'I didn't agree. Raven thinks you are wounded, returning home to lick your wounds.'

Kate shrugged but there was a flicker of something in her eyes. Recognition of the truth?

'What are you doing here?'

'I apologize for inflicting my polluting presence on England.'

He squeezed her hand in warning. 'No one said you weren't welcome. But you don't risk coming back without a reason.'

Kate sighed. 'I can't manage this.' She pushed the hot chocolate away.

Nathan moved it back. 'Try. You seem to want to survive, so don't do your enemy's job for them by fading away.'

With a grimace she took a quick gulp. 'My granddad died.'

Finally, she was admitting something important. 'I know. I'm sorry.'

'I'm Gran's only relative. I had to check she was OK.'

'I saw her.'

Kate's eyes shot to his face. 'You didn't . . . didn't tell her anything, did you?'

He shook his head. She clearly had a very low opinion of him if she thought he would plague vulnerable old ladies with fears for their granddaughter. 'No. We had a chat and she said I looked like Clark Gable.'

'Who?'

'I had to look him up afterwards. The guy from *Gone with the Wind*. I'm nothing like him. He had this really stupid little moustache.' He touched his top lip and was delighted to raise a faint smile from Kate. 'I promised to take you to the "pictures" and look after you.' His tone turned serious. 'I might not get to do the cinema thing but I do intend to keep you safe.'

Kate rearranged the sugar sachets in the bowl on the table. 'Do you really mean that?'

'Yes.'

'Will you listen to me then?'

Alarms started ringing again. Here came another pitch for pity. 'I don't know. I suppose it depends what you have to say.'

A look of upset and disappointment rippled across her face. Briefly closing her eyes, she turned to him. 'I know you don't trust me but just hear me out. The reason I don't want to come in with you is that it's a death sentence for me. Look at my wrist.' She twisted her right hand free of his left and pulled away the length of the short chain. There was a little black scorpion on her inner arm.

Nathan swore, instinctively wanting to get away, but he had chained them together. 'You're one of them?' Human trafficking, drugs, gang murders: how could she get herself mixed up in that? Had her last shred of decency died? Nathan then realized that Kate's expression hadn't changed. She had expected this reaction. That made him reconsider. Had he jumped to the wrong conclusion?

'No, I'm not one of them.' Her voice was flat. 'Why do you think I'm running if I was?'

'Then why wear their gang sign?'

She shifted her wrist to hide the scorpion. 'You don't understand the first thing about me or what's happened, do you? I'm wasting my breath.'

'Try me.' He was angry now, because he suspected he had reacted badly to the tattoo. What had he been thinking?

'It's a sign to say they'll sting me wherever I go—an over-the-top gesture but oddly effective. Part of their power rests in this kind of mystique. Gang members have the same tattoo somewhere on their body, usually the wrist. I was forced to have mine done.'

'How can you force someone to have a tattoo?' Scepticism still lurked.

'It's easier than you think. You chain the person down,' she rattled the cuff ironically, 'and order it done.' Her eyes drifted to the window. 'You tell your victim that they are now yours for life and no one will want them back after their betrayal. Gani was right about that part.'

'You're wrong.' Nathan felt his blood boil at the mention of Kate's ex-boyfriend. 'We want you back.'

'No, you don't. You want me "solved", tidied away. That doesn't matter. What this means,' she flexed her wrist, 'is that the Scorpions will kill me when they catch up. They've made several attempts already.'

Nathan nodded. He had seen the CCTV footage.

'If you take me in, they'll get to me.'

'That's where you are wrong. You'll be safe at headquarters.'

'You don't get it, do you?' Her tone was almost mocking.

Nathan bristled. 'Get what? You've deluded yourself that these guys are all-powerful. The YDA will protect you.'

'I knew I was wasting my time,' she muttered.

'I've been listening but so far you've not told me anything to change the facts of the situation.'

'OK, how about this for a fact?' Her temper was flaring but it was the rage of an animal caught in a trap, snapping and biting at the bars. 'I think there is a Scorpion contact embedded in the YDA. If you take me there, Isaac will start talking to the police and other officials, doing things the right and proper way; that spy will have time to tell their masters and at the first opportunity I'll be killed. The YDA is a college—not a fortress.'

'A spy at YDA?' Nathan refused to believe it. Even the suggestion made him want to howl with fury. How dare she accuse the people who had spent so much time training her and looking after her! 'But the team are handpicked by Isaac. I'd swear to every one of them being loyal.'

She shook her head, expression grim.

Nathan couldn't bear that she had attacked the best thing in his life, the people who were his true family, the ones who had taken him in. 'The only person with dodgy loyalty is you. Don't start slinging mud at others, Kate, just because you want to hide from what you've done.'

She said nothing but he could see that her lip was trembling. No, she wasn't going to weaken him that way. Jim had warned him she would turn on the waterworks, play the damsel in distress. *Toughen up, Nathan.*

'OK, we're going. I have to report in. I'll ask the guy here if we can borrow his phone. You behave, OK? You gave me your word.'

Silently, she followed him to the counter where Nathan quickly explained what he needed.

'Can you believe it? I dropped my phone in the sea.'

The man was sympathetic and offered his landline for Nathan to use. He waved off payment and went to clear their cups, giving Nathan privacy for his call.

The phone was answered by Isaac's PA.

'Mrs MacDonald, it's Nathan. Can you put me through to Isaac?'

'He's on the other line, Nathan, talking to the rest of your team. They were wondering what had happened to you. You've not answered your phone.'

'I know. It met with an accident.'

'Shall I interrupt the call?'

'Yeah, please.'

There was a brief pause, then Isaac's reassuring deep voice came on the line. 'Nathan, I'm relieved to hear from you.'

Nathan glanced at Kate. She appeared to be examining a glass dome covering a plate of cakes, but from her expression he could tell she was battling tears.

'I've caught up with Kate.'

'Excellent. Is she with you?'

'Yes.'

'Put her on the line.'

The barista walked by with a tray of empties. 'We're closing in five minutes.'

'Thanks. We won't be long.' Nathan passed the phone to Kate. 'Isaac wants a word.'

She shook her head.

'Go on.' He held the phone to her ear. He let Isaac speak for a few moments but Kate wasn't replying. Finally, he took it away. 'She's not very keen on the idea of coming in, sir.'

Isaac sighed. 'I told her she didn't have to worry.'

'Yeah well, I've told her the same. She's been dragging her heels ever since I caught her. That's what happened to my phone. There was a struggle and it got trashed.'

Isaac sucked in a breath. 'We told you, no violence. Be kind to her.'

'It wasn't exactly violence, sir, and the only thing that got hurt was my phone. She knocked it out of my hand and into the North Sea.'

Isaac chuckled, relieved. 'She always was good—does the unexpected. Remember that. Now get yourself a taxi and get back here. I'll call the others into HQ. You'll want to know that they followed the two men who went after Kate at the fair and they're now watching a house in East London. I'll put someone else on to that. I'll see you back here at midnight— that should give you enough time to drive from Suffolk.'

'Sounds a plan. See you later.'

'Be careful.'

'I will. I won't let her get away.'

'I meant be careful *with* her.'

Ending the call, Nathan quickly used one of the numbers pinned on the notice board behind the counter and rang for a mini cab. He arranged for the driver to pick them up at the pier entrance.

'Thanks for the loan of the phone, mate.' He towed Kate to the door.

The barista nodded. 'Your girlfriend all right? She's very quiet.'

'She's feeling a bit sad, that's all.'

The barista winked. 'Cheer up, love. It might never happen.'

From the look of Kate's face, Nathan guessed that it already had.

Kate's silence was getting on Nathan's nerves. She had climbed in the back of the mini cab with no protest and said nothing as Nathan gave the instructions for the drive to central London. The driver had demanded the fare upfront for such a long journey, so Nathan had handed over his YDA credit card before they left the car park. They had been driving for fifteen minutes, heading down a winding road to join the route to London, and Kate still hadn't said a word.

'You OK?' Nathan cursed himself for giving in to the silence first. He had told himself not to take any notice of her sulk.

'No: my wrist hurts.'

Looking down, it was too dark to see if her skin was chafed by the cuff but she had been wearing it a long time. His own wrist was feeling the strain. He had only meant it as a temporary measure but thanks to her chucking his phone in the sea, it had been well over an hour. In any case, where could she go in the back of a moving car?

'I'll take it off if you behave.'

She didn't reply, her little nose stubbornly pointing away from him. He had to give her points for doing snits properly. If only she would admit that this was for her benefit.

Taking the key from the inner pocket of his jacket, he released the cuff from his wrist first and then hers, keeping their hands low so that driver wouldn't notice.

'Better now?'

She dipped her chin once. He supposed it was too much to expect thanks.

The mini cab drew up at a T junction and joined the main road south to London. The driver accelerated. Another five minutes of silence passed.

'You want the radio on?' called the driver over his shoulder.

'No, thank you,' Kate replied quickly before Nathan could.

'Suit yourself.' The driver sounded disappointed. He filled the quiet with tuneless humming. Nathan would have preferred the radio.

'I'm sorry,' Kate announced suddenly and very loudly. 'I can't do this.'

'Can't do what?' Nathan grabbed her hand but she tugged it free. The driver was frowning at him in the mirror. 'We're just going to London as we agreed.'

'But if I move in with you, I won't finish sixth form. You go to college this year, but what about me?'

'What are you going on about?'

'Driver, pull over please. Look, Nathan, sorry but I've changed my mind. I won't move in with you. I need to get my A levels. Mum and Dad will kill me if I drop out now.'

'Don't listen to her. Keep driving.'

'It's fine: you take the cab to London. You'll miss lectures tomorrow if you don't. I'll get a bus back home from the other side of the road. I haven't missed the last one yet. I'll come see you next weekend.'

The mini cab was slowing. 'What do you want me to do, people?' asked the driver.

'Stop,' said Kate.

'Carry on,' said Nathan.

The driver sighed and indicated that he was pulling over. 'Look, I'm not taking anyone somewhere if they don't want to go. You sort out your differences. How old are you, love?'

'Seventeen,' Kate said swiftly. 'I'm kinda worried about that too. I didn't tell my parents where I was going.'

'Right, I'm stopping.'

'She's lying!' Nathan felt his temper rising. He grabbed her wrist again, squeezing tightly.

'Ow, Nathan, that hurts!'

'You'd better let her go, mate.' The driver was now completely on Kate's side. 'There's a bus stop over there, love. You'll be OK?'

Kate opened the door. 'Yes. Thanks. Sorry, Nathan.'

He slid across the seat, shoving his foot in the gap to prevent her slamming the door in his face.

'Do you want me to take you to London or not?' shouted the driver as Nathan raced after Kate.

He didn't pause to reply: she was getting away. Again. Rather than cross the road to the bus stop, she had vaulted the fence and was now running flat out down the side of a meadow, sheep scattering like ghosts into the dark. He jumped the fence, finding some grim humour in the situation. She was so damn good that he was in serious danger of losing her. Pushing for extra speed, he began to close the gap, his long legs an advantage on the flat. Kate leapt a stile at the far end of the field, stumbling as her foot caught in the muddy groove on the other side. She only got five metres into the next field before he caught her around the legs in a flying tackle. Kate fought to get free but he solved that by letting her take his full weight on her back.

'I've had enough of this.' He grappled her arms behind her and put the cuffs on both wrists. Lifting himself up, he heaved her off the ground by taking hold of the material of her jacket between her shoulder blades. 'Every time someone helps you, you make it worse.' He shook her but she refused to look at him. He swore, hating her for doing this to him, and himself for falling for it. 'Any injuries?' No response. 'Then I'll have to check myself.' He turned her round. It was nearly pitch dark so he ran his hands briskly over her arms and legs, cutting off an attempt to knee him in the face as he bent down. 'You don't give up, do you?' He pushed her in the back to start walking. 'Isaac told me to be gentle, but I don't think he really knew what you are like. You are the most infuriating girl alive.'

When they neared the road, Nathan was not surprised to see their mini cab driver had driven off. He had been paid so had no reason to wait to sit through a lovers' tiff.

'That's just brilliant. Miles from anywhere and no lift. We'll have to hitchhike.' Nathan dragged her the last few metres to the curb.

'Good luck with explaining why you've got me hand-cuffed,' she spat at him like a cat doused with muddy cold water. 'First gallant lorry driver on my side and you're toast.'

Nathan let rip a string of German curses—a favourite language for swearing in. His father had served with the British Army in Lower Saxony, so he'd picked up some choice words which he had shared with his son during particularly gruelling training hikes. Kate was right, of course. He pulled her back behind the hedge, giving himself a moment to think. They had to be at least twenty miles from Ipswich, the next big city south of here. His best bet was to walk to a phone box in one of the villages close to the main road. Wouldn't that be fun with Kate in tow? He supposed he could chain her up to something immoveable but he wouldn't put it past her to have lock-picking skills. Given enough time she might get free. Could he leave her attached with her back to a pole, hands cuffed behind her? He could see her in his mind's eye leaping onto the rooftop in Bath without a second thought. She'd probably find a way of shimmying up the obstacle like Mulan with the weights in the Disney film. He just didn't trust Miss Houdini to stay put. If she got free this time, she'd never be found again.

'Let's go,' he growled.

'Where?'

'To the next place with a phone: where do you think? If you don't fancy the walk, well too bad: this is entirely your fault.' That wasn't true. Nathan was blaming himself. Isaac had warned him she would do the unexpected; that was the only predictable thing about her.

'All right.'

All right? What was this? Another trick. *Brace yourself, Nathan.*

She faced up to him, her five foot and a few inches to his almost six. You had to allow that the girl had courage. 'If

I don't make you drag me there, will you consider making a deal with me?'

'Babe, there's nothing you're offering that I want.' What a lie. He started walking, hand gripping her upper arm.

She ignored his insult. 'You don't believe me about the source in the YDA so you need proof. OK, there's an easy way to give it to you. You make the call, tell them where to fetch you, we hide and watch who turns up first: your colleagues or the guys after me.'

Nathan considered the offer. He had no fear that he would lose the deal if a source in the YDA was really the only way they were tracking her. But her logic didn't stack up: the YDA hadn't known where she was before and the Scorpions had got there first twice.

'There's one problem with that: your guys always seem to know where you are, so that's not much of a test.'

'They're not my guys,' she said quietly, 'and the word is *knew*. I found a tracker in the lining of my jacket today.'

'Really? Where is it?'

'In pieces in a bin back at the pier.'

Did he believe her? 'You walked around for months with it on you and didn't notice? They should've caught you long ago.'

'*Should* have. But I moved a lot and there wasn't always a tracking signal in the places I've stayed.'

It was a very convenient excuse. He summoned his inner Jim to prevent gullibility. Maybe all these delays were an elaborate trap so the Scorpions would catch up while he was alone with her. She might think to get away while he put himself on the line to defend her. 'So you won't mind if I check you now?'

She gave a bitter laugh. 'Why all this patting down, Nathan? Still got a thing for me?'

Yes. 'In your dreams.'

'You've no idea who is in my dreams. Go on: search me. I'm clean.'

Under the faint light of the street lamp the other side of the hedge, he could see she was pretty much plastered down the front with mud. He grinned. 'Honey, you are many things, but none of them is clean.'

She snorted, half amused despite herself.

He kept his search strictly professional, taking particular care with the puffa jacket. His fingers found the rip in the seam.

'This where the tracker was?'

'Yes.'

She said nothing more, letting him draw his own conclusions. Her other pockets were empty apart from a little money. He transferred that to his own wallet.

'Stealing from me, Mr Wolf?' she asked.

'Taking precautions, Miss Houdini. You'll get it back. OK, I'm going to do a body search now.'

Gazing straight ahead, she stood very still as he checked her jeans' pockets, then ran his hands along her arms and legs with more care for the details than when he had been checking for injuries. He couldn't help a little flicker of desire as he smoothed the fabric over the fragile cage of her ribs, curve of her waist and hips. This was why a search should be done by someone of the same gender.

Kate was no fool. 'Having fun?'

'Have to get my kicks where I can.' He brushed off his hands as if it hadn't affected him. Neither bought the act but it was better than blushing like a schoolgirl. 'OK, as you said, you are clean. I'll accept the story about the tracker.'

'Gee, thanks,' she said wryly.

'And I'll take the deal. You come to the phone box. We'll make the call and see who turns up. If it *is* the YDA, you'll get in the car with no more fun and games?'

She bit her lip, not liking this extra condition. Now was the test of how much she believed her own story. 'OK. If the Scorpions don't show, I'll try my luck with you.'

'Deal.' He undid one of the cuffs and fastened it back on his own wrist. That had to be more comfortable for her than stumbling along with her arms behind her.

Kate glared at their joined wrists. 'Can't bear to be apart from me?'

'Honey, I'd be heartbroken.'

Chapter 8

They did not have to go far as they found a petrol station a mile down the road with a pay phone. Kate listened as Nathan put in the call. She was beginning to trust him but it would be foolish not to check he kept his word.

'Yes, she did it again, sir. We're stuck on the side of the road near Yoxford. Can you send a car to get us? I don't want her near another mini cab driver.'

Kate could guess Isaac's reaction from the grimace on Nathan's face. She had a gift for annoying people she liked.

'Thanks, sir. Yeah, I'll keep a tight hold on her until then.' He put the phone back on the hook. 'And now we wait.'

What was he thinking? she wondered. She didn't really know him, did she? From the past, she recalled something about him being the YDA kid—the one who had grown up there and never had to apply for a position. That had been handed to him by his adopted father, Sergeant Rivers, the scary guy who kept the Wolves on a short leash. She had to remember that: she was saying things to Nathan that contradicted everything he knew. *Keep things in business mode, Kate. He'll listen to evidence not pleas.*

'Shall we get something to eat?' Kate had noticed there was an ATM inside. She would need some money to tide her over if she was proved right about who was coming for her. 'It might be a good idea to get some cash.'

'You're very cool about this whole hanging-around-wait-ing-for-disaster thing, aren't you?' He sounded more bemused than annoyed now. Decision made, he was content to postpone their quarrel.

'Months of practice. Will you?'

'Will I what?' Nathan held the door open for her, a slightly odd gesture as they were manacled together.

Kate almost laughed, thinking this was in danger of being mistaken as one of those weird stag/hen night pranks: the couple chained together for a lark. 'Get some money. Just in case.'

'I've got about a hundred on me.'

'Please.'

With a put upon sigh, Nathan went over to the machine and fed in his card. 'How much?'

'What's your limit?'

'Two hundred.'

'If you've got that much, then it's better to be prepared. You can always pay it back in if we don't need it.'

Kate gave him full marks for doing as she asked. He was being very reasonable considering what he knew about her. To him, she was the high-risk prisoner he was humouring to persuade her to come quietly. The ATM whirred. Nathan shielded his PIN and waited for the slot to cough up. The crisp bundle of notes was folded away and tucked into a different pocket from his wallet. Good strategy. She never carried all her eggs in one basket either.

'Satisfied?' he asked.

'Thank you.' She noticed, not for the first time, that he had kind brown eyes. He acted tough but he was a sweetheart really, she could tell that about him, quicker to laugh than fight. After Gani's rough treatment, she found his gentleness very appealing. She'd been lucky that it was Nathan rather than one of the others who had stayed behind as the sweeper.

He nodded to the shelves of groceries. 'Ah, I see we 'ave a selection of ze finest English cuisine.' It really was the most ridiculous French accent ever. '*Zut alors!* We 'ave the white bread, the baked beans, and the pot noodles. What would madame like?'

A hug would be nice. A kiss even better. She was surprised by the thought, having never seen Nathan in that light before today. What had he asked? 'Sorry?'

He dropped the accent. 'What do you want to eat? Or do you want something to drink?'

Concentrate, Pearl. 'Um, let's get a hot drink to take away, some biscuits, chocolate and a local map.' She picked up the Ordinance Survey map of the area; they were by far the best for a serious escapee.

Nathan glanced over his shoulder and then up at the security camera. 'How long do you think we've got?'

'If the Scorpions are coming from London, then about an hour and a half. Depends how many speed limits they break.'

Working now as a team, Nathan held the basket while she selected some groceries to tide them over. He raised a brow when she added a pint of milk, teabags and some bread. 'What do you want with them?'

'Think about it: we arrived on foot. What are two young people doing at a service station late at night? You always need a story just in case. Plausible excuse is that we live nearby and been sent out for emergency supplies. Maybe we just got back from holiday to an empty fridge.'

'Then why the map?'

'You're right. Perhaps I should put this back?' She really didn't want to sacrifice such a valuable tool to keep her cover.

He lifted the basket out of reach. 'It's OK; just spin the

story a little more. We've arrived on holiday here. Car broke down up the road. Parents waiting for roadside rescue while we stock up.'

'So what: you're my brother now?'

'Yeah, little sis.' He walked over to the till and placed the basket down.

The assistant looked up from his portable TV. His Chelsea shirt stretched over a sizeable belly; it bumped into the edge of the desk when he reached to pull the groceries closer. 'Petrol?' He glanced over at the empty forecourt.

'No, just this—and two coffees, please. How did Dad want his?'

'White, no sugar. Same as Mum,' Kate said quickly, taking her cue. She huddled to his side so the handcuff was hidden.

The man programmed the drinks machine and began ringing up the goods, trying to make sense of his customers. 'Walked here, did you?'

'Yeah, the car broke down. Heap of junk.' Nathan was doing well for a Wolf; he had injected just the right tone of disdain.

'I've got numbers for a local tow service.'

'Thanks, but the RAC are coming.'

'Okeydokey.' The assistant put the drinks in a cardboard carrier. 'We're open all night if you need anything later.'

'Good to know.' Nathan handed over the cash, pocketed the change, then picked up the plastic bag. Kate took the drinks.

Even before they walked out, the man was back to watching his programme.

'Well done,' Kate whispered as the door bumped shut behind them.

'For what?'

'You played that just right.'

'How do you know?'

'He's not watching us. When you get it wrong, they watch.'

They left the lights of the forecourt and headed up the road, consistent with their story that they were returning to a broken down car. When she judged they had gone far enough, Kate stopped.

'OK, now we cross and find somewhere to keep the petrol station under surveillance.'

Nathan shrugged. 'It's your party.'

After a quick survey of the roadside, probing the dark hedge with a stick for ways through, Kate hit the jackpot. An old World War Two pillbox, a gunner's lookout, lay half buried in the undergrowth at the edge of the field. Hexagonal, low roofed, and made of concrete, it had tiny slot windows that gave a clear view of the petrol station. Stamping down the brambles, she located the entrance. Local vandals had kicked in the door so they could crawl inside.

Nathan ducked his head under the lintel and drew back. 'Smells of piss.'

'Welcome to my world.' Kate pulled him in. 'Believe me: you can put up with anything when you have to.'

'Mind the floor: I can hear broken glass under my shoes.'

'No surprise there.'

'Do you want to go back over and buy a scented candle?' he joked. 'I think I saw one in the souvenir section: Suffolk beeswax.'

'Great idea: find a perfect hiding place then light it up so anyone can see.'

'Might be worth it to protect my delicate nose.' For all his banter, Nathan had moved into the pillbox with the efficient movements of someone trained to survey his environment. Kate had felt the pull on the manacle as he checked the dimensions and swept the floor with his feet, searching for obstacles that would hamper a quick escape.

Kate was hardened to most things but she couldn't bring herself to sit on this ground. 'Let's wait by the entrance. We can move to the window when there's something to see.'

'Good idea.' Exiting the dank pillbox, Nathan dragged a log out of the ditch and placed it across the doorway. It was wet, but a wholesome damp of rain and mud, not the stuff inside. Kate listened to the rustle of the plastic bag and then felt something placed in her free hand. 'Have some milk.'

'Don't really like it.'

'I'm not carrying it and it would be a shame to waste it.'

'OK then.' She was thirsty but drinking coffee didn't really help. She was tense enough as it was without shovelling more caffeine into her system.

'You need it.' Nathan had started on one of the coffees. 'You're really thin. Ever since I saw you today I've been wanting to feed you up.'

'Fattening me for the kill?' She regretted the joke even as she said it. 'Sorry, that's unfair. I know I'm in bad shape. Money's been tight.'

'You'll be OK from here, I promise.'

'You can't promise that, Nathan, but thanks for the thought.'

They sat listening to the night sounds. An owl hooted. Cars swished by on the main road behind them, about one every minute or so. No one slowed to enter the petrol station.

'What time do you think it is?' she asked.

Nathan checked his watch, dial lighting up, a little firefly glow in the dark. 'One thirty.'

'Do you still have it?'

'What?'

'My watch.' Kate feared the answer. She had carried that with her when she had left so many other things behind.

'It's with the rest of your stuff in the bag. That must be at HQ by now.'

One less thing to worry about: it hadn't been lost or thrown out. 'Good.' The YDA would keep it for ever if necessary. She could dream of a day when it would be safe to collect it.

Nathan scuffed the twigs at his feet. 'Why keep a broken watch? Was it his?'

'Whose?'

'Gani Meosido's.'

The boy had a way of springing a punch on you when you least expected it, Kate thought. 'Definitely not. He wouldn't have worn anything like that—Rolexes, or at least good knock-offs, were his style.'

'Then it belonged to . . . ?'

'To me.'

He sighed, as if disappointed in her evasion.

'No, really. Before that it belonged to my father. It's the only thing of his I have.'

'Not much use broken though, is it? We could get it fixed for you.'

He was still trying to sweeten the pill for her, persuading her that the YDA was her best option. 'Don't do that.' She was going to have to explain. 'Look, it broke when he was killed. Motorbike on a wet road. I kept it because of that. The time he died.' That sounded macabre, she knew, but she hadn't meant it like that; it had been her tribute, a vow to remember that life was short and maybe even shorter than you suspected.

'OK.' Nathan cleared his throat awkwardly. Kate supposed that her words had been a bit of a conversation stopper.

'So, Nathan, how is everyone at the YDA?'

'You want to know?' His voice echoed his surprise.

'Why wouldn't I?' Kate felt a little hurt that he assumed she no longer cared for the people she had trained alongside.

'I just . . . yeah, why wouldn't you want to know?'

90

Nathan squeezed her hand in apology. 'They're good, thanks. Remember Kieran?'

'Mr Computer Brain? Yeah, I saw him in Bath, didn't I? How is he?'

'Really well. The girl you met—Raven—has taken him in hand and he's never been happier.'

'Aw: sweet.'

'She's really good for him. And Damien—well, Damien's the same guy.'

'What? Cold and calculating under his charm?'

Nathan shrugged. 'He can be, but he's not really like that, you know? That's just the job.'

'No, I don't know. We never got on.' Kate thought back to those days at the YDA. They seemed impossibly far away, separated by the chasm of the events in Jakarta. 'We were sent on a mission once, did you know that? We were supposed to keep an eye on the American ambassador's daughter at a gig. There were rumours of bad people circling her, drug-pushers. Didn't work out.'

'Yeah, he said you almost got him thrown out of the YDA.'

'Did not! I just dragged him out of there when he tried to protect her by chatting her up! He totally took it too far and they were wrapped around each other like octopuses before I knew it. The Secret Service guys looked like they were going to kick the stuffing out of him.'

Nathan laughed. 'So that's what really happened! Yeah, that sounds like him. He has a very creative approach to how he interprets his missions.'

'What about your other friend, Joe Masters?'

'He's taking a break. Visiting his parents in America.'

'I always liked Joe.'

'He always said you were the best of the Cats.'

Another person she had let down. 'That was kind of him, but wrong. He was pretty good himself.'

A car slowed down. Nathan put the drinks to one side and tugged her wrist to follow him inside the concrete bunker. They knelt by the little letterbox sized slot that looked out on the forecourt. A black Toyota had parked in one of the bays reserved for shoppers.

'Not our team,' admitted Nathan.

The front doors opened. Kate let out a hiss of breath, scared even though she had been right. It was the two guys from the residential home incident—the Indonesian man and the thug.

'It's the Scorpions.'

'Yeah, I recognize them from the CCTV.'

The men went inside the shop and had a talk with the Chelsea-shirted assistant. They could see through the brightly lit window that he was shaking his head. One of them produced a photo and handed it over. The guy scratched his chin, took a glance at the men, gauging the threat they posed, then gave a reluctant nod. She didn't blame him: he was on his own in an isolated service station in the middle of the night. She wouldn't ask for trouble either. He jerked his head down the road in the direction she and Nathan had walked when leaving the garage. The men took back the photograph and left quickly in their car, following his directions. Back in the shop, the assistant's hand hovered over the phone as he contemplated reporting what had just happened. Finally he let his arm drop, giving in to his second thoughts of not making trouble for himself.

Kate felt a tug at her wrist and the cuff came off, leaving her free. She rubbed the skin. 'Thank you.'

'I wouldn't have believed you without seeing it for myself.' Nathan sounded devastated, voice a faint echo of his normal tone.

'I know. I understand.'

'I have to tell Isaac.'

'Yes, but please wait until I've got away.'

They retreated into the fresh air. Kate's mind ran through the possibilities. She would ask Nathan for some money and then lie low for a few weeks, head up to the fair in Lichfield. After that she would hook up with some fairground folk going abroad and tour for a while.

But Nathan had other ideas. 'You aren't going away.'

Uh-oh. Trouble. 'Can't you see I have to? I'm not joking about the death threat.'

'I know. But I can't let you face this alone.'

Of all the stupidly brave people in the world, he had to be the worst! 'This is no time to play hero, Nathan. You go back and sort out the YDA. I'll be fine.'

'Kate, you've been almost killed twice in two days: that's not a definition of fine.'

'But you can't come with me. You're still a member of the YDA. Isaac's ordered you to bring me to him and I'm not coming in until that leak in the YDA is discovered and plugged.'

'I know.'

'So you can forget about dragging me over to your mates when they arrive to collect us. I'll fight you.'

'I get it.'

'We had a deal.' She stopped as she realized he hadn't been denying anything she said. 'You what?'

'I understand. I'm not going back on my word. I'll let you run but only if I come with you.'

Chapter 9

Nathan would have laughed at Kate's surprise if he hadn't been still recovering from the shock of discovering she had been right about the traitor in the YDA. Kate stood in front of him, chin raised, hands on her hips, trying to look intimidating. He found the stance strangely adorable, even though there was a high risk she'd kick him where it hurt most if he told her.

'You can't come with me,' she said fiercely.

'I can and I will.'

'But you'll tell Isaac where we are.'

'Give me some credit for intelligence, please.'

'Then he'll boot you out of the YDA for disobeying orders.'

'He might.'

'Nathan!'

'Kate!' he echoed.

'Aaargh!'

From the sound it seemed Kate had just kicked the log they had sat on earlier. At least it hadn't been his essentials. It gave Nathan some little satisfaction to find he was annoying her as much as she did him. This was a crap night: he was damp, devastated, exhausted, fighting Kate, but at least he wasn't the only one suffering.

'You're an idiot. I'll just go,' she announced, making a good attempt at flouncing off.

'You have no money. I have around three hundred.'

She stopped and turned on him. 'Give me back my fifty quid.'

'No.'

'Thief.'

'And your point is . . . ?'

'I hate you.'

'Good to know.' He glanced over at the garage. 'Look, do you want to argue or shall we get going? My team will be here soon and if I'm going to ignore my orders, I'd prefer not to explain myself to them right now.'

Kate gave an exasperated huff. 'You're certain about this?'

He had won. 'Yes.'

'All right, all right: let's go then. Ruin your career, why don't you. I can't stop you. We'll find a barn or something. Sort things out in daylight.'

Nathan gave a dry laugh. 'This isn't the nineteenth century, Kate. The countryside round here isn't full of picturesque barns stuffed with hay. The farming is industrialized—plastic-covered round bales and locked storage units. Probably alarms and cameras to protect the premises.'

She raked a hand through her hair. 'Yeah, I forgot. It's just that I slept in lots of barns in Romania.'

Nathan tried not to think too much about that. The idea of her sleeping rough across the length and breadth of Europe gave him the chills.

'So, er . . . ' She swallowed her pride. 'What do you suggest?'

Finally, she was showing some sense. 'Give me that map.'

She handed it over. Nathan angled it so some of the street-light fell on the surface. 'I think we're here. Yeah, I was right. I know a place we can stay for a while.'

'Where?'

'Holiday cottage.' He pointed to a coastal hamlet a few

miles away. 'It belongs to Damien's uncle. I went there two years ago. It's empty most of the year.'

'Won't Damien know where we've gone?'

'I don't think he'll suspect that I've run off with you. He'll assume you gave me the slip and I'm chasing you again. When he does work it out, he won't give us away without first finding out what's happening.'

'You sure? It's my life you are betting on your friend's character.'

'I'm sure.'

Kate was still undecided. He tried to make the offer more attractive. 'There will be hot water, a bath, a proper bed, a change of clothes. It really is the last place your enemies will look for you.'

She rubbed her face wearily.

'Please Kate: trust me.'

Letting her hands drop, she stood up straight again. 'OK. How far?'

'Ten miles.'

'It would be.'

'But on an OK surface. It's a minor road but better than going cross country.'

'And we can get there before we're spotted?'

'We just need to cross the main road again and take the next turn-off to the north. If we walk quickly, we should get away before everyone stops looking for us in the London direction.'

Kate had made her decision. 'Fine.'

Nathan held out his hand.

She took a step back. 'You're not going to cuff me again, surely?'

'No, I was just going to offer to help you over the ditch.'

She laughed darkly. 'Sorry. Old habits.'

Nathan jumped over and was pleased when she accepted a

hand up the bank. His mind was in a spin but at least there was one fixed point: he was going to help Kate as he had promised. Right now, finding her shelter was his number one priority, even before the YDA. The Yodas could look after themselves; Kate needed him.

'I think I've a blister the size of Suffolk on my heel,' Kate grumbled.

'Not much further now.' It was easier to ignore his own tiredness while he was aware that Kate had to be so much more exhausted than him. They were walking down a narrow road that led to the bird sanctuary where Damien's uncle, an avid twitcher in his spare time, had bought his cottage.

'Are we going to break in?' Kate asked.

'I know where he keeps the key.'

Kate chuckled darkly. 'Don't you just love the country?'

The moon had risen in the small hours, giving them a little light to navigate the tree-shadowed roads. Nathan glanced sideways. Kate's face was mysterious, shuttered against everyone, a faint wash of silver over her cheeks, her eyes unfathomable. Damien was right: she had changed, but Nathan was beginning to suspect that the alteration had been into something even more interesting than the bubbly, careless girl she had been before.

A row of roofs appeared ahead, a blacker ridge against the dark sky.

'I think we're here,' he announced.

Kate stopped to listen. 'I can hear the sea.'

'It's just over there to our left.'

A hoot echoed in the darkness.

'And an owl.'

'This is a bird sanctuary.'

'I can't hear any people.'

'There are plenty about during the day. People come for

97

miles to visit Minsmere, where the birds are. I think there's also a visitor's centre and tearoom.'

'Now you give me the good news!' Amused, she grinned up at him. 'If you'd promised cake, I'd not have started moaning about blisters.'

He felt a wash of tenderness for her. 'I'll buy you cake tomorrow, but just now, unless there are other people staying in the fishermen's cottages, there will be no one else around this late.' He took her hand. 'Come on.'

He was pleased that she didn't refuse. They had spent so many of the last few hours hand-in-hand, he wanted to continue the contact. It felt natural.

'If anything goes wrong, Nathan, and I don't get a chance, I just want to say thank you,' she said softly.

'Nothing's going to go wrong. Careful now: there's gravel up to the back door. Let's not make too much noise. I'd prefer our arrival to pass unnoticed.' They walked cautiously down the path to the rear of the house. He reached up and felt along the lintel. An old key lay there, just as it had when he'd stayed a few years back. Kate stifled a giggle. He could tell she found the owner's trusting nature hilarious. With a flourish, he put it in the lock and turned. Easing the door open, he ventured in, checking the kitchen was empty. Anyone staying would surely have taken the key inside, so he was fairly sure the cottage would be unoccupied. Kate followed him, closing the door behind her.

'Wait here.' Without turning on any lights, Nathan walked through the living room and then upstairs to the tiny bedroom and bathroom. All clear. He came back down, taking less care of noise now he knew they were alone. 'It's fine. Let's close the curtains, and then we can risk some light.'

Kate locked the back door while Nathan wrestled the blind down over the sink. The stupid thing didn't seem to want to move.

'Let me.' Kate took over the strings and gave it a sharp yank sideways. The blue blind rattled obediently down. 'I obviously have the magic touch.'

She absolutely did. Nathan turned on a table lamp. 'We'll keep the main lights off. With any luck, no one will notice we're here.'

Kate sat down on a chair and unlaced her shoes. She placed them by the back door then took off her socks. 'You can't imagine how good that feels.' Her small toes wriggled in the fresh air.

'You can wash your stuff if you like,' said Nathan, his head in a cupboard as he worked out what he could offer by way of food and drink. 'There's a machine over there.'

'That would be wonderful.' Kate pulled her hoodie off, then paused. 'Did you say something about spare clothes?'

'Go look in the bedroom.'

She disappeared upstairs and he could hear her opening drawers and moving about. He filled the kettle, having found the teabags. By the time the water had boiled, she was back, swathed in a huge dressing gown.

'Oh yeah,' he smirked, 'Damien's uncle is an extra-large.'

She stuffed her clothes in the machine. 'Tell me something I don't know. Damien really should have a chat to him about security. Anyone could just walk in here.'

'He wouldn't mind. Uncle Julian is a fanatical bird watcher. He figures only people like him come down here; it's not as if it's on the way to anywhere.' Kate snorted and poured some liquid into the soap dispenser. 'Hang on a second: I'll put my stuff in with yours. I don't have a change of clothes either.' He undid the button of his jeans and stepped out of them.

Kate shielded her eyes. 'Jeez, Nathan, go get a robe.'

'You don't have to look, sweetpea.' Turning his back to her, Nathan carried on stripping off, then wrapped a towel around his waist. It was only a hand towel, so didn't do a very good job. He scooted the clothes across the floor to her. 'Back in a moment. Pour the tea if you don't want it too strong.'

He dashed upstairs, wondering why he had done that. He'd wanted to tease her, he supposed. Had to be the tiredness making him a little reckless. He found some spare clothes in the dresser, suited to birding. Nathan pulled on a pair of canvas trousers with zips at the knee to convert them to shorts. He secured them at the waist with a belt. An ochre shirt completed the outfit. Maybe he'd start a new trend for twitcher chic? He glanced in the mirror. Maybe not.

When he returned to the kitchen, the washing machine was tumbling away and two mugs of tea steamed on the table. Kate had found some UHT milk and sugar. She was sipping hers thoughtfully, watching the clothes slosh in circles.

'Hungry?' he asked.

'Not so much. Maybe something light?'

He emptied the groceries they had bought at the garage onto the table. 'Biscuits or toast?' He opened the fridge. 'There's butter in here and I saw honey in the cupboard.'

'Biscuits are fine. We can have toast for breakfast.'

He sat opposite her and offered her a chocolate chip cookie. They ate in silence, lulled by the whirr of the machine. Nathan watched her out of the corner of his eye, wondering what she was thinking. Her face was sad again, hazel eyes distant.

The now familiar urge to comfort her was back. 'It's going to be OK.'

She mustered a smile. 'Yes, of course.' Her sleeve fell back as she raised the mug to her lips, revealing the scorpion on her wrist. She shook the material back down. 'Thank you for bringing me here.'

'It was the least I could do. Now, if you've finished your tea, shall we sort out where we're sleeping?'

'I'll take the couch,' she said quickly.

'No, you take the bed upstairs.'

'It's a two person sofa, Nathan: you'll never fit.'

'I'll put the cushions on the floor. That's how I slept when I stayed here with Damien. You need to rest.' And he didn't want her to be left alone downstairs in case . . . well, just in case.

'But . . .'

'No. You are my guest.'

'This isn't your cottage.'

'It's more mine than yours.'

'That's false logic.'

'I invited you here.'

'It's Damien's uncle's, bless his innocent cotton socks.'

'And if he were here, he also would insist a lady sleeps in the bed.'

'You . . . you are the most stubborn person I've ever met.'

'Pot calling kettle black?'

She huffed a laugh. 'Possibly.'

'Then go on up. You can have a bath if you like. I'll have one after you. I turned on the water heater.'

'Bath? That sounds like heaven.'

He knew the thought would distract her from their argument. 'Don't hog the tub for too long.'

'I'm going.' She put her mug on the draining board.

'If you hear the door, don't worry: it'll just be me having a scout around to see who else is here.'

'Fine.' Thoughts already fixed on a hot soak, Kate vanished upstairs. At least she was learning to trust him and not asked for details of where he was going.

Nathan waited until he heard the water running, then slipped outside. Kate had remembered not to turn on the main light in the bathroom. He could see her dark silhouette moving against the frosted window as she reached up to pull the blind. Walking round to the front of the cottages, Nathan counted the cars. The only other occupied house appeared to be the one at the other end of the row. A Range Rover with mud-splashed sides sat in the little driveway; lights out in the building. The other two cottages had no vehicles, which was an almost sure sign they were empty. Only lunatics and those running for their lives would come here on foot. Nathan decided he had to be the lunatic in their pairing. He had just thrown over years of training and loyalty, putting Kate's needs before the YDA. Jim was going to be furious and his mum, Maisie, disappointed. As for Isaac's reaction, that was not something Nathan wanted to contemplate. He would have to find a way of contacting Jim or Isaac without involving anyone else in the YDA. Until the leak had been found, he would have to go outside procedures.

Life would be so much easier if his phone hadn't ended up in the sea. He hadn't realized how much he had come to rely on it. Tomorrow he would borrow a mobile and ring home rather than headquarters; that way his information would be secure. He couldn't help that his parents would have a night of worry about him. Regrettable, but they would survive.

Alone in the dark, his brain circled round to the question he had been avoiding. Who was their traitor? It had to be someone who had been with them at least a year and had access to mission data. Kate's job in Indonesia had been common knowledge to the students because they had all got to know Tina. That meant any of the older recruits could be passing on news to someone outside. However, the truth had to be faced: it was unlikely that a student could have acted so fast tonight unless they were one of his team, Kieran or Damien.

No, that was absurd: he would trust both of them with his life.

That left the staff. It was hard to believe any of them would risk one of their own. They were nothing if not devoted to their trainees, even if that loyalty was exhibited in a brand of tough love by trainers like Jim and Isaac.

Yet he had seen the evidence with his own eyes. The Scorpions had been there to sting first.

Maybe he had been misled by that? Maybe it wasn't a person but a listening device or some kind of spyware that Tina had managed to plant at headquarters that had tipped them off. He preferred that theory. He would suggest that to Kate in the morning.

Nathan walked as far as the cliff edge and looked out to sea. The nuclear power station was visible on his right, much closer here than at Southwold. The white dome lit up at night, a jarring note in this wild place, a space-age egg. A ship's light twinkled on the horizon, marking where sea met sky. He took a deep breath. Yes, this was a good place to bring her, safe, like a nest for them to hide in while they sorted out the mess. He might have destroyed his career at YDA with his insubordination but he was secure in the knowledge that he had made the right choice.

'The only choice,' he added under his breath, turning back to the house where he had left Kate.

Chapter 10

Kate woke to the smell of coffee and toast. Opening her eyes, she saw Nathan standing in the doorway with a tray, tea towel over his arm.

'Breakfast is served, my lady.'

Amused by his butler act, she sat up, then remembered with dismay that she must look a wreck. Her hand went to her hair, pushing the straggly bits out of her eyes. Nathan smiled, one eyebrow arched knowingly, and put the tray on her lap.

'Here: I thought you needed spoiling. Don't get used to it though.'

Kate rubbed her eyes. 'What time is it?'

'Ten thirty.'

'Wow. I don't think I've slept in so late for ages.' She stretched, luxuriating in the unfamiliar comfort of clean cotton sheets, warm covers, soft mattress, and safety.

'No rush. Eat that and come down when you're ready.' Nathan turned to leave. 'I'll just go out and see if I can borrow a mobile from someone.'

From semi-awake, Kate lurched to full attention. 'No!' The tray rattled. He put out a hand to steady it.

'Don't panic: I'm not phoning HQ. I was going to phone home to call off the search for me.'

Sense of safety vanishing out of the window, Kate picked up the tray and swung her legs out of the bed. 'I can't stop you, but if you're going to do that, then I'd better get going.'

He took the tray from her. 'Get back in bed.'

'I'm serious. You don't know these people like I do.'

'I know my parents. You can trust them.'

'No, I can't. Sorry, but I just don't have your faith in others. They might say something—give me away without meaning to.' She wrapped the dressing gown over the T-shirt she had slept in. 'I'll get my clothes and then I'll hitch out of here. Just give me an hour's head-start, please.'

Nathan dumped the tray on the floor and grabbed a fistful of her robe. 'Look, wait a moment. Your clothes aren't even dry.'

'I'll live.' She jerked the material, but he wasn't letting go.

His face took on that familiar exasperated look she had the peculiar talent of provoking. 'OK, OK, you eat your breakfast and I promise I won't go anywhere. We'll talk first and I'll explain what I've been thinking.'

Kate stopped tugging to get free. 'You promise?'

'I'll even stay where you can see me. Get back under the covers and enjoy your breakfast.' He waited. 'Please.'

Warily, half expecting him to bolt when she returned to the bed, Kate took off the dressing gown and pulled the quilt over her cold feet. Nathan picked up the tray and placed it on her lap. He then sat on the upright wooden chair by the window.

'Second attempt. Breakfast in bed,' he said wryly.

'Thank you.' Kate felt terrible putting him in this position. She was rapidly learning that he always tried to do the right thing by everyone, even giving a chance to the girl about whom he only knew terrible things. She now had the dubious honour of being the bad girl to corrupt the YDA's most loyal boy scout. 'I appreciate what you're doing for me.'

'You're welcome.' He tugged the curtains aside, filling the room with sunshine. 'It's a beautiful day. You've got a view of the sea, did you know?'

'I'll enjoy it later, but just now I think toast and honey calls louder.'

Nathan rocked back on the chair as she made inroads to the breakfast he had brought her. She still hadn't quite adjusted to the new Nathan—the sprouted-to-nearly-six-foot version. He was a rare mix: decent instincts, comedic skills wrapped up in a seriously gorgeous body. She entertained herself thinking how quickly he must have grown out of his trousers and shirts when he hit his growth spurt. She imagined it like one of those fast-forward time-lapse nature films of plants, David Attenborough narrating. Nathan speeded up would be like watching a mini version of the Hulk, apart from the green skin, bad haircut, and anger.

Perhaps that was a thought better kept to herself.

'This is the best toast I've ever eaten,' she said instead.

He grinned, eyes full of laughter which seemed never far from the surface. 'Yeah, I'm a natural at it. Have to warn you: anything more complicated is above my pay grade. The thought of tackling an omelette makes me shudder. Fortunately, Mum is an excellent cook.'

Kate had a vivid memory of her gran cooking in their trailer home, whipping up amazing meals on a two-ring hob while the view outside the window changed each week. She had been spoilt once too. 'Tell me about them, Jim and . . . what's your mum's name?'

'Maisie. Jim and Maisie Rivers.'

Kate sipped her coffee. It was the real deal and smelt heavenly. 'Your dad always scared the living daylights out of me.'

'I'd like to say that underneath it he's an old softie, but he's really not.'

Kate choked on her coffee. 'I see.'

'Mum's a sweetheart. They kind of balance each other out.'

Kate trawled back through the little she knew about him from before. 'They adopted you, didn't they?'

'Yes.'

'But you didn't change your surname. How did that happen?'

Nathan shrugged. 'I thought everyone knew.'

Kate realized that she had not paid much attention to the lives of other students at the YDA, too wrapped up in her vain attempt to impress. 'I don't. Sorry.'

'No need to apologize. Why should you know?'

Because I stupidly missed out on knowing an amazing boy when I had the chance.

'I'd like to know—if you want to tell me.'

'I was abandoned as a baby in a public park.'

'Oh.' She'd walked into that one.

'Yeah, I guess my mother must have been very young and scared to do that. She left a note with me—just the name she had chosen for me: Nathan Hunter. I often wonder why she bothered when she didn't give me anything else.' Some of the sunshine in his expression dimmed; this wasn't easy for him to talk about, despite his matter-of-fact tone.

'Perhaps she felt she didn't have a choice,' Kate said carefully. Her recent experience seeing desperate girls trapped in the trafficking network had taught her that terrible situations could happen to anyone. 'She guessed someone else would give you the chance she couldn't.'

Nathan shook his head, eyes without their sparkle. He had clearly made up his mind long ago; she could understand his resentment.

He just didn't know what it was like to see no escape. He had had a bad start, true, but after that he had been given a good break being placed with the Rivers. 'She might have been scared of her family—so desperate she couldn't think straight.'

He fixed his gaze on the view outside. 'You don't know she was like that. She could've just not cared.'

'Then why name you? Why leave you where you would be found? I hate to make the grim point but there are other ways to get rid of a baby, places no one will look.'

He scratched at the windowsill. 'I suppose. I guess I hadn't really thought about that. And yeah, I worked out that she was probably a child too at the time.'

'Maybe younger than you are now.'

'That's . . . that's hard to take in.'

'I feel sorry for her; don't you? You've had a good life with decent people and she won't know that. She'll worry what happened to you.'

'You're right.' His expression brightened. 'Funny really: I've always judged my biological mother without seeing that moment from her side. You know, Kate, I think you might be good for me.'

Kate put her empty mug on the tray. 'I'd not rush to that judgment about me either, Nathan. I don't think I'm that good for you. Your parents and Isaac would certainly say I'm poison. And my relationship with my own mother is a disaster. You shouldn't be throwing away your career for me.'

Ignoring her warning, he stood up and took the tray. 'Why don't you get dressed and meet me downstairs?'

'You're not . . . ?'

'No, I'm not going out to call anyone. We work on this together, OK? You don't go tearing off on your own and I won't drop any nasty surprises on you.'

Kate waited until he had gone before getting out of bed a second time. She had been prepared to put on damp clothes in an emergency but not now. She opened the drawers where Damien's uncle kept spares. Right at the bottom she came across a pair of shorts and a smaller T-shirt. Looking at the tags she found labels with Damien's name on them. Aw, cute. They had to be old school kit from a few years back, left behind when he grew out of them. She wriggled into the shorts and changed T-shirt. She laughed when she saw the school logo on the front: Applewood Primary. Calling into the bathroom for a wash and toothbrush (Damien's uncle thoughtfully stocked spares), she then headed downstairs. Nathan was doing the dishes. She stood in the doorway, hand on one hip.

'What do you think? Would a primary school have me?'

He turned round and almost dropped the mug he was holding. 'Where did you find them?'

'Must be an old set of Damien's.'

'You look great.'

'They're a bit tight.' She twisted to see how stretched the material was over her butt, teasing him a little. 'And the top's turned crop.'

Nathan grinned. 'As I said, you look great.'

She felt absurdly pleased by his flattery. She hadn't flirted for so long it was an odd feeling, like lemonade bubbles in her stomach. 'So, let's plan our next move.' She picked up the tea towel to dry up the crockery he had stacked on the draining board.

'Fine.' He tipped away the sudsy water. 'Let's start with what we agree on. We agree there is a leak in the YDA.'

'Yes.'

'We agree we need to keep you out of the hands of officials until we can be sure you are safe from the Scorpions.'

'I'll never be safe.'

'OK, little edge of disagreement there, but basically we are on the same page. I was wondering last night if the leak might be technical. I'm struggling to imagine anyone inside betraying us. Why would they?'

'Money, blackmail, fear, love, loyalty.' Kate listed the reasons. 'Whoever it is, their motive will show that they have something that matters more to them outside the YDA.'

'As you did?'

'Yeah, as I stupidly thought I did. They got to me; why not someone else?'

He dried his hands on a towel. 'OK, that's possible, but so is my suggestion.'

'I thought Isaac had the whole place regularly swept for bugs?'

'There is always someone getting ahead in the spy game. We just might be looking in the wrong place and not seeing the information bleeding out from somewhere else—a computer server, an unencrypted phone—the possibilities are endless.'

'OK, I'll let you have that, but that doesn't change how I have to behave. I'm not safe if you contact the YDA.'

'But Isaac needs to know his communications are compromised.'

'And he is the one they'll be watching most closely.' She shook out the damp tea towel and hung it over the radiator. 'I'm sorry: I just can't risk going to him. You could go back and tell him in person: I'd be fine with that.'

'But let me guess: you wouldn't sit here and wait for me to return?'

She shook her head.

'You'll not even let me make a phone call?'

She leaned with her back to the stove, watching him prowl by the back door. 'Think about it: they'll be listening for you. As soon as you contact them, they will triangulate the mobile or trace the landline and would have a shrewd idea where we are hiding. The only way to make the call safely would be to leave me here and not come back.'

Nathan looked as if he would like to shake her out of her stubbornness but Kate stood her ground. He hadn't lived the year she had just survived. She had to be extra careful if she wanted to see eighteen.

He threw up his hands. 'OK.'

'OK what?' she asked warily.

'We'll do nothing today. My head is spinning. I need a break from this and you probably could do with a rest. Why don't we decide today is outside of all of this—a holiday? We are completely safe here, next to no chance anyone will find us; the sun is shining and I promised you a visit to the tearoom.'

Kate rubbed her elbows, tempted beyond caution. 'You mean we just enjoy ourselves?'

'Why not? I've bolloxed my career with Isaac, pissed off my parents, so I might as well enjoy the decision before I have to face them. I'm fed up with dragging you places you don't want to go. I'd like to spend the day on the beach with you.' He stuck his head into the cupboard under the stairs and pulled out a bucket and spade. 'See: another relic of Damien the Younger.'

A glorious laugh bubbled up inside Kate. It would be so amazing to take a day off from fear. Her nightmare had lasted for so long she had forgotten what fun felt like.

'You're on. What's first: cake or beach?'

Moving to the back door, Nathan leant over to put on his trainers. 'Beach. Let's work up an appetite so we can do the cake justice.'

They didn't take the bucket and spade in the end; they settled for stone skimming and paddling. The shoreline was a mixture of pebbles and golden sand, the sea a muddy blue. A fringe of green topped the sand dunes, protecting the mere where the birds nested from the wave-battered strand. Most people on the beach were runners, or walking dogs, so they had a stretch to themselves with only the occasional enthusiastic collie to visit. Kate found the simple of challenge of getting her stone to bounce more times than Nathan's a good way of unwinding.

'Five!' she declared, lying only a little.

'Rubbish: that was four.' Nathan let his missile fly. It bounced twice.

'Ha! What was that?'

'Not my best attempt, it must be admitted.' He spent a few minutes looking for the perfect flat pebble while Kate threw a three and a one. 'Ah-ha! I feel good about this little beauty. Yep, this is it.' He was holding a flat black disc, about the size of an oyster shell. Kissing it, he sliced it sideways. One, two, three, four, five, six. A breaking wave caught it before it could manage seven. Nathan whooped.

'Complete fluke,' Kate taunted.

He ran at her and lifted her off her feet. 'Admit it: that was so skillful, you are now in awe of my talent!'

Laughing, she shook her head and batted his shoulder. 'Put me down!'

'Not until you say, "Nathan, you are awesome!"' He spun her in a circle.

'Nathan, you are awesomely . . . ' he started to drop her, 'big-headed!'

'Right, that does it!' He lifted her over his shoulder. 'Into the sea with you.' He waded in, threatening to dump her.

'Nathan!'

'Kate!' he echoed.

She hit his back. 'I don't have any other dry clothes.'

'True.' He pretended to consider that. 'Oh well, can't be helped.'

This time she really thought he was going to drop her. She shrieked, clinging on to his shirt to save herself. He caught her a hair's breadth above the surface and carried her to dry ground. Once she was back up the right way, she saw he was grinning, very pleased with his joke.

'You are a bad man, Nathan Hunter.' He looked so

wonderful standing there with the wind playing with his dark brown hair, his eyes twinkling with merriment. She wanted to reach up and kiss the dimples that popped up in his cheeks when he smiled so broadly. He had really expressive eyebrows, slightly arched at the outer edges. 'Really bad.'

'I know.' He leant down and kissed her lightly on the lips. 'Forgive me?'

She put her fingers to her mouth and nodded. Her skin was still tingling from the brief contact.

He seemed a little embarrassed by what he had just done, caught by surprise as she had been. He turned away from her. 'That's good. I'll buy you that cake I promised to make up for the scare.'

'Sounds reasonable.' If he could act as if nothing had happened, then so could she. Kate picked up her shoes by the laces and tiptoed painfully over the beach to a flat rock where she could brush the sand from between her toes.

'Kate, something's been bothering me.' Nathan shook out his trainer.

'Apart from the obvious disaster that I've brought into your life?' she asked wryly.

'Not your fault, and being here is my choice.' His tone was firm. 'Something else. Do you have any idea why the Scorpions haven't just given up on you? Surely chasing you is mega-expensive? It doesn't make business sense to spend a whole year pursuing one girl.'

Kate tied off her right lace. 'I've wondered about that too. My best guess is that Gani Meosido told them I knew more than I do. They've tried to kill me, so my silence must be what they're after.'

'But you don't think you know anything?'

'Nothing worth killing for.' She stuffed her toes in her left shoe, not bothering with socks. 'It could also be a saving-face thing. None of us are supposed to get away and I did, eventually.' A cloud passed over the water, turning the brown-blue surface grey. Those last days with Gani when he had given her the tattoo felt like a stain on her soul. She would never be free of that ugliness. It wasn't fair on Nathan to drag him into her troubles. 'Nathan, you should really go, you know?' A stray tear dripped off the end of her nose. Had to be something in her eye—she wouldn't let it be anything else. Annoyed with herself, she mopped at her face with the bottom of her T-shirt. Nathan wouldn't separate from her if she acted so weak around him. Squaring her shoulders, she forced her tears back. 'Leaving me—that would be best for us both.'

A hand appeared in front of her eyes.

'What's this?'

'Take it. That's my answer.'

She shook her head. 'Don't do this.'

'Offer you cake? Come on: you know you want some.'

'This isn't about cake.'

The hand didn't move.

'Has anyone ever told you that you were the most stubborn person in all creation?'

'You did—but you are wrong. You carry the prize in that particular category. I'm sure they have brownies.'

'Stop it.'

'Fresh baked scones. Chocolate cake. Millionaire's shortbread. Carrot cake with cream cheese icing.'

Her mouth watered despite her resolve. Her shoulders slumped. 'I have the self-control of a rabbit in a bed of lettuce.' She put her hand in his.

He converted their touch to an arm around her. Bending down he dropped another kiss, this time a friendly one on the top of her head. 'You are the best looking rabbit I've ever seen.'

And he was the kindest boy she had ever met. 'I give up.

You are a hopeless case. I'm just trying to save you, not get rid of you.'

'I know, Kate, but I'm not bailing on you. That means we'll just have to save each other.'

Chapter 11

Nathan kept his arm around Kate as they walked back to the fishermen's cottages along the path that followed the top of the dune. On the land side, the reeds in the mere rippled in the wind like hair smoothed by an invisible comb. Birds skimmed and dipped in the dark water, small ones with curved wings and forked tails. Swallows? Another creature that knew about escaping, though naturalists called it migration. That would be Kate given half a chance.

'What's that?' Kate was pointing ahead along the ridge. In the distance there was a flutter of colour like a fairground stall covered in bunting.

'Let's go and see.'

They reached the structure perched on the crest of a dune. It was made of driftwood lashed together into a rough kind of teepee. Plastic bottles and scraps of plastic bags had been attached to the poles. Nathan knelt down and brushed away the sand to read the sign the nature wardens had screwed onto a rock.

'It's called the Chapel of the Sea. Everything in it was washed up on the beach below and they invite us to find something and tie it on.'

'Cool.' Kate ran her fingers over the multicoloured flags of shopping bags. 'Oh look: someone's made a wind-chime out of cans and metal things.' She let it clang together. 'We've got to add something. Gran always did when we visited churches on our travels. She usually lit a candle but we could put something on the sculpture.'

Nathan was surprised by the interest she was showing in this, her eyes bright with excitement. 'You want to?'

She looked a little embarrassed, lids dipping to hide her enthusiasm. 'Yes, like an offering to the sea. It is a chapel.' She twisted her fingers in the belt loops of her shorts.

Clearly, this was important to her. 'OK: let's find something.'

They scrambled down the bank, slip-surfing on the loose sand, and walked along the beach for a hundred metres. Nathan found a hank of rope like a snake and Kate hit the jackpot with an old boot. They hung their offering from the poles, the boot positioned so when the wind blew it would kick the cans.

'There: that's our offering made,' said Nathan. He had enjoyed the installation art feel to their exercise and was pleased that Kate had persuaded him to pause. When had he last stopped to do something so creatively playful? It had been too long.

Kate sat with her legs curled to one side in the middle of the open structure, admiring their handiwork, her blonde hair whipping about in the breeze. 'I love it here. It feels clean and right.'

Nathan thought she looked like a mermaid washed up on mortal shores sitting there, but he kept the fanciful idea to himself. 'It's perfect: I wish I had a camera to keep the memory.'

She rubbed sand from her suntanned legs. 'Just make an effort to remember and the picture comes back when you need it—that's what I do. It helps in the bad times.' Her expression shifted inwards.

So often he would watch her mood nose-dive like a kite dipping from exulting flight to crash into the ground. What had caused that? Before Indonesia, she had always been so positive, bobbing high as if nothing would bring down her confidence. He wished—no, he *needed*—to do something to help her. He knelt on the sand beside her. His gut was telling him he could use this moment. 'Kate, you are . . . I don't know how to say it without sounding stupid.' He wished he knew what he was doing.

'I'm fine with stupid.'

He framed her face in his hands. 'I keep seeing this terrible sadness in you.'

She pulled away, retreating from what he was saying. 'Well, then you'd be right. I'm not a happy camper.'

He rested his hands on her knees so they were face to face. He wasn't going to let her get away with being flippant. 'Will you tell me what it's about so I can help?'

She turned her wrist over. 'Isn't this enough?'

He covered the scorpion with his palm. 'It's part of it, but I don't think you've told me everything.'

She dropped her chin so he could only see the top of her head.

His intuition nudged him to guess what it might be about. The injury was personal—intimate. 'I won't hate you no matter what you tell me.'

'I hate myself.' Her voice was a scrap like the plastic fluttering around them.

She was carrying around a huge burden; she needed permission to put it down. 'Your gran went to chapels, so she was religious, right?'

'She was open to all kinds of spirituality.' Kate bit her lip. 'I mean, *is* open.'

'Then she would tell you that you've made your offering to the Sea Chapel, handed over your troubles. See your boot?' He twisted round to sit on the sand beside her.

She nodded, her expression wistful.

'There it is: all that bad stuff. You're leaving it here when we walk away. If it tries to creep back, you can remember your boot kicking those cans. This Sea Chapel has taken it from you and turned it into something wonderful.'

She blinked rapidly, keeping emotions at bay. 'It's easier to imagine God forgiving me than me forgiving myself. I let things go too far with Gani before I knew if he could be trusted.'

On the mention of Meosido, Nathan changed inside from meek counsellor to rampant warrior. He wanted to fight dragons for her, but the target had already paid the ultimate price for his choices. *Rein it back*, Nathan told himself. *She doesn't need your anger.*

He kept his voice level. 'You just made a mistake, Kate. We all do.'

She scratched at her bare forearms. 'I fell for him—slept with him. He said I was his girl, and for a short while I wanted to be.'

Nathan had sensed that there was something at the root like this, and now he understood her self-loathing. 'No one else would blame you for that. He exploited you.'

'But I was so stupid. I feel like dirt—worse than dirt.'

'All that dirt is hanging up there with that boot, the bits of mud and grit in the sole. See them? Now we are going to get up, turn away and leave the boot there. It's not coming with us.' He matched his words with actions, pulling her to her feet. She was still facing towards the boot. 'No, don't look. It isn't yours any more.'

'Are you suggesting my *soul's* now clean and that *sole's* dirty?'

He hadn't seen the pun but was happy to claim it if it amused her. 'Exactly.'

She took a final look at the boot then took a step away. 'I'm not sure this is going to work.'

He squeezed her hand. 'It won't harm you. When things calm down, you should talk to a professional—you know, a therapist or counsellor.'

She hugged his arm, resting her cheek against his bicep. 'I like talking to you.'

'Thanks, but I'm winging it here. The more help you get, the better. You've been dragged through hell.'

Kate smiled up at him. 'It feels pretty heavenly just now.'

They had been sliding towards this moment for a while. It had probably been inevitable since he first fell in love with her over a year ago. Nathan stopped and pulled her against him, arms looped behind her. 'Is it OK if I kiss you?' With the shadow of Gani Meosido still fresh in his mind, he had to know she was happy with this.

'Be my guest.' Her eyes were laughing at him.

A slight worry that he wouldn't measure up to those who had kissed her in the past nagged at him as he bent his head. When their lips made contact, anxiety vanished and sensation took over. She felt perfect, her body yielding just the right amount to press against him, chest, stomach and thighs. Her mouth was so warm and welcoming. With the sea breeze ruffling them both, every inch of his skin tingled. They were speaking a new language of touch, one where both wanted to dissolve barriers and merge. He became aware of her fingers stroking his back, tracing the muscles of his shoulders, leaving fire in their wake.

He broke away while the feelings were still singing in his chest. He couldn't afford to lose control or go too far when she had been so hurt. He looked down at her tenderly. Her eyes were closed, her cheek pressed against his chest. This had either been the greatest mistake or the best thing he had ever done. Maybe both.

'Thank you,' he murmured.

She lifted her lids, brandy-gold eyes glimmering. 'You are so very welcome.'

Kate spent the rest of the day in a wonderful haze. After months of being alone, the rapid development of closeness with Nathan was a total shock. It was the last thing she had been expecting when he had handcuffed himself to her, though looking back that should have been a clue. From the sweet moment in the Sea Chapel to the stunning kiss, from the tea and cakes to the lazy afternoon reading novels, she was learning to have faith in him. She didn't give her trust easily but he was persuading her he deserved it.

The sun was setting, spotlighting the chair in which she had curled up. She had just finished a military thriller—not her taste but the cottage bookshelf didn't yield much in the way of reading material unless you were interested in birds. Nathan had given up on his doorstop-sized adventure story and had taken to sketching her instead in the little pad he had bought in the visitor's centre.

She yawned. 'Let's see.'

He glanced up, frowning. 'It's not ready yet.'

His defensive expression warned her that this was a hobby he took seriously. 'I didn't know that you're an artist.'

'You might not think me one when you see what I've done.' He held the pad further away. 'I can't get your nose right.'

She was tempted to cover the feature in question with her hand. She had always considered it a ridiculous part of her face—small and a little bit snubbed at the end.

Nathan made a couple more flicks of the pencil. 'I'd better stop or I'll ruin the few good things in it.' He turned it round for her inspection. 'What do you think?'

It was amazing. Not a careful beginner's sketch but a loose bird's nest of lines that resolved themselves miraculously into her face. 'You have a real style of your own, don't you?'

'Is that a polite way of telling me you hate it?'

'No! It's great.' He had caught her face brilliantly, though she found it unsettling that he had also captured her vulnerability. Now it was on the paper for all to see. 'Can you do a self-portrait?'

'Why would I do that when I've you to sketch?' Smiling, he put the pad down on the rickety coffee table and checked his watch. 'Do you want to go first in the bathroom like last night?'

'How did you know I'd like a bath?'

'I'm omniscient. I'll see what I can find for supper. A girl cannot live on cake alone.'

'But she can make a very good attempt at it.' Kate got up, shaking out the pins-and-needles from sitting still for so long. 'Don't start cooking: I'll prepare the meal while you have your bath. You just find the things we can use.'

He headed for the kitchen. 'So I'm demoted to *sous chef* after my toast confession this morning? You know, I think I could probably manage to boil some pasta and sauce without screwing up.'

'I just thought I should pull my weight.'

'OK then: you cook later while I soak. Off you go, wench: have your bath.' He flicked the tea towel at her butt to get her moving up the stairs.

Laughing, she took the steps two at a time. 'Button it, *sous chef*. Remember who's in charge in this kitchen tonight.'

Kate lay in the tub, winding the cold chain of the plug around her big toe. The visitors were heading back to their hotels and homes, cars pulling out of the parking area, voices retreating. The gravel crackled and crunched under tyres. The shyer birds were coming out of hiding, singing their evening songs now they didn't have fifty binoculars trained on them.

122

Nathan had given her an enormous gift by bringing her here: he had allowed her to feel peaceful for the first time in so long. The little ceremony at the chapel with that ridiculous boot had helped. The guilt hadn't totally gone and would probably creep back, but it was a relief that he knew the truth and thought she should let go of the shame. She closed her eyes and imagined her boot kicking the wind-chime, each tap another mistake blown away on the breeze. Gran had always said that in times of trouble God sent people to be his stand-ins. Kate wasn't certain what she believed—it sounded a bit too much like a line from *The Sound of Music* to her—but if someone so utterly good and kind as Nathan could remain with her after knowing the worst, then maybe she wasn't a completely worthless husk of a person?

There was a tap on the door. 'Oh, bathroom hog? Are you OK in there?'

'Uh-huh.'

'Any chance of me getting a go before the return of Halley's comet?'

She sat up, water streaming off her shoulders. 'Are you inferring, Mr Wolf, that I am taking a long time and if I don't hurry, you'll huff and you'll puff and you'll blow the door down?'

'Well, I am getting hungry.'

So was she, but her appetite was for another of his kisses. 'All right, all right, nag, nag, nag, day and night. Never a moment's peace.'

He snorted. 'I think you've had quite a few moments, sweetheart.'

She treasured the name coming so naturally from him. That earned him free run of the bathroom at least. 'Just getting out now.' She wrapped a big towel around herself, pulled the plug and opened the door. 'All yours.'

He looked down at her with a cheeky grin. 'I wish.'

'I meant the bathroom.'

'Yeah I know.' He stepped aside to let her pass. 'I put your clothes on the bed. They're dry now.'

'Thanks.'

She sniffed her T-shirt as she put it on, enjoying the scent of washing powder on the fabric. It had been so long since she had her things properly clean. Quick hand-washes in sinks weren't enough. The day had been a spectacular success. She hoped she could rustle up a decent supper to round it off. It would be lovely way to say thank you.

'What did you find to eat?' she called out as she passed the bathroom.

'Pasta and red sauce. There's a tub of parmesan too,' he replied over the thunder of the water falling into the bath. 'I left it all out on the table.'

'Thanks.' She jogged down the stairs, batteries fully recharged, head full of plans for the meal. Maybe she would find something for dessert? There had been a tin of peaches in one cupboard and a little tin of evaporated milk. Gran used to serve that as a cheaper alternative to cream. Granddad's favourite, she always said. Kate decided she could also fold some napkins, fancy the table up a little, add a candle.

Entering the kitchen, she walked straight into Damien. He was holding the sketch book and his expression was beyond angry.

'You!' he spat.

She turned to flee out the front door, mind tumbling from happiness to hurt. Had Nathan betrayed her after all? She didn't make it to the entrance. Damien seized her elbow and yanked her back.

'Don't even think about running.'

'Let me go!'

He hauled her back to the kitchen, not caring if she got bumped in the process. 'I get why you might want to keep out of Isaac's way, seeing how you messed up so badly, but now you've taken my friend with you—worked on his weakness for you!' He shoved her into a chair.

Kate sprang up immediately and darted for the back door. Damien swore and tackled her. They both went down. Kate's head rapped on the side of the fridge. She fought dirty to get free, kicking and biting.

'You vicious little cow!'

Kate sank her teeth into Damien's forearm. He gave a howl of pain but still didn't let go of her.

Then a chair flew out of the way and Damien's weight was lifted off her. Shaken, Kate shuffled back into a corner between the fridge and the food cupboard. Nathan was wrestling Damien wearing nothing but a towel around his waist, wet footprints showing he had leapt out of the bath to come to her rescue. The boys were well-matched, and it wasn't until Nathan pushed Damien out of the kitchen, and over the arm of the sofa that the fight ended. Damien rolled and got back on his feet deftly, fists raised, ready to go another round.

Nathan held his hand up, the other keeping his towel secure. 'Enough, Damien.'

'You moron. What the hell are you doing here with her, other than the obvious?' sneered Damien.

'I'm going to get some clothes. You,' Nathan stabbed a finger at his friend, 'don't move from that spot.'

'We need to talk, Nat. Without her listening.'

'I mean it, Damien: don't move!' Nathan strode into the kitchen and approached Kate in her corner. 'Did that idiot hurt you?'

Kate shook her head.

'I can see a lump on your forehead. Wait a moment: I'll get

a flannel.' With a warning glance at Damien in the living room, Nathan hurried upstairs. He must have dressed in record time as he was back within a minute, jeans and T-shirt on, damp cloth in hand. He coaxed Kate off the floor. 'Sit at the table and hold that to your head.'

Still too shaken to speak, she did as he asked. She had worked out while he was upstairs that he must have no more expected Damien to arrive than she did. He hadn't betrayed her trust. Damien had just put two and two together quicker than expected. 'Is he alone?'

Nathan turned to his friend who was glowering at her from the doorway. 'Are you?'

Damien nodded.

'You haven't reported in?'

'Not yet.'

Kate closed her eyes, feeling a wave of relief. She could still get away if it was only Damien they had to get round.

'How did you guess?' asked Nathan, gently smoothing Kate's hair.

Damien glared at the hand. 'Because we've been friends for years. I saw the CCTV from the petrol station—you guys buying an OS map of the area. We waited for you to ring last night and this morning I found myself saying, *no, surely he couldn't be so fricking stupid*? By this afternoon, with Isaac blowing steam out of his ears, I decided I had to go check.'

'Does he know you're here?' Nathan glanced out of the window, stance alerting Kate to the fact that he half expected several YDA cars to roll up and the whole team descend to take them into custody.

Damien's blue eyes flashed fire. 'What do you take me for, Nat? I wouldn't land you in it.' He shoved his hands into his pockets in exasperation. 'Look: we can still pull this off. I'll say I found you stranded somewhere—twisted ankle, couldn't move.

126

Got injured chasing Pearl. We already know you didn't have a phone. That might just persuade Isaac not to kick you out.'

Nathan took the flannel out of Kate's hand and put it under the cold tap. He passed it back. 'Thanks for trying to cover for me, but no deal.'

Kate thought it sounded a good idea. At least she wouldn't be responsible for the ruin of a second career at the YDA. 'Nathan, you should go with him.'

Damien flicked his hard gaze in her direction. 'You've got the wrong impression, cutie pie: we're not going anywhere without you.'

'She's not coming in.' Nathan spoke before she could.

'Have you completely lost your mind, Nat? She's been playing you, stirring up your protective instincts.' Damien turned to Kate. 'No offence, Miss Pearl, but you're a stone cold bitch using him that way.'

Kate choked. 'You say "no offence" then call me a bitch? I thought Cobras were supposed to be charming?'

'You don't deserve the effort it would take to charm you.'

'Stop it, Damien. You don't know what you've walked into here,' said Nathan.

Damien folded his arms. 'Oh, I know exactly what's going on; it's you who's blind to what she really is.'

'And what am I?' asked Kate bitterly.

'A failure.' He poked a finger at her to underline each accusation. 'Possibly a murderer, or at least responsible for several deaths even if you didn't kill them; a manipulator.'

'She's none of those things,' said Nathan, his fists clenching and unclenching as he struggled to keep a grip on his temper.

'Wake up, Nat! Look at her: yesterday she was running from us, now she's running at you, throwing herself into your arms with her *"what can I cook for you, darling?"* routine and her *"oh, big strong Nathan protect me from horrible Damien"*.'

'Shut up, Damien.'

'Why? Don't you like hearing the truth?'

Kate twisted the jar of red sauce on the table in front of her. Damien was only saying things she had thought about herself but she was a thread away from heaving it at his head.

Nathan eased the jar out of her grip. 'Kate, why don't we start on supper? Give Damien a chance to cool down.'

She got up and walked to the sink, tense as a bow strung with an arrow. Choosing a big saucepan, she filled it halfway with water. Even though her back was to him, she was aware of Damien's eyes following every move she made.

'Do you want to eat with us?' Nathan asked politely, getting out the plates.

Damien gave a hollow laugh. 'Yeah, why not? Let's see what the fugitive whips up for us: a plate of bull sprinkled with crap.' He took a seat at the table, but sat sideways so he could leap to intercept if she made a sudden bid for freedom.

Nathan brushed her nape, over the sore spot that had been troubling her. 'Kate, I apologize for my friend. He's worried about me.'

Kate knew that already, that's why she hadn't thrown the jar at him.

'Don't apologize for me—and definitely not to her.' Damien ripped open a packet of breadsticks and crunched down on one.

'You'll regret what you said when you know what's going on.'

'No, I really don't think I will.'

Kate could feel his hatred boring into her rigid back. She ignored him and tipped the pasta into the water.

Nathan emptied the sauce into a smaller pan, scraping out the container with a spoon. 'Kate isn't handing herself in because there is a leak at the YDA.' He gave the side of the pan two decisive taps to dislodge the tomato mixture.

'Oh yeah? And I suppose she told you this, did she, in between batting her eyelashes at you and stroking your ego?'

'You are well out of order, Damien.' Nathan threw the spoon into the sink. Control only went so far.

'*I'm* out of order? I'm not the one who's ignored his instructions and run off with the suspect he's supposed to apprehending!'

Nathan planted himself between Damien and Kate. 'I disobeyed orders because I saw proof with my own eyes that she's right. We watched the service station and the Scorpions got there before you did. If you'd run that CCTV footage a few hours longer, you'd've seen them for yourself. How could that happen unless they knew almost immediately after you got the call to head back to Suffolk and fetch us?'

'You're kidding me?' Damien snapped the remains of his breadstick in half.

'No, I'm not. I promise.' Nathan sat down opposite his friend.

'Why didn't the guy at the till tell us?'

'I guess he was warned not to. For all he knew they were still watching him.'

Damien pulverized the stick with his fist on the tabletop. The accompanying swearing was fluent and vivid. Kate allowed herself a little smile. She turned down the heat to stop the pasta boiling over and put a lid on the pan.

'So things really aren't what they seem,' said Nathan. He reached for her and pulled her onto his lap, large hand warm on her thigh. 'Kate has good reason not to trust us. We thought she was the one who betrayed us but it was the other way round. She was set up either because our security isn't good enough or . . . '

'. . . Or because one of us is a traitor. Crap.' Damien passed her the box of breadsticks. 'Here: take one and imagine that's me eating my words.'

She pulled one out. 'I still don't like you.'

'Yeah, I'm not so hot on you either, babe, but I get that I jumped to the wrong conclusion. I'm willing to give you a second chance. But let's be clear: if you hurt my man, Nathan, I'll make you regret it.'

Kate waved the breadstick at him. 'You know, that's the only thing you could've said that actually makes me forgive you for being a jerk.'

Damien laughed, taking the insult on the chin.

'Now hostilities are ended, shall we eat?' asked Nathan. 'Then we've got to work out what we do next.'

Kate shrugged. 'It's obvious, isn't it? I've got to keep running.'

Nathan's embraced tightened. 'Sweetheart, you've got a Wolf and a Cobra on your side now.'

Damien made a derisive noise but didn't voice his disagreement.

'And that means?' asked Kate.

'Nat here hunts the bad guys and then I take them out. Simple.' Damien leaned back in his chair, oozing confidence.

That kind of attitude would kill her, and possibly them. 'Nothing about the Scorpions is simple. You might be a Cobra but they are like the Hydra—cut off one head and six more grow.'

'Greek mythical references: classy,' Damien said to Nathan.

'Yeah, she is.' He rested his hand on her waist.

'So what's she doing with a pleb like you?'

'No idea.'

They were teasing her. At least Damien didn't sulk. 'You know what I mean.'

'I think it's ready.' Nathan pushed her up so they could serve the pasta. 'Of course we know what you mean, Kate, but we'll just have to make our plans Hydra proof.'

'Don't forget we have home ground advantage,' added Damien.

Kate groaned. 'When we get to sporting metaphors then I know we're really doomed. The YDA was always riddled with them.'

'Oh, ye of little faith,' mocked Damien. 'You've got a premier league team behind you.'

'Tell him to stop,' Kate begged.

'You want me to show him the red card?' said Nathan, tipping pasta out onto three plates.

Kate would have hit him if he hadn't been holding her meal. 'You'll both drive me crazy.'

'Payback for running rings round us in Bath and Southwold,' said Damien brightly. 'Pass the parmesan.'

Chapter 12

Over peaches and evaporated milk, the conversation turned to the central issue standing in their way.

'Who do you think we can trust at headquarters?' asked Damien. He poked his dessert, not looking convinced by the combination Kate had served up.

'Isaac,' Nathan said immediately, 'but he's also the one whose communications are compromised. We can't talk to him in the office.'

'Agreed. Who else?'

'I trust my dad.'

Damien narrowed his eyes. 'He hates all other recruits.'

'Strongly dislikes maybe, but he would never betray them—us. That goes right against his moral code.' Nathan glanced sideways at Kate to see how she was taking this discussion. She was keeping her expression shuttered, slicing the peaches in her bowl into neat chunks. 'I think the problem with Dad is different: he's rigid about sticking to the rules. He'll be all for bringing Kate in, as per procedure. Isaac would allow us a little more leeway when he understands.'

'I think Sergeant Rivers would be concerned most about protecting you,' said Kate quietly. 'He won't like me on principle.'

'There is that.' Nathan rubbed his chin, registering he could do with a shave. 'As for the others involved in this, I trust the team: Kieran and Raven.'

Damien helped himself to another spoon of peaches. 'No question there.'

Kate shook her head. 'Raven is new so she's in the clear, but what if someone got to Kieran and tried to blackmail him? He's from a well-off family, isn't he? He might be trying to protect them—giving up information for their sake.'

Nathan and Damien exchanged looks. They were among the few who knew Kieran's secret; that his background was anything but privileged.

'Kieran's not worried about anything like that. You can trust him, Kate,' Nathan assured her.

'I don't trust anyone easily.' Her mouth took on an obstinate line.

Seeing Nathan wasn't making headway, Damien stepped in. 'But Kate, you do know Kieran is awesomely intelligent?'

'Of course. That's all everyone talked about when Isaac recruited him.'

'Can you really imagine a guy with Kieran's brain power letting some scummy gang blackmail him for over a year without thinking of way of taking apart their organization? He'd nuke their communications—pocket their money.' Damien turned to Nathan. 'That's not a bad idea. We should put him onto it.'

'Later. First we need to know that Kate agrees who's in and who's out on this operation.'

'You still in charge then?' Damien arched a brow.

'Isaac hasn't recalled me, so yes.' Nathan knew that was only semantics. Isaac was going to sack him on sight; not just for failing to bring Kate in yesterday, but for breaking the rule about relationships.

'OK, boss.' Damien tapped his forehead in a mock salute.

'Kate, are you happy for us to reach out to Kieran and Raven? We can't do this alone.'

Reluctantly, she nodded.

'Good, that's agreed then. My idea is that we head back to London, stash you in a safe house and go see Isaac. Damien, we can say that Kate's still on the run. Once we've started that story, we get Isaac out of the building and tell him what's really happening.'

'You won't tell him where I am, will you?' asked Kate.

Nathan could imagine the likely path of the conversation too vividly to promise that. 'He might insist.'

'I can't risk it.'

'How about we check with you first before we tell him anything? We could arrange for you to meet up in a neutral venue, protect where you're staying.'

Kate chewed her lip, wanting to reject the idea.

'Come on, Kate: you know Isaac. He feels responsible. I know he'll want to check you're OK.' Even if Kate denied it, she would need Isaac's help eventually.

'All right, but I've got to have a way out. I won't be cornered again. You promise me you'll take my side if he's determined to bring me in?'

'I promise.'

Kate turned to Damien. 'What about the Cobra here?'

Damien slapped his hand to his chest. 'Cross my heart, I'll take your side.'

'Can I believe him?' Kate appealed to Nathan.

Nathan drummed his fingers on the table, eager to leave. 'Yeah, you can. He may be annoying, but his word is good.'

'You mentioned a safe house: where is it?'

Damien stretched his arms above his head, fingers laced together. 'That's my major contribution to the plan. Nathan can't park you with his folks for obvious reasons, so you're going to my place.'

'I'm not sure I'd feel happy about that. I don't know your people.'

'You're already staying at our country cottage so I can't see that our city pad should be any different. I live with my uncle when I'm not at the YDA.'

'The birdwatcher?'

'He's also a commodities broker. Works in the city. He'll take your presence in the house in his stride and not ask too many questions. He'll only get interested in you if you show a passion for ornithology.'

'And the advantage is that no one would imagine you'd be staying at Damien's,' added Nathan. 'Damien's made no secret of the fact he isn't your biggest fan.'

Damien spread his arms proudly. 'See, my cynical attitude works to your advantage. You should be eternally grateful.'

Kate flicked him a hand gesture that suggested her feelings were not running in that direction.

'Right, now we've got that settled,' said Nathan quickly, 'let's head out. I take it you drove here, Damien?'

'Yep. The car's parked outside. I borrowed the new little BMW. It's a sweet ride.'

'Can't we wait till tomorrow?' asked Kate.

'I'm afraid not. Damien's due back and the longer I leave reporting in, the more Isaac is going to question my story.'

Resigned, she got to her feet. 'Then we'd better tidy up and go.'

Having very little with them, they were ready in five minutes. Nathan locked the back door and returned the key to its laughable hiding place. Like Kate, he was reluctant to leave the cottage. It had become a very special place for them both and felt safe. Where they were heading was going to be anything but.

'Nat, you drive while I phone ahead to my uncle.' Damien got in the passenger seat, leaving Kate to take the back, subtly reminding them that on a mission he was Nathan's lieutenant, not Kate. 'Then I'll report in, give Isaac the heads-up that we're coming his way. If you're right about the leak, that'll give the Scorpions the wrong scent to follow. Where do I say we think she's heading?'

'Lichfield,' said Kate.

Damien swivelled round in his seat. 'Where's that?'

'North of Birmingham. There's a fair on this week and it's where I'd be going if Nathan hadn't caught me.'

'OK, that's good—the reasoning is convincing and it's miles from where you'll really be.' He checked the location in the car atlas.

Nathan started the engine. 'Are we good to go?'

'Yep.'

Kate dipped her head. Her reluctance was like a hot sun beating on the back of his neck but he couldn't think of a better solution.

'Well, then. Let's do this.' He turned the car towards trouble.

Kate listened carefully as Damien made his calls, checking he wasn't double-crossing them. Nathan was ready to trust his friends but she hadn't the same instincts. Once bitten . . .

'Yeah, Uncle Julian, just for a few days. No, she's not my girlfriend—I told you: she's Nat's. Yeah, she's pretty.'

Nathan caught Kate's eyes in the driver's mirror and grinned.

'No,' continued Damien, 'she won't be impressed by an overweight birdwatcher in his fifties. And no, I don't stand a chance with her either. Wouldn't want to. Mates before dates.'

Nathan laughed. 'Your uncle never changes.'

Damien rolled his eyes. 'Yeah, I am sitting next to him right now. His parents aren't into the idea of him dating this girl so he doesn't want to take her there.' Damien held the phone away from his ear. 'My uncle says she's welcome to stay as long as she needs.'

'Thanks, Julian!' Nathan called so the man could hear.

'See you in a couple of hours. Bye.' Damien ended the call. 'That was the easy one. Don't take any notice of him saying you'd fall for him, Kate. He likes to tease Nat and me about our girlfriends, even more so because he's in a long term relationship with a guy called Paul.'

Girlfriends? It suddenly struck Kate that she hadn't ever asked Nathan if he was already with someone. Her heart sank. She would have to ask him. Still, Julian sounded good value. 'Will the boyfriend be there?'

'They don't live together. Paul says he'd kill my uncle if they had to share a kitchen.'

'Oh?'

'Paul's a chef. Takes his cooking seriously. Nice bloke. Knows about knives.' Damien swore under his breath. 'OK, here goes call number two. I don't need to tell you to keep quiet, do I, Kate?'

She shook her head emphatically.

'Hi, Mrs Mac, can I speak to Isaac? It's Damien. I think he'd be happy to be called out of his meeting—better still, patch me through. Yeah, I've news.' Damien tapped his knee in a nervous beat. 'Isaac? It's me. I'm heading back in with Nat. Sorry: I can't pass the phone to him as he's driving. He's OK. Pearl gave him the slip again and he was left stranded without a phone in the back of beyond. He finally reached civilization and rang me for a pick up.'

Damien went quiet while Isaac lectured him on the other end. 'I know that's not procedure, but I went as his friend. He realizes he's messed up.'

Nathan shook his head but kept silent.

'Kate Pearl? Nat thinks she might be heading for Lichfield: that's where the fairground people she knows have set up this week. Yeah, yeah, I understand. We're coming straight in. We know there'll be consequences. Uh-huh. Thanks. I'll tell him. See you in a couple of hours.' Damien ended the call. 'Crap.'

'He'll come round when he knows why we did what we did,' said Nathan. 'You won't be in serious trouble, Damien: you were the one who worked out where we were.'

Damien said nothing.

Nathan couldn't let him brood. 'Good hunting, by the way. Want to transfer to the Wolves? I think there might be a vacancy opening up.'

'No way. I couldn't stand the pace you guys set. That reminds me: your dad was there. He wants you to call. In fact, he said to pull over and swap drivers so he could shout at you.'

'Funnily enough, I don't feel much like taking a break.'

'Perhaps you should get it out of the way,' suggested Kate. She hoped the father/son tie was strong if Nathan's career had gone pear-shaped. She had enough guilt to carry as it was without adding that to her burden.

'I suppose you're right.'

Scanning the roadside, Nathan found a place to stop. Rather than take the front seat next to Damien, Nathan climbed in the back with her. Damien chucked him the phone.

'You guys make me feel like the damn chauffeur.' Damien pulled out and put his foot down, taking the car up to the speed limit. He drove like a rally driver, confident and controlled.

Nathan put his arm around Kate and drew her to his side. 'I need to remember why I'm doing this,' he told her.

She nestled as close as she could, giving him her silent support.

Nathan dialled the number. 'Hi, Dad? Yeah, it's Nathan. Sorry I didn't call earlier but I've been really . . . er . . . busy.'

Kate could hear fragments of Jim's reply. Words like 'idiot' and 'kicked out' featured heavily.

'Yeah, I know. I'm sorry,' said Nathan after letting Jim run out of steam with his complaints. 'No, I'm all right. We'll talk when I get back. I promise I'll give Mum a quick call. Yes, love you too.' He ended the call. His thumb stroked the screen meditatively.

'Was that as bad as it sounded?' Kate asked.

He rolled his shoulders, shaking off the dark mood. 'Not really. You see, I know I did the right thing. That helps.'

'You think he'll understand eventually?'

'Maybe, but he'll respect that I took my own decisions and stand by them. He likes that in a person, even if he disagrees.' Nathan tapped in his home number. 'Hi, Mum, it's Nathan. Yes, I'm fine. Things didn't go the way I expected on the mission, that's all. I'll see you at the weekend, sooner if they kick me out.'

The voice on the other end rattled away.

'I don't think Isaac will react well to you slapping him sensible, Mum.'

Kate smiled into Nathan's chest.

'Don't blame the girl, Mum: she was just desperate and good at giving us the slip.' Nathan rubbed the back of Kate's neck. She flinched when the pad of his finger touched the bite. He gave her a quizzical look but she shook her head, not able to explain in case his mum heard. 'Yes, I love you too. See you soon.' He put the phone on the central console within Damien's reach. 'What's the matter with your neck?'

Kate lifted up her hair. 'I've got a bad bite there: it won't heal up.'

He tipped her head forward. 'I can see it. What did it, do you know?'

'A mosquito maybe—but I've had it since Jakarta. I thought it would clear up on its own.'

'You need to see a doctor. Could be some weird tropical insect beneath the skin,' Damien chipped in.

'Oh God.' Kate felt herself go quite green.

'Don't listen to him,' said Nathan. 'It just looks like there's some kind of lump that's got infected. I'm sure a GP would be able to sort it out for you with some antibiotics. We'll ask Julian who his doctor is and get you an appointment for tomorrow if they've space.'

'Good idea.' Kate shuddered. Damn Damien for planting horrible thoughts in her head.

'Relax, Kate. It's nothing.'

'If you've had it a year and nothing's hatched then you're probably OK,' agreed Damien cheerfully.

'Can I gag your friend?' Kate asked Nathan.

'Not while he's in charge of a moving vehicle, sorry. We still need him for another hour or so.'

'He can drive perfectly well without the power of speech.'

Damien growled something rude about who should be gagged in the car.

'Then I think I'll just go to sleep and ignore him: is that OK?'

'Fine by me.' Nathan settled her more comfortably in his arms and held her as she drifted off.

Not far from the southern bank of the Thames, Uncle Julian's apartment was on the second floor of an eight-eenth-century terraced house that looked out onto the grassy sweep of Greenwich Park. Black railings separated the property from the street, with steps up to the front door. The house was the bricks-and-mortar equivalent of a neat gentleman: black-and-white trim, windows polished to a shine, flowerpots on sills like a carnation in a lapel. Kate hadn't imagined Damien living in a quaint place like this:

he seemed more suited to modern architecture and stainless steel, things with sharp edges that wouldn't allow you to get comfortable.

'I'm sorry we can't stay long,' Nathan said as Damien fitted his key into the door. 'We're on the clock with Isaac.'

'It's OK, really.'

'Hi, Uncle Julian, it's just us!' called Damien, going through the doorway.

A large man bowled out of a room to their left like a ball headed for ten pins—though in this case there were only three of them. 'Damien!'

'Uncle!'

Julian was an impressive person: about the same height as the boys but twice the girth. A swept back mane of tawny-grey hair and dark eyebrows gave his features drama, well matched to his manner. He had the bearing of an opera star. 'Damien, Damien: why during term time do I only see you when you want something?'

'Because I'm a heartless nephew.' Damien was enveloped in a hug.

Julian gave him a squeeze then released him. 'You'll do. Nat, you're next!'

Nathan got the same hug treatment. Kate braced herself, not sure what was coming her way.

'And this must be my guest.' Julian held out a hand and gave her a conventional shake, putting the brakes on to his exuberance. 'Delighted to be of assistance in your hour of need.' His eyes twinkled with friendly warmth.

'Thank you, Mr . . . er . . . ?'

'Mr Castle, but you must call me Julian. I am only Mr Castle at work. Now, I've made up the bed in the spare room. Where's your case?'

'Oh. Uh . . . '

'I'll bring her stuff tomorrow,' said Nathan quickly. 'We weren't sure you'd say yes to having her to stay.'

'Of course I was going to say yes! The more the merrier. Now let's put on the kettle and you can tell me all your news.' He led them into the kitchen, which was a homely place with pale lemon units in a simple Shaker style. A clock in the shape of a flamingo added an exuberant exotic note over the sink. 'For a start, what have your parents got against this lovely young creature? She seems more than acceptable to me.'

Where to begin? Kate cleared her throat but Damien was there first.

'I'm sorry, Uncle, but it upsets Kate to talk about it. Can we leave it until she knows you better?'

Julian looked a little offended at this brush-off. He bustled to the counter to switch on the kettle. 'But I thought I might be able to help. I could have a chat with Maisie.' He patted Nathan's arm as he passed him. 'Even I wouldn't dare raise the subject with your father—terrifying man!'

'Please don't. I'm handling them but it's tricky.'

'Ah, that I understand. Delicate negotiations.' He tapped the side of his nose. 'I know a thing or two about those as well. Now, what's your poison, my dear? Ask away. If it exists, I probably have it. I completely lose my head when I go into the local deli. Tea, coffee, rooibos, something herbal?' He opened a cupboard and a packet of mint tea fell out.

'That'll do, thanks.' Kate helped him pick up the bags that had spilled on the floor.

'Boys?' Julian put one of the sachets in a cup.

'I'm sorry, but we can't stay. It's really late and we're way past curfew at the YDA. We'll be back tomorrow.' Nathan gave Kate an apologetic grimace.

'Don't worry about me. I'll be fine.'

'She certainly will be.' Julian put a second tea bag in a mug

142

for himself. 'You go and say your goodbyes and I'll make the drinks.'

Damien turned to go.

'Not you, Damien. I can't think Kate is interested in saying goodbye to you.'

'Uncle, you shock me.'

Leaving the two of them to their teasing conversation, Nathan led Kate out into the hallway.

'Do you like him?'

'He's great. Nothing like Damien.' That sounded bad. 'You know what I mean.'

Nathan laughed. 'I know. Damien's one of a kind. He's even less like his parents, if you can imagine that.'

'They're still alive? I thought living here that maybe . . . ?

'They're both doctors with a charity working in Uganda.'

'Crumbs.' That didn't fit with her image of sardonic Damien at all.

'I'll be back tomorrow when I can, but until then you'll need some stuff.' He peeled off some of the notes he had drawn out of the ATM and tucked them in her back pocket. 'That should get you started.'

'Thanks. I'll keep the receipts and pay you back.'

'Shut up, Kate.' He bent his head and kissed her. 'It's a gift.'

'I can't . . . '

'I said, shut up.' He kissed her again.

'Are you going to do that every time I protest?'

'Yes.'

She opened her mouth then closed it.

'Shame.' Nat brushed her lips with a fingertip. 'Oh well: I'll just kiss you anyway. Can't waste this perfect opportunity engineered by the excellent Uncle Julian.'

This kiss lasted much longer than the preceding ones. Kate's fingers wandered under the T-shirt just above his waistband, stroking the surprisingly soft skin below his ribs. His hands shaped her body to fit to his, one pressing gently in between her shoulder blades, the other across her hips. They eased apart, aware they would soon have an audience.

Embarrassed by an intense wash of emotion, Kate made a joke. 'So, is my hug as good as Julian's?'

'Much, much better.' Nathan held his forehead to hers.

'Time to go!' called Damien.

Kate made herself release Nathan. 'Goodnight—and thanks, both of you.' She blew Damien a kiss which he received with an ironic smile.

Kate watched the door close behind the boys, wishing things were different and that she could go with them.

'Tea's ready!' called Julian.

Squaring her shoulders, Kate went to tell polite lies to her host.

Chapter 13

Damien entered the code to lift the barrier blocking the entrance to the YDA underground car park. As he drove to the space reserved for his borrowed vehicle, Nathan noted that there were quite a few staff cars there despite it being the middle of the night.

Damien's phone buzzed. He checked the screen. 'Isaac's losing patience.' He tapped in a reply. 'I told him we've just arrived.'

Nathan nodded. All areas of the YDA headquarters were monitored by CCTV, so they had already agreed that they wouldn't mention detours. 'Well, we got here as fast as we could.'

Damien summoned the lift. 'We absolutely did.' He exchanged a wry look with Nathan.

'You're a good friend,' Nathan said in a low voice as the lift doors opened.

'Thanks.' Damien gave him a punch on the arm. 'Don't worry: it'll work out.'

The doors opened outside Isaac's office on the top floor of the building. Damien knocked.

'Come.'

He opened the door, entering ahead of Nathan. 'I'm sorry you've been waiting. Sat-Nav let me down,' Damien said, trying to draw fire to himself and away from his best friend.

Nathan followed close on his heels. The first thing Nathan saw was the bank of windows in front of him. Located in an old warehouse on the South Bank of the Thames facing St Paul's cathedral, Isaac's office had a fantastic view of the city. It was hard to think of vistas when he saw who else was in the room: his dad; Jan Hardy, wily mentor for the Cats; Taylor Flint of the Cobras, as hard as his name suggested; and studious Dr Waterburn of the Owls—the complete senior management team. And Isaac, of course: their commander-in-chief. Ice-blue eyes were not giving away any of his private thoughts as he sat at the head of the table.

'Damien, Kieran and Raven are waiting next door for a debrief. Please would you leave us.' It wasn't a request.

'Yes, sir.' Damien gave Nathan a commiserating look and headed out to the conference room.

The beginning of Nathan's dressing-down was delayed by Mrs MacDonald coming in with a tray of coffee.

'Would you like me to take minutes, Isaac?' she asked, placing a cup before each mentor, already poured to their preference. She was good at remembering details.

'No, thank you, Tamsin. I'll write this up myself. You get on home. Thank you for staying late.'

Mrs MacDonald patted Nathan's arm as she passed him. 'Glad you're back in one piece,' she said in a whisper.

'Thanks, Mrs Mac.' She had known not to give him a coffee—this was not a social call.

The door closed, a very final sound.

'Nathan, take a seat.'

Nathan sat down next to his dad. Jim was here in his capacity as mentor to the Wolves, so could not act as Nathan's father, but that didn't stop him checking Nathan for any sign of injury.

'You're really OK?' Jim murmured.

'Yes, Dad.'

'So, Nathan, are you going to explain exactly what happened?' asked Isaac. 'Last we heard you had Kate Pearl restrained and were waiting for us to pick you up. Then you disappeared for almost twenty-four hours.'

Nathan wished he was anywhere but here. 'It's complicated.'

Isaac gave him a humourless smile. 'We can do complicated, Nathan. We aren't idiots. We have all worked out that Kate Pearl managed to run rings around you.'

That seemed as good an explanation as any. 'I have to admit that she's amazing—so resourceful. I tried my best but she slipped off before I could stop her.'

Jan Hardy sniffed. 'You should have planned for that, Nathan. She is highly trained.'

'And so is Nathan,' said Jim. 'He's my best Wolf. I can't believe you would make such a basic mistake, Nathan.'

'But even the best have an Achilles' heel, don't they?' Isaac twisted a pen in his fingers. 'You confessed to having feelings for the girl a year ago but you assured me you were over them. That appears now to be a less than honest assessment.'

Nathan had to give them something. 'I didn't know I still had a thing for her when I took on the mission.'

'Maybe not, but my guess is she played on your emotions and persuaded you to let her go.'

That was close to the truth. 'I admit that I wasn't on my best game. She continually wrong-footed me. You know that already as I reported in after the mini-cab incident. She pulled another trick at the service station and I pursued her. By the time I realized I had lost her completely, I was miles away.'

'And then you broke with protocol and summoned Damien rather than call me or Jim?'

'Yes.' Nathan kept his gaze on his folded hands on the table. He knew his guilt would be readable to those who knew him well.

'Nathan,' murmured his dad.

'But the hours elapsed do not match your account of your movements,' said Isaac.

'It took me a while to reach a phone. I'd . . . I'd twisted my ankle in the dark.'

The lie lay heavy in the room.

'You seem fully recovered now,' observed Taylor Flint. In his late forties, the dark sleek hair of the Cobra mentor gleamed in the lights, adding to the overall polish of his appearance, hard and unrelenting.

'You were driving when Damien called in,' added Isaac.

Nathan kept silent.

Isaac sighed. 'Nathan, I'm not satisfied with your explanation. I think you're hiding something from us.'

He did not fill the pause with an explanation. The only sound was Dr Waterburn typing rapidly on her laptop, taking notes or writing a research paper on string theory—hard to tell with the elusive mentor of the Owls. Her long brown hair was held in a bun by ebony chopsticks, pale round face tense with concentration.

Isaac's forefinger caressed the edge of the folder on the table in front of him—Nathan's personnel file. 'I see. You are off the case.'

He hadn't expected any other outcome, Nathan reminded himself.

'In the event that you were telling us part of the truth, I've sent another team to Lichfield. They are working under Miranda Yang's leadership. I hope for their sake—and yours—that this isn't a wild goose chase.'

'It is my best guess as to where Kate would go next, sir. She let slip a few hints.' He didn't even have to lie this time to mislead. Kate had given them the destination herself.

Isaac's face was granite. 'But what I can't accept from one

of my agents is a failure to be honest with me. I have no choice but to suspend you until you come up with a full and frank account of what you've been doing in the last twenty-four hours.'

An amazing kiss on the beach came into Nathan's mind. That wasn't going in any official report.

'Do you have anything to say, Nathan?'

'May I have a piece of paper?'

Jim made a move to intercept, clearly thinking Nathan was about to write his resignation. He trapped Nathan's hand under his. 'Give it until tomorrow to think about it, Nathan.'

'It's OK, Dad. It's not that.' As the mentors looked on curiously, Nathan wrote a quick note, shielding it from other eyes and the CCTV.

I apologize for the holes in my account but YDA communications are compromised. I have more to tell you but it can't be here. Will you give me a chance to explain by meeting me outside at the entrance on Clink Street immediately after this? Please do not mention my suspicions to anyone else. Kate's life depends on it.

Nathan folded the paper and passed it to Isaac. Mouth pressed in a cynical line, Isaac shook open the message. His eyebrows winged up on reaching the first sentence. He refolded the note and put it inside his jacket pocket.

'What did he say?' asked Jim, glancing at Nathan, hurt not to be included in the confidence.

'An apology.' Isaac shrugged as if it were no matter. 'As you suggest, Jim, I think it would be a good idea to leave this for tonight. We've done all we can here. Nathan, you can sleep in your usual room, but tomorrow you'll have to vacate the premises until your suspension is resolved.'

'Yes, sir.' Isaac was giving no sign that he believed the note. Was he going to meet him as requested?

'Does anyone have anything else to say before we end?'

The mentors shook their heads.

'Thank you for staying on, ladies and gentlemen. We'll meet at seven-thirty in the morning to plan our next steps in this mission. The Lichfield team should be in place by then. There's also the smaller matter of Damien's behaviour—going to fetch Nathan without permission—but we can postpone that conversation. Nathan, you are dismissed.'

Nathan got up, confused as to what Isaac intended. Jim stood up at the same time.

Isaac's gaze swept over Nathan, taking in his dad's protective stance. 'Jim, you can see Nathan tomorrow. I know you have questions for him but I think he should get to bed. It's been a long day for us all.'

'Goodnight, Nathan.' Jim gave him a bone-crushing hug, using his touch to say what he couldn't speak out loud.

'Sorry, Dad.'

'We'll sort this out, you'll see. You're a good lad.' His voice sounded thick with emotion. Jim would see being kicked out the YDA as the worst kind of failure. Funny how Nathan's own priorities had shifted so far that it no longer seemed very important.

'See you tomorrow.' Nathan left the room still wondering if Isaac was going to act on the note. He was a hard man to read.

Damien, Kieran, and Raven were waiting for Nathan in the corridor. Raven ran straight at him and hugged him hard. This was his night for being embraced, it would seem.

'You OK? Really?' She patted him on the chest in a comforting gesture.

Nathan nodded. 'I'm OK.'

'I was doing my nut about you! So was Kieran, weren't you?' She stretched out a hand to pull Kieran closer.

Nathan was aware that Kieran was examining him closely. His gaze was even more terrifying than Isaac's because he had the uncanny ability to read secrets from a crumb or speck of mud.

'Interesting,' Kieran said, green eyes narrowing as he considered the evidence.

Raven nudged him. 'Say you're pleased he's OK.'

'I'm pleased you're OK. Damien said there was more to your story than he could tell us here.'

Nathan held Kieran's eyes and then looked up deliberately to the CCTV in the corner.

'Is that so?' Kieran rubbed his jaw. 'I would have thought it impossible.'

'Let's not discuss this in the corridor,' said Damien.

Nathan headed for the lift. 'I've been suspended—I'm off the mission.'

'It was inevitable. You went off the grid,' said Kieran.

'And sent to bed without my supper by them.' Nathan gestured to Isaac's office.

The doors opened and they piled into the lift. Nathan pressed the button for the ground floor.

'So why are we heading out?' asked Raven.

'Because I've got a bedtime story to tell.'

'You passed the note?' asked Damien.

Nathan nodded.

'You guys are being very mysterious,' grumbled Raven. 'What note?'

'I think you'd better not say anything more, Raven,' said Kieran.

'What? I've got questions—I won't be told to be quiet!'

Kieran clearly thought as Nathan did on these matters: action was better than argument. He gave a sigh then hauled Raven into his arms for a kiss. It didn't finish until they reached the ground floor.

'What was that for?' she spluttered. 'Not that I didn't enjoy it, but still!'

'Kiss her again,' said Damien. 'She doesn't get it.'

Kieran bent to her ear and whispered. Her dark eyes flicked to the cameras. Cheeks flushed from kissing, she flapped her hand at her face. 'I need a breath of air after all those meetings,' she announced. 'You guys going to come with me to keep me company?'

Thank you, Raven. 'Happy to,' said Nathan.

They headed out on to the street. Nathan felt the pressure of minding his words lift from his shoulders.

'You think the system has been breached?' asked Kieran immediately. As he had had a large hand in devising the communications and IT network, he had a vested interest in Nathan's reply.

'Sure of it, Key. The Scorpions knew about the phone call I made to Isaac, probably before you did.'

'I'm confident of my design.'

'I'm not saying the fault has to be in the system.'

'Someone on the inside?'

'That's what Kate thinks. Or a new bugging device we've not yet seen.'

'Where is she? She's here, isn't she?' Raven looked up and down the street as if she expected Kate to jump out on them.

'We've left her somewhere safe.'

'But the other team have gone north—is she there?'

'They won't find her.' Nathan grimaced. Miranda Yang was not going to like it when she found out what he'd done, sending her team off to Lichfield and, committed to Kate, he no longer had the option to kiss and make up. 'I'm sorry about that, but we had to say something to put the Scorpions on the wrong track. Isaac can call Miranda's team back in when he knows what's going on.'

'And here he is now,' murmured Damien as Isaac slipped out of the main door. He headed for them, hands shoved deep in his jacket pockets. Nathan breathed more easily; Isaac was giving him a chance.

'Cafe opposite Borough Market is open all night,' Isaac said briefly, striding past them.

Giving him a moment to get ahead, they followed at a discreet distance, giving the impression to any watchers that they were merely going for the walk Raven had suggested. When Nathan was sure they weren't being shadowed, they turned into the little cafe. It catered mainly for the market stall owners who made their deliveries in the early hours of the morning, so this was the quiet period. There was a practical roughness to the decor. The bench tables were wipe-clean Formica, coffee served in thick white mugs: a comfortable place for a guy in boots and overalls to hang out after offloading veg without being afraid he'd damage something.

Nathan ordered a round of drinks from the man at the counter and joined the team at the table at the rear. Isaac was already in occupation, a black coffee on the table in front of him.

'I see the whole gang's here,' Isaac said wryly, nodding to Kieran, Raven, and Damien.

Nathan nodded. 'Yes, sir. I can vouch for every member of my team.'

'I thought I just kicked you off the mission.'

'You did, but I have respectfully reinstated myself until you've heard the whole story.'

Isaac appreciated the irony of having his orders ignored with the greatest respect. He toasted Nathan's cheek with his mug. 'This better be good.'

'Kate's mission was compromised last year by a leak from within the YDA. That's why she didn't come in. She doesn't know the source, but she has had plenty of experience since to show that her fears are not groundless.'

Isaac brushed the edge of his jaw with his knuckles, thinking. 'Are you sure, Nathan, that this isn't just a clever fabrication on her part? We trained her to shift story to suit her ends. I'm not blaming her but it would be the kind of excuse a Cat would invent.'

'I took that view myself until she confronted me with the evidence.'

'What evidence?'

'I called you from the service station in Suffolk. The Scorpions arrived before the car you sent for us.'

'You're sure it was them?' Isaac shook his head, correcting himself. 'Of course you are, or you wouldn't have gone AWOL for a day.'

The waitress arrived with a tray of drinks. Raven struck up a bright conversation with Damien about a midnight cruise on the Thames in a stronger American accent than her usual, providing them with cover for their presence in the cafe in the middle of the night. Nathan paid the tab so the waitress wouldn't be tempted to return to the table and eavesdrop.

This little pause gave Isaac time to regroup from the shock of finding his organization had been infiltrated. 'Kieran: your assessment?'

Kieran steepled his long fingers together, tapping the tips. 'Unlikely to be a hardware issue. The system is top of the range. Nat thinks I might have missed a new kind of bug but I think that implausible. I've looked into what the research teams in the world's various secret services and military are doing in this area and we are up with the frontrunners.'

'But have you checked on the hostiles? This could be Iranian, Russian or Chinese design.'

'Sir, I was thorough.' And if Kieran said he was thorough, then that meant he had explored everything there was to be known on a subject.

'And I'm best off not knowing how you did it, I suppose,' said Isaac. 'Still, I want you to run a discreet check of the entire system as your priority. If you do find the bug, don't deactivate it, but bring it privately to my attention. We can use it to our advantage once we know where it is.'

'And if there is no bug?' asked Damien.

Isaac twisted his mug, thinking. 'Then we have someone undercover in the YDA. I thought we'd rooted that out when we got rid of Tina. Does Kate have any idea who?'

Nathan shook his head. 'No, she suspects everyone.'

'Good girl,' Isaac murmured.

'Apart from you.'

Isaac smiled bleakly. 'That's a relief.'

'She knows that the leaks are close to you though. If something has got into the system, it's monitoring your communications. Taking last night as an example, that means the senior management, your office staff, and my team are all under suspicion.'

'I could have done it,' said Kieran without sounding too distressed that he was in the frame. 'Indeed, if I were a hostile, I'd target me. I know the comms and I have access to everything, including the things I'm not supposed to have access to.'

'You are digging a hole here, Kieran,' warned Isaac.

'Just telling the truth, sir.'

Raven elbowed him. 'No one thinks it's you, Ace.'

'I'm just exploring the theory.'

'Well, you can discount yourself, can't you, without running it through the logic?'

'I suppose I can. And you.'

'Thanks.' Raven smiled up at him.

'Because you weren't here last year.'

She opened her mouth to protest, then realized he was teasing her. 'Thanks,' she repeated sardonically.

'Before Kieran dissects us all with his logic, I can say that all of you at this table have my full confidence.' Isaac rubbed his face wearily. 'I'm going to have to think the unthinkable and examine the conduct of my closest colleagues. Kieran, I hope you are wrong: I hope it is a listening device.'

There was nothing anyone could say to that with Kieran's earlier denial still fresh in their minds.

Isaac changed the subject. 'Will Kate see me? I need her help working out what's been going on. I'm still unclear what happened at the end of her mission.'

Nathan and Damien exchanged a look. 'She . . . she is wary of meeting you,' Nathan said cautiously.

'Understood, but I still need to see her. I can ensure no one knows where I am; there'll be no risk.'

Nathan had known Isaac would insist on this. 'She's more than wary, sir. She's changed.' She was ashamed, but Nathan didn't want to throw that out there for public consumption.

'Nathan, when the chips are down, she's my responsibility.'

'She doesn't hold you to that. She considers her disappearance was her resignation note.'

The expression in Isaac's eyes hardened. 'I don't agree. She's still one of mine—you all are. You aren't the only one who cares what happens to her.'

'I know, sir.'

'Are you telling me your first loyalty is now to her, rather than to the YDA?'

Raven had the tact to look away, embarrassed to be listening to this part of the conversation. Kieran's expression was of polite interest; Damien was scowling.

'I . . . yes, sir,' Nathan admitted. 'It is.'

Unexpectedly, Isaac grinned. 'Good. She needs a champion. Tell her to meet up with me tomorrow. She can set the time, place and conditions. She can even have her defender with her. I don't care what it takes, just make it happen.'

'Yes, sir.'

Isaac pushed away his empty mug. 'Right: until this mess is cleared up, you are still on the case reporting directly to me and no one else. Not even Jim, Nathan. I'm sorry, but it is going to have to look as though you're still suspended. He's going to give you grief about that.'

Nathan shrugged. 'I can handle that. But you can trust Jim Rivers—I swear it.'

'I'm making no exceptions. I would have said the same of everyone close to me. OK, guys: get some sleep. I'll see you all tomorrow.' Isaac got up and exited the cafe, disappearing into the shadows outside. He was headed away from HQ.

'He's upset,' said Raven astutely.

'The YDA is his brainchild; of course he's upset.' Damien zipped up his jacket and stood. 'We could've just delivered the fatal blow to the agency. If the rot goes all the way to the top, we're doomed.'

'That's a happy thought,' said Nathan.

Raven looked shaken, not having realized the seriousness of the threat.

Kieran took her hand and pulled her after him. 'In that case, let's see what we can do to save it.'

Chapter 14

Kate woke early, a shaft of sunlight finding its way through the curtains and falling on to her face. Blinking, she sat up, taking a few moments to remember where she was. Greenwich. Julian's guest room. Green and blue decor. Masculine. Safe.

She opened the curtains to see the view looking out over the trees of the park. A few were turning brown and there was a chill in the air which gave away that autumn was nibbling at the trailing hem of summer. Up at the top of the hill was the Greenwich Observatory. Odd to think how the relatively modest brick building split the entire world with the international timeline. Rubbing her forearms, Kate made a quick plan for the day: get some clothes, make an appointment with the GP, sort out her life and avoid being killed.

See: easy.

She smiled, having long ago decided it was either that or cry, and she was done with tears. At least for the moment she had Nathan on her side. With tiny steps, he was coaxing her to think their relationship could be more than temporary—making her want this when she had never thought she would trust a boy again—but she didn't dare raise her hopes too high. Her life was full of sudden endings.

Her musings were interrupted by a loud voice coming from Julian's living room.

'He's a complete tit if he thinks he can pull a fast one like that! The contract note is already in place. Yeah, yeah, I'll sue the shirt off his back if he tries that. Where is it? Singapore? What the hell is it doing there? It should have been in Shanghai last week.'

She wandered to the door and peeked in. Julian was already dressed, standing by the birdwatcher's telescope he had positioned in the bay window, phone clamped to his ear. He bent down, adjusted the sights, and continued his harangue of the unfortunate bearer of bad news.

'You get the effing package on the plane. Tell the guys in Jakarta to sod off. I'm not buying.'

Jakarta. Kate went cold and backed away. Her plan to run was ruined by bumping into an umbrella stand. It clattered to the tiles of the hallway.

'Yeah, you too, mate.' Julian ended the call and threw the phone on the coffee table. 'You all right, Kate?' His voice had entirely changed from strident to his normal jolly self.

Shakily, Kate righted the stand she had pushed over. 'Yes, fine, Julian.' Was he involved? He dealt with the Far East— prime candidate for Scorpions to involve in their schemes or blackmail. Damien would do anything to protect his loved ones—you could tell that about him by the way he looked out for Nathan.

Julian joined her in the corridor and picked up the walking stick that had fallen out. Kate readied herself to dodge a crack across the skull. Instead, he twirled it like a majorette and threaded it back in the stand that was shaped like an old fashioned telephone box in screaming red.

'Ugly thing, isn't it?' he said happily, a different man from the butt-kicking broker of the phone call. He gave the umbrella stand an affectionate pat. 'Damien gave it to me as joke and I repaid him by putting it in pride of place. I think he is mortified every time he sees it.'

Her fear ebbed a fraction. It was hard to believe a man who had a ridiculous umbrella stand could be plotting to hand her over to the Scorpions.

'Are you feeling all right, my dear? You look a little pale.'

Kate rubbed her cheeks. 'Oh, um, yes, I'm fine.'

'Come and see what I've found then. I was having such a lovely morning until that idiot in Hong Kong rang.' Julian bustled into the living room, returning to the telescope. 'Take a look at that!' He sounded absolutely delighted.

The telescope was focused on an orangey-brown bird with a long beak strutting on the muddy tidal shore of the river. It had to be almost half a mile away but the lens gave amazing definition. She'd only seen equipment as top spec as this at the YDA. She couldn't work out if that made Julian more or less of a suspect.

'See it?'

Kate flinched as she felt Julian's hand rest on her back but he was only nudging her to get a response.

'What is it?'

'A black-tailed godwit.'

'Yes, I see it.' He had to be innocent. Anyone who got excited about a bird with such a silly name at six in the morning had to be above suspicion. She wasn't sure if Damien was also off the hook: there could be a complicated deal going on to protect his uncle's business interests. She would have to consider that—and fast. Even if Damien was the source, she couldn't see him bringing Scorpions to his uncle's door. The danger would come when she left this haven. 'It's . . . lovely.'

'Isn't it? It shouldn't be here, you know; godwits feed further out in the Essex marshes. I last spotted one when I was on volunteering on a bird tagging programme with the RSPB last year: wonderful creatures. I guess this specimen took a wrong turn at the Thames Barrier. Ah, life is good!' He got out a notebook from a battered canvas satchel leaning up against the telescope legs and made an entry. 'Last one logged this far up the Thames in . . . yes, here it is: 1997! This is a great day, Kate. You've brought me good luck.'

She relinquished the place at the scope. Julian was clearly itching to get back to watching his bird superstar. His phone rang. Julian glanced at the screen, frowned and swiped the screen to answer.

'What is it, Armaldo? I don't care—just get it done. That's what I pay you for. Look: something important's come up. Don't bother me for an hour. Got that?' He ended the call and returned to the scope. 'Nothing more important than a wonder of creation; certainly not some annoyingly lost contract to move ten thousand barrels of oil.'

So the package had been normal business, a contract, nothing sinister. 'Can I make you a drink? Tea? Coffee?'

'Er, tea . . . or coffee. Doesn't matter.' Julian fiddled with the fine focus.

Kate headed into the kitchen to put on the kettle. She could probably serve him dishwater and he wouldn't notice. Hunting through his vast collection of teas, she came across a breakfast blend. Loose leaf. She had fun finding the little metal scoop and tea strainer. Her gran would love this. A proper cup of tea, she would call it. Granddad had preferred supermarket teabags. A twist of longing to see him again caught her unawares. She hadn't even visited his grave, didn't know if he was buried or cremated.

She could not do anything about that now. Time to start on her list of chores.

While the tea brewed and the bread toasted, Kate went through the notes pinned to the board over the radiator. As she had hoped, there was a leaflet for the local GP surgery and opening times. Telephone appointments could be made from eight o'clock.

Kate added mobile phone to the list of things she would like to buy. She needed a way to keep in touch with Nathan if she had to run again.

'Kate, quick!' Julian shouted from the front room.

Kate's heart thumped double-time in her chest. She ran in, expecting to see a police car, at least, parked outside. 'What?'

'There's two of them!'

Bloody godwits. 'Oh. That's good.' She sagged against the sofa.

'You have to see—I've never seen two together down here.'

Obligingly, she went to verify that, yes, there were two brown birds prodding their way up and down the mud. Her hands were still trembling when she stood up from the scope. Julian noticed—he could hardly fail to as she was making the telescope rattle.

'Are you sure you are all right, my dear? You are shaking like a leaf.'

'I . . . I'm recovering from something I caught abroad.' Life meltdown. 'I was wondering: can you recommend one of the local GPs?'

'Not malaria, is it? I caught that once in Kenya while watching flamingoes on Lake Nakuru. Damn serious, it was.'

'I'm not sure.'

'Dr Chaudri's your man. He sorts me out every time I go to see him.'

'Thanks. I'll just get your tea.'

Julian intercepted her. 'No, no, I'll do that. You stay there and keep an eye on the godwits for me.' He pulled a low arm-chair over so she could sit comfortably at the window. She could imagine him spending many happy hours in this spot with his beloved birds. The cushions held the curved shaped of his body.

'You don't have to . . . ' She was guided firmly to sit down.

'Greater love hath no man than he give up his bird-watching to look after a house guest,' declared Julian histrionically.

Kate applied her eye to the scope, forcing herself to concentrate on the innocent capers of water birds. When he had gone into the kitchen, she quickly checked the satchel for any more suspicious equipment. The only thing that gave her pause was a case of syringes—that was until she read the instructions on tagging birds with radio frequency identification using microchips that turned out to be about the size of a grain of rice. Her gran's cat had had something similar done by the vet. OK: nothing to worry about. She returned the satchel to where she had found it.

The next hour passed peacefully. She shuffled the chair back when Julian brought in the tea and toast and he continued to bird watch while entertaining her with snippets about the birds he spotted. He let his drink go cold. She had never realized there were so many wild creatures living in London.

'People don't. Most are blind as bats to what's going on under their noses,' Julian agreed. He cast her a shrewd look which she didn't welcome. It was easy to think him a bird-obsessed buffoon, but he wasn't that at all.

The doorbell rang. Julian glanced down at the doorstep.

'Ah, it's your young man. Buzz him in, won't you? He'll like to see the godwits.'

Feeling a wonderful ripple of anticipation in her stomach, Kate went to open the door. Nathan took the stairs two at a time and scooped her up off her feet.

'Missed you,' he said, head buried in her neck where he could kiss the sensitive curve between neck and shoulder.

The shivering this time was entirely welcome. 'Missed you too.'

'You OK?'

'I'm as jumpy as a turkey at Christmas, but I'm fine. Did it go OK at the YDA last night?'

'Yeah. I'll tell you later.'

'Nathan, dear boy!' called Julian.

'You'd better hurry. He's got something important for you,' said Kate, pushing Nathan towards the living room.

Looking serious, Nathan rushed in. Kate smiled to herself and went to make him coffee.

After making sure that Nathan was suitably impressed by the godwits, Julian declared he had to leave for work.

'Here's the spare key, my dear. I won't set the alarm today so you don't have to bother entering the code.'

'Thanks, Mr Castle.'

'Julian.' He held the key out of reach.

'Sorry—yes, Julian.'

He chuckled and dropped it into her palm. 'Have fun.' Picking up his briefcase he strode quickly out of the door.

Nathan waited until they heard the downstairs door close, then gathered her into another hug. 'How are you getting on with him?'

'He's sweet.' She debated whether she should mention the Far Eastern connections, but as it cast doubt on Damien it wouldn't go down well with Nathan. Better to explore that on her own rather than confuse Nathan's loyalties any more than she had already. 'He recommended his GP. I'll just give them a ring and see if I can get an appointment.'

The receptionist was helpful but explained no space was available for a non-emergency problem until the following day. Kate looked at Nathan and he nodded. 'OK, I'll take that one then. Ten thirty you say? Thank you.' Putting the phone down, she crossed her arms. 'So, that leaves me the whole day free. I really need to do some shopping.'

'Great. I'll come with you.'

164

'Don't you need to be at the YDA?'

Nathan shrugged. 'I'm suspended and trying to avoid awkward questions, so no. I left a message to tell my dad I'd gone to get a new phone. He can't moan about that.'

'I'll just get ready then.' She returned to her bedroom and put on her old clothes. She couldn't wait to have a new outfit; she was heartily sick of the jeans and T-shirt she had been wearing for the past few days. She could hear Nathan moving about in the kitchen, stacking the dishwasher and humming to himself.

'What are you singing?' she called.

'A song about not giving up.'

'And you don't, do you?' She brushed her hair with a soft bristled brush. Her fine hair started to lift up with the static, so she gave up and tucked it behind her ears.

'I certainly don't. Can I come in?'

She opened the door. 'Sure. I'm decent. Just need to put my shoes on.' She held them up and a trickle of sand escaped. 'I think I wrecked these when I waded in the sea under the pier.'

'Let's get you sorted then—new shoes too.' He cupped the back of her head as she sat on the bed and leant over to do up the laces. 'Wait a moment: let me look at this thing on your neck.'

Kate held still. She couldn't see it herself, only feel it. 'What does it look like?'

'It looks more like a scar than a bite.'

'A scar?'

'Did you cut yourself there?'

'Not that I remember, but maybe when I was running away. I might not have noticed if I had other things on my mind.'

'Like staying alive?'

'Yes.'

'I'm glad you've got that appointment.' He let his fingers brush the underside of her hair tenderly.

Kate sat up, giving herself a moment to let the blood rush subside from being upside down—or maybe it had been the effect of his caress? She noticed that Nathan was looking down at her warily. 'What?'

He smiled and shook his head. 'I can't hide anything from you for long, can I?'

She shrugged. 'Cats are trained to see these details. It's how we survive.'

'It's just that someone else has made an appointment with you.'

'Isaac?' .

'Yes. He made me promise to bring you to him today—the place and time are your choice.'

Kate bit her thumbnail then shoved her hand down on her lap. Another bad habit she had to break—that, and getting into life-threatening situations. She would have liked to refuse to see Isaac but she knew that was because she was ashamed, not because she couldn't think of a secure way of meeting him.

'He needs your help, Kate. I told him about the leak and he's having to ask some very difficult questions about the people he works with. You could give him the right direction to explore.' Nathan sat beside her and bumped her with his shoulder. 'Remember you've got Damien and me on your side.'

Kate wasn't ready to trust Damien after hearing his uncle's conversation this morning. 'If it's OK with you, I'll see Isaac but just with you. I don't want to get Damien tangled up in my business more than he is already.'

'He doesn't mind. Isaac's sanctioned his role in this so he isn't in trouble.'

Kate flexed her thumb, looking at the ragged skin around the nail. 'Still, let's just keep it to you, me, and Isaac. We need a place no one will expect us to go—with lots of exits. Any ideas?'

'There's a cafe in Covent Garden I know. It's in the covered market area but you can get out easily, and then you're close to several underground stations. If we have to run, no one will know which way we've gone.'

'Sounds good. Let's set that up. But how are you going to get a message to him?'

'Are you OK with me using Raven as a messenger? You know for sure that she isn't involved in the spying as she's new.'

'That's fine.'

'I'll ring her and ask her to pass the message on in person.' He started to rise.

Kate tugged his sleeve. 'She knows not to say anything out loud?'

'Sweetheart, she's good at what she does. Stop worrying.' He cupped her face briefly, letting his fingers linger a little as he removed his hand. 'How I wish I could make you trust us.'

'I do trust you.'

He smiled wryly. 'You do, in the sense of not betraying you, but you don't trust us not to mess things up. You've forgotten how to be a team player.' He left the room to make the call on Julian's phone.

Kate got up and straightened the duvet. Nathan was right about her trust issues but she had never been much of a team player even before the disaster, feeling an outsider in the YDA despite acting super-confident. The last time she had been in a team she had been betrayed by her partner, so it was hard to let down her guard. But she wanted to be different. She wanted to be like Raven: happy, part of a friendship group, in love. Kate was afraid that the only part of that she was experiencing was the last and, without the security the other two provided, falling in love was more a torment than a source of comfort.

'Ready to go?' Nathan was back in her doorway.

Pulling herself together, Kate nodded. 'Yes, let's hit the High Street.'

Shopping with Nathan proved to be more fun than Kate expected, mostly because clearly he was bored rigid by it and trying to hide the fact. The shopping centre near Stratford had a fabulous selection of shops, so she was indulging the chance just to do something normal: be fussy about her clothes. She came out of the changing room in her fifth pair of jeans to ask his view and found him surfing the news channels on his new phone.

'What do you think?' she asked, displaying the light blue skinny jeans.

Nathan nodded. 'Great. But so were the last pair—and the one before that. You look good in anything.'

'Thank you. I think I'll get these and the grey ones.'

'Good idea.' His eyes were drifting back to the phone screen.

'Or maybe I should look some more?'

She could almost hear the 'give me strength' cry inside Nathan's head. 'Whatever you think best.'

She smiled brightly. 'Just joking. These are fine.'

'Joking?' He tucked his phone away, not quite hiding his relief.

'I can see that for you clothes shopping is a huge pleasure.' She went back into the changing room and sorted out her purchases. When she came out to hand the rejects to the assistant, Nathan was looking pensive.

'Shopping's not that bad,' he said gamely.

He was such a boy scout, trying to be the perfect guy for her. She nudged him. 'Don't lie; you hate it.'

'It's just that jeans all look the same to me.' His eyes

sparkled. 'Now, if you wanted to get a dress or something like that, then I'd really pay attention.'

Maybe not so much a boy scout after all. 'Dresses aren't practical.'

He put his hand on her hip, pulling her closer and behind a tall rack of clothes in the designer section. 'Exactly—but think how much fun we'd have choosing one. I've not seen you wear anything . . . you know . . . '

'Pretty?'

'I was going to say "special".' He lifted the two pairs of jeans from her hands. 'Find something you really like, something to go out in.'

'I go out in jeans.' She had to, in case she had to run again.

'I mean, wear on a date.' He thought for a moment. 'With me.'

'It'll be a waste of money.'

'No, it'll be an investment. I fully expect in the near future to be able to take you somewhere on a date so I want you to be ready. A club. Or maybe a gig. What do you like?'

She wasn't sure as her life hadn't really been normal of late. 'I suppose I like live music—a big concert, like at the O2, would be fun. Shame to live in Greenwich and not go.'

'I'll get tickets. So something you can dance in then. Go choose. I'll wait here.'

Taking a seat outside the changing room, Nathan got out his phone again.

'You sure?'

He just raised an eyebrow.

'OK, I'm going.' Humming to herself, she browsed the racks and picked a few dresses that would work for a concert. They would need tights and boots too: would he realize that? Brushing a kiss on the top of his head as she passed him on the way to the changing room, she quickly tried on the various

169

options. She decided on a poppy flower tunic dress which she could also wear with leggings when not dressing up. The colours reminded her of the fairgrounds she had known: bold and bright. Her gran would like it as much as she did.

Nathan stood up as she came out. 'You're not going to show me?'

She shook her head. 'Nope. It'll be a surprise when you get those tickets.' She handed back the three unwanted dresses and thanked the assistant.

'Do you need anything else—stuff to go with it?' Nathan asked.

He had noticed, 'Like what?'

'You know—other things.' He gestured to the underwear section of the shop.

'Yes, I do. Do you want to sit outside that changing room too?'

He tugged at his collar. 'I was thinking I might go down and look at the men's section.'

She giggled. 'Yes, Nathan, you go and look at manly things like socks and ties. I'll go deal with lingerie.'

Looking somewhat relieved, Nathan took the escalator down. Kate chose some underwear and tights in her size then went to find him. He was perusing the racks of T-shirts.

'Seen something you like?' she asked.

'This trip is about you.' He shoved the T-shirt he was holding back on the peg.

Kate took it out again and held it up against him. 'This would suit you. That blue really works.'

'You think?' He looked pleased at her endorsement of his taste.

Kate added it to her collection. 'Let's get it. You can wear it to the gig with me.' This wonderful, impossible dream concert.

'OK, it's a deal.'

170

Clothes bought, then new plimsolls and boots purchased, Kate felt absurdly pleased with her morning. The only thing she didn't like was being weighed down with bags when they were going to meet Isaac. If she had to flee then they would have to abandon their new things.

'Do we have time to go back to Greenwich?' she asked.

Nathan checked his watch. 'Not if we're to get there before him. I want to watch him arrive to make sure no one is following.'

He was right: that would be a good idea. 'I'm worried we might have to dump our stuff.'

Nathan scratched his jaw, thinking. 'I see.' Kate could have kissed him when he didn't tell her to stop panicking. 'Look, just give me a moment.' Nathan left her on a bench while he went into an outdoor wear store. He came back with a light-weight backpack. 'Let's put everything in there.'

'Thank you, Nathan.'

'For?'

'For understanding me.'

His hand paused over the drawstring to the central compartment. 'Kate, I get it that you've learned to expect the worst. I don't imagine you can drop your caution so soon, and with such a real threat hanging over you.'

His kindness made tears well up. *Stop it, you idiot*, she told herself. She looked hard at her new Rocket Dog boots while he packed away their purchases.

'You don't need to do that, you know,' he said quietly.

'What?'

'Hide when you're upset.'

'I'm not upset.'

'Then what are you?'

She passed her wrist over her eyes. 'Emotional. Stupid and weak.'

Dropping the backpack on the ground, he gathered her into his arms. 'You are not stupid and weak. You are wonderful. You are a survivor.'

That made the surge of feeling even more acute. 'Nathan, I don't deserve you.'

He hugged her tight to his chest. 'You deserve better, but it's me you've got so . . . ' He kissed her, soft warm lips, cruising along the line of her mouth to the corner and back to the centre. They were in the middle of a busy shopping centre but it felt like they were the only people in the world. Kate felt some of the tension slip from her shoulders. She put her hands up to his cheeks, shaping her palms to the smooth skin from where he had shaved that morning. It was becoming a little rough again as the bristles grew back; his jaw felt firm, determined to face down all threats. His eyebrows were silky soft, as was the hair over his ears.

A wolf whistle interrupted their kiss. They broke apart to find a couple of guys in hard hats and reflective jackets passing by with a takeaway tray of coffees. Kate blushed, embarrassed to have so forgotten herself that she had ended up half-wrapped around him.

Nathan grinned. 'Don't mind them: they're just jealous. Who needs caffeine when you've got Kate to get the pulse racing?' He shouldered the backpack and held out his hand for her to take.

Chapter 15

'Is Isaac on his own?' Kate peered over the rack of scented soaps in the small perfume shop. One door opened out to the street to the north and there was a clear escape route to Covent Garden Tube station; the other went south into the market with its pavement cafes, arched glass roof and bold pigeons. Crowds of tourists flowed through the space, providing cover for them but also for any potential watchers.

Nathan stood by the market exit, pretending to browse the essential oils. His hunter instincts were fully deployed, eyes focused on the passers-by, body held poised for fight or flight. Kate felt a strange flutter in her chest—part professional admiration, part desire. He just looked so . . .

Mind on the mission, she reprimanded herself. She wasn't too worried about this meeting as she knew Isaac would not betray her. He had military training and would surely know how to shake off a tail if he suspected he was being followed.

'Looks clear,' said Nathan. 'He's sat down at the table and is ordering.'

'Shall we?'

Nathan moved his hand out to block her exit. 'I asked him to order three drinks if it was safe, only one if he wasn't sure.'

Kate bit her lip. The waiter seemed to be taking forever to fulfil the order. Finally, he went back to the table and put two coffees and a tea on the table. 'That's three.'

'OK, let's go. But if I say run, you get away from here.' Holding her collar, he tugged her jacket straight. 'Don't go to Covent Garden station—it has a lift down to the platform and you could be cornered. Get to Leicester Square or Charing Cross and disappear. We'll meet up later as we agreed.'

'Yes, sir.' Kate did not hide her smile. Nathan had been running over the details of their escape plan repeatedly since they arrived in Covent Garden like a nervous commanding officer sending a recruit into battle for the first time. The nearer to the appointment, the more agitated he had become. She had felt the opposite. It would be good to settle her debt to Isaac. It had never sat right with her to abandon her mission but at the time she hadn't seen any other way. Judging the time was right, she took Nathan's hand and tugged him towards Isaac.

Her old boss looked up as they approached, his face registering a brief snatch of pleasure to see her before resuming its usual serious expression. He had the bluest eyes of anyone she knew—formidable like a dragon's stare, if such a creature were to exist. His light blond hair was cut short as usual but he looked more careworn than she remembered. Kate flopped down in the chair beside him, playing the teenager out shopping with her less enthusiastic father.

'The shops round here are so great!' she said loudly as the waiter passed their table. 'I saw an antique hip-flask on a stall over in the next aisle that you might like.'

There was a flicker of appreciation for her blending skills before Isaac joined in. 'I hope you've not spent all the money I gave you already? Anyway, I've had enough shopping today. Here: have a coffee—or would you like tea today?' He had ordered one of both as he hadn't been able to guess her preference. Nathan preferred coffee so Kate picked the tea.

'Thanks.' She dunked the teabag-on-a-string a few times then lifted it out.

'Are we good?' Isaac asked in an undertone.

Nathan had been scanning the crowd while Isaac and Kate did their little opening act. 'No one is paying us any attention. I saw no sign of a tail.'

'I didn't sense one either.' Isaac reached across the table and took Kate's hand briefly. 'Good to see you alive and well, Kate.'

She swallowed. 'Thanks.'

Noticing the catch in her voice, his tone softened. He was being so gentle with her—that alone made her want to weep. 'I'm sorry for what happened to you. I had no idea.'

She tried for a brave shrug. 'Of course you didn't. I'm sorry too for making so many mistakes.'

'I think you only made one: trusting the wrong man.'

She looked away, fixing her gaze on a pigeon strutting along one of the roof beams. 'But people died.'

'If there's a leak at the YDA, then they would've been betrayed another way eventually. I don't want you to hold yourself to blame for that. If you think of it as a line of dominoes, you weren't the one to set the run going: you were the first domino to fall.'

Kate hadn't seen it like that. If only she could persuade her head to absolve herself, but that was impossible. She knew she had made bad choices. 'Thanks for saying that, Isaac.'

He sat back and studied her pensive expression. 'But you don't believe me. I wouldn't in your place, but that's for us to sort out later when we've got you out of this mess.' He leaned closer, getting down to business. 'I need to know anything you know about the source of the leak.'

Kate poured a little milk into her tea and watched the golden brown turn to beige. 'It's close to you.'

'Yes, I got that.'

The waiter passed and conversation lapsed. Nathan stirred his coffee. Kate checked her new phone for imaginary texts. Isaac flicked through a tourist brochure for the area.

Once the man was out of earshot, Kate continued:

'Gani said something about how easy it was to plant his sister among your students—that you weren't suspicious enough—thanks to what was going on under your nose.'

Isaac's jaw clenched. 'That's going to change. I'm bringing in outsiders to vet everyone who works for me and the students.'

Nathan put his coffee cup down. 'You mean you think there might be more like Agustina?'

'I just don't know, do I? As you'll have noticed over the years, we have frequent exchanges with other international agencies training up young detectives and law enforcement officers—that's why Agustina Meosido was accepted. It looked routine to me. We rely on the references provided by the agency that send them to us. I suppose that end was infiltrated too—a message the Indonesian police are just going to love when I tell them. We had not seriously considered that young people at the start of their career could be compromised: that now looks hopelessly naive.'

'When did that exchange programme start exactly?' asked Nathan.

'Five years ago. Why? You on to something?'

'Maybe. And the link to Indonesia: was Agustina the first from there?'

'First and last. We normally work with agencies we know well—Americans, other Europeans and so on. Going to Jakarta was a new departure for us.'

'Can you remember who suggested it?'

Isaac tapped his forefinger against his lips. 'No, I can't but there will be minutes of the meeting. The original approach from Jakarta came via SIS, and Jan Hardy or Taylor Flint would've been the liaison. I'll ask Tamsin to dig out the notes.'

'I think you should do it yourself,' Kate said. 'No one is above suspicion.'

The creases on his brow deepened. 'You're correct, of course. It's just that Tamsin has been with me for years—from the beginning. She is the mother of a soldier under my command who was killed in combat in Iraq. Joe was a good friend.'

'I'm sorry but I think you should start to ask difficult questions about everyone: your PA, your cleaning staff, your caterers, the other mentors. Mrs Hardy, for example, she was closest to the mission—she must have been in a position to compromise it without anyone realizing. She didn't answer any of my calls in the last few days before things went badly wrong.'

'There were no messages from you on record, Kate.' Isaac's gaze narrowed, watching for any telltale signs that she was lying to excuse her behaviour.

'Well, then, that's your first clue. I promise you I was desperate for guidance but didn't get any.'

An awkward silence fell as Isaac absorbed the implications.

'Have you been able to rule out the technical leak yet?' asked Nathan, trying to lighten the mood.

'I left Kieran running a deep search. So far nothing. He is quite insulted that we could even question his system.' Isaac smiled wryly.

'It'll be more insulting to find out it's one of us.'

'That's what I told him.' Isaac turned back to Kate. 'I know we can't cover everything now but I'd like you to write down a full report of what went on in Jakarta. The betrayer is going to be found in the details—the timing—I'm sure of it. Leave nothing out.'

Kate couldn't repress a shudder. Nathan squeezed her leg under the table. She was immensely grateful that he understood how horrified she was at the prospect of admitting the full details of her relationship with Gani. She cleared her throat. 'It's not going to make pleasant reading.'

'Kate, I'm not going to be shocked by anything you write.' Isaac held her gaze with his steady blue eyes. 'The only thing I require from you is the truth. The other problem we have to solve is why the Scorpions have tracked you down so far from their home territory. Even though they are a relatively new organization on the international stage, I know they have influence here too, but that's nothing to their strength back in Indonesia. The sensible thing for them to do was forget you ever existed.'

That was the same point that had been on her mind. 'I don't know why. It makes no sense to me.'

Isaac took another slow survey of the market. The crowds gathered around the street magician were clapping his act; a couple of entertainers waited to take over his spot, tightrope and stands leant against the wall, juggling clubs bunched in their hands. Nothing appeared out of place. 'You should know that Alfin and Yandi Gatra are in the country.'

'What? The big bosses have come all the way here?' Kate half rose from her chair. If the leaders of the Scorpions had both come, this was even worse than she had thought. 'Why?'

'It seems to be about you. They're unhappy that it's taking so long for their men to locate you. They've set themselves up in a suite at the Dorchester. The police have put eyes on them but they are too canny to get caught out that way.'

'This is just stupid! Why come all this way for me? I know nothing!'

The flick of Isaac's gaze to their surroundings warned her to keep her voice down. 'I agree. But you have to see that it is also an opportunity.'

Trust Isaac to have an eye on the benefit. He was ruthless as well as fair-minded.

'What do you mean?' asked Nathan.

'He means that if we can catch them doing something illegal here, we could cut off the head of the organization—kill the Hydra, or at least seriously damage it,' said Kate.

'And here they won't be able to buy their way out of the system,' added Isaac.

Kate gave a sceptical snort.

'Or at least they will have far more difficulty doing so,' Isaac amended.

'What kind of illegal thing?' asked Nathan suspiciously.

'Attempting to kill a seventeen-year-old girl would do it,' said Kate flatly.

'You can't use her as bait!'

'Nathan, I'm already bait and not because of anything Isaac did. It's just the situation, and he is trying to exploit it. It's what we're trained for.'

'I thought you'd resigned.' Nathan was not happy.

'She's still YDA,' said Isaac firmly.

It was sweet to hear him claim her but unrealistic. 'I'm no longer a Yoda, Isaac. I lost the right to be one in Jakarta.'

'Who runs the YDA, Kate: you or me?'

She shook her head, knowing where he was going with this. 'You, Isaac.'

'Then if I say you are still one of us, then you are. End of story.'

So it turned out that Isaac was as stubborn as Nathan. Kate sighed. 'Shall we put this in the "to be resolved later" pile?'

'There's nothing to be resolved. I don't accept your resignation as I believe the grounds on which you offered it were flawed. You think you failed and I think I failed you.'

'Isaac, do you have to be so . . . so decent about everything?'

'I train you to be capable, honest investigators. In return, you can hardly expect me to treat you in any other way.' He signalled the waiter to bring the bill. 'Kate, your orders are to continue to lay low and write up that report for me. Leave the rest of the team to do the leg work on this.' He handed the waiter the cash with a healthy tip included.

'What do you want me to do?' asked Nathan when the waiter had moved off.

'See Kate to wherever you've stashed her.' Isaac's eyes twinkled with intelligence; Kate would lay money on him having a shrewd guess at the address of the safe house. 'Then report in to the YDA. We still need to go through the motions of the disciplinary process. You have to pack up your stuff and take it home.' Nathan grimaced. 'Consider it as part of your punishment.'

'Punishment for what?' asked Kate indignantly. 'I thought you agreed that he wasn't at fault for his actions to protect me?'

Isaac stood up. 'I'll leave Nathan to explain. We've new rules at the YDA since you were last there. See you later.'

Kate watched him stride off, his emphatic gait out of place among meanderings of the soft civilian crowd. 'What rules did Isaac mean, Nathan?'

He picked up the backpack. 'Oh, nothing important.'

She snagged his arm. 'Clearly it is, if you're being punished.'

'Just not to, you know, get emotionally involved on a mission.' He looked a little embarrassed by the admission.

A bubble of happiness welled up inside Kate. 'Are you saying you're emotionally involved with me?'

'Whatever gave you that impression? Was it the decision to throw over my career for you? Or maybe the amount of kissing that we've done in the last day or so?'

She went up on tiptoes and pressed a kiss on his cheek. 'Both. Thank you.' She started walking away, knowing he would follow. Nathan looked so gorgeous when he was hot and bothered. 'But you should challenge Isaac on the punishment thing,' she said over her shoulder.

He caught up. 'On what grounds?'

My, didn't he sound grouchy! As much as he tried to say otherwise, the smudge on his record evidently annoyed him. 'Well, if I'm still YDA, I'm technically your colleague and he lets Raven and Kieran work together. I'm not the mission—I'm part of the mission team even though I didn't know it.'

'You're in the wrong job, Kate. You should be a defence barrister, getting the client off on technicalities.'

She linked her arm through his. 'I'll give it some thought. I need an alternative career. For all Isaac's reassurances I don't think I'll be welcomed back by others at the YDA, do you?'

Nathan dumped his rucksack on the black-and-red tiled doorstep of his family's Victorian terrace home in Battersea and fished in his pocket for the key. Was it too much to ask for his mother to be out? It had been bad enough having to lie to his father and pack up his belongings under Jim's beady eye. Only Damien running interference had prevented a full grilling. He owed his friend for that.

Opening the door released the enticing smell of freshly baked muffins. One question answered.

'Hi, Mum!'

Maisie came out of the kitchen. A part-time art teacher at the local college, she was on one of her at-home days. 'Nathan, darling!' A tall woman with shoulder-length brown hair, she squeezed him in a hug. 'Let's go through and you can tell me all about it.'

Let's not. 'You've made cakes?'

'Of course. They're your favourite.' Leading him through to the kitchen, she took a plate off the rack over the sink and put one of the warm muffins on it. 'Sit down, love.'

Resigned to another round of untruths, Nathan took a seat at the breakfast table under the glazed roof. His parents had extended the narrow kitchen with a conservatory, turning the back of the old terrace into an airy and bright modern room. His mother's landscapes decorated the walls, as well as some of Nathan's own pictures. These ranged from embarrassing scribbles that his mother claimed showed his early promise to his more recent works, on which he was not ashamed to sign his name. His flare was for portraiture, his best being a picture of his parents sitting in deck chairs and laughing—a side of Jim that other YDA students would find hard to credit.

'So they suspended you?' Maisie filled the kettle, letting the water splurt into the jug. She snapped the lid shut and put it smartly down on the base.

'Yes. Isaac said he'll review my case in a week.'

'Don't mention that man! I thought he would know better than this.' Next kitchen object to feel her wrath was the teapot as it was clunked down on the side and the lid yanked off. 'All those years you've studied there without the least cause for complaint and he suspends you on the first little mistake! Jim always said that Isaac had great holes in his judgement, blind spots that would lead the organization into trouble.'

He had to divert her from this subject. 'I did break the rules, Mum. He is treating me like anyone else.'

'Don't you defend him to me!'

'Let's not talk about this now, Mum: it'll only upset you. Tell me what you've been doing. How's the picture of Richmond Park coming along?'

'Oh that. Almost done.' Nathan half-listened as his mum chattered on about her latest projects, but the other part of his mind was with Kate. She had nothing like this behind her, no parents fighting her corner, no home to go to. She was right when she had said that he had had a pretty cushy ride since he had been adopted by two such decent people. He felt a surge of anger at Kate's mother, old enough now to do more than palm her daughter off on her in-laws. When talking about her background, Kate hadn't expressed any hurt or expectations of more, but if he had his way he'd make sure Maya Hubble took more interest in being family for her older daughter.

And how are you going to do that exactly? mocked an inner voice. *Force a mother to love her child? How does that work?* Nathan knew he had a tendency to think he could be the one to solve all the world's problems. This was one thing beyond his control. All he could do was offer Kate his love and hope that was enough.

Love.

The word sat there in his mind, glittering, diamond-edged. Rolling his shoulders, he decided he was comfortable with the acknowledgement that he had fallen for Kate. He had already been predisposed, thanks to his hopeless crush, but now he knew her, not just the image, and had far more substantial reasons on which to base his feelings. The real battle he anticipated was persuading Kate to love him in return when so many had let her down. She liked him, he felt sure of that, but love?

'You all right, darling?' Maisie asked, refilling his mug from the teapot.

'Er, yes.'

'It's just that you look a little funny.'

'Funny how?'

'Stunned, like you've taken a knock to the head.'

He had to smile at that diagnosis. Love was a bit like that: sneaking up on you, bashing you over the head and leaving you reeling. 'I'm fine, really. I haven't told you enough, but I really appreciate all you and Dad have done for me.'

'Oh, darling, you don't need to say that.' His mother

cuddled him to her chest, ruffling his hair. 'You're a wonderful boy. We're your greatest fans.'

Nathan gently extricated himself from her embrace. 'Show me your picture and then I have to go out.'

Disappointment showed in her eyes. 'Again? So soon?'

'I'm meeting up with friends.'

'Damien, I suppose.' Maisie tutted. She wasn't as opposed to Damien as Jim, but neither was he a favourite.

'And Kieran and Raven.'

Maisie cheered up. 'Such a nice boy, Kieran. I'm so pleased he's found himself a lovely girl. You could do with one of those, you know.'

'I'm working on it.' Nathan put his finger to his mother's lips before she could ask the obvious questions. 'Early stages. Not yet ready to share.'

Maisie beamed. 'When the moment's right, you know you can bring her home. I won't embarrass you, I promise.'

'I know that. Studio?'

'Come on then.' Maisie headed upstairs to her room in the attic with the good light for painting. 'I don't want to hold you up but I've been waiting to ask your opinion on it. You always see things clearly.'

He hoped she was right. Someone needed to see through the mess at the YDA before more people suffered.

Kate couldn't stay in the flat once Nathan had dropped her there. Still not settled in her mind that she could trust Damien, she decided not to spend long stretches of time inside when Uncle Julian was out. Just in case. She had survived a year following instincts so opted not to risk everything by changing her habits now. Finding a quiet corner of Greenwich library in a study carrel far from the librarians' desk, she set out her pad and pen. The white page, faintly lined, glared at her. It was like looking down at a pool from the top of a high board. Just to break the surface, she picked up the pen and scribbled on the first sheet, tore it up and balled it up for later disposal. Right: down to business. Isaac wanted a full and frank report, did he? That was what he was going to get, even if the thought made her want to howl. Forcing herself to face the past, the memories flooded back.

Getting off the plane in Jakarta had been her introduction to the humid heat of the Indonesian capital. The walkway between the plane door and the terminal wasn't air conditioned and she had immediately been doused in the tropics. First time out of Europe and in one of the world's largest countries by population, Kate had found the sensation incredibly exciting. Even the breathing was different here.

'Good to be home?' she asked Tina.

Her friend smiled, quiet brown eyes lighting up. 'Really good. I've spent the last six months feeling cold.'

'But that was our summer!'

'Exactly. I can't wait to show you around my city.' Tina frowned, correcting herself with her usual caution. 'I mean, if we get time.'

They separated for the passport check: Tina to the queue for locals, Kate for foreigners. Kate's line went more rapidly as the flight from Europe held mainly well-travelled business men and package holidaymakers, whereas Tina's queue had a large number of returning migrant workers whose status had to be checked. Meeting up on the other side, Kate felt the bubble of anticipation expand. This was it: the start of her first mission! It was everything she had ever dreamt of: an exotic location, an important task, something she felt well up to handling.

'OK, from here on we are on the job,' murmured Tina. 'Remember the cover story at all times: I'm a poor girl from one of the islands come to make good in the city and you're a westerner, travelling the world on your gap year, who has run out of money and luck. We meet by chance at the airport and get the bus into the city.'

Rescuing her luggage from the carousel, Kate stuffed her heavy puffa jacket into the top of her backpack. She wouldn't be needing that again. 'Got it. Lead on.'

Tina had a little room in a low rise building in an area called Blok M in South Jakarta. A mixed area of main roads, flyovers, foreign and local businesses, and mid-range housing, it was rumoured to be the centre of the Scorpion network in Indonesia. The noise in the flat was constant, either from the road construction workers or the heavy streams of traffic that never stopped, day or night. Lights flashed and pulsed on the bars and hotels of the area, illuminating the darkness with their feverish energy. Street kids hid in back alleys, swarming out when they spotted anyone who looked good for a few coins. Offers to shine her shoes numbered in their hundreds, even though she was wearing canvas plimsolls.

'Good try, but no thanks,' she replied, knowing not to encourage the beggars by handing out loose change.

After a couple of days of acclimatization, Tina and she prepared for their first night on the job. They were to hang out at Bar Z, an extremely dodgy operation that attracted shoals of ayams, as the local prostitutes were known, as well as shady businessmen and drug dealers. The intelligence on the Scorpions was that they snapped up innocents who foolishly wandered into their territory. Kate, with her western passport and youth, would be attractive as a possible drugs mule so it was unlikely they would let the opportunity slip.

Squeezing into the tight black skirt and lacy top, Kate applied a thick layer of makeup and tied her hair back in a tight ponytail. She checked her reflection in the wall mirror: she looked like a character from a soap, one of the dippy ones who end up on the wrong side of the law or with a violent boyfriend. Mascara running down the face for the cheery Christmas episode. Perfect.

'You ready?' she called to Tina, who was still in the bathroom. Her own visits there were as brief as possible as it smelt and attracted cockroaches.

'Two minutes.'

Having nothing to do but worry, Kate distracted herself by pulling out the copy of 'The Quiet American' the Yodas had given her knowing she liked Graham Greene. That wiry joker, Nathan, had pressed it into her hand just as she was leaving for the airport. Her classmate was a cutie but she hadn't encouraged him, not knowing what to do with his devotion. She was essentially a loner. Her eye fell on the middle of the page she had read last night. 'You say that we've always tried to tell the truth to each other, but, Thomas, your truth is always so temporary.' She got out a pencil and underlined it with a wry smile. Temporary truth – that summed up her role to deceive the bad guys.

Tina emerged in a satin high-necked dress and heels.

Kate grinned. 'You look cheap.'

Tina wasn't smiling, her face apprehensive. 'And you look gullible.'

'Great.' Was Tina really worried? 'This is going to be fine. Really it is.' She squeezed Tina's cold hand, waiting for the nod of agreement. Even though Tina was older, Kate felt protective of her. She had a much more dangerous role to play than Kate. 'Right. Let's check in and let them know we are going out.' Leaving Tina to contact the local intelligence handler who was supposed to be monitoring them, Kate texted Jan and Isaac back at the London HQ.

Mission launched.

The bar was beginning to fill up with the after-work crowd. No one asked for proof of age so they passed inside freely, tottering on too-high heels. Many of the Asian girls hanging out in the lounge area looked younger than Kate and Tina—no more than thirteen or fourteen. Kate felt sickened. She had known about child trafficking and exploitation but to see it brought it home. That slim girl smiling up at that obese man in a suit: what was her life like? Unbearable. The importance of the mission was even greater than she imagined: Kate vowed to make this succeed; she would bring down this network and save a few lives from being sucked down the traffickers' plughole.

Ordering a drink at the bar, the two girls sat on the high stools and waited, making occasional conversation, though the level of the sound system made even that hard. Kate surveyed the place, hoping to spot the intelligence agents who should be guarding them. The atmosphere in the bar was brash and brutal; it would be a comfort to know where their bodyguards were but she daren't ask Tina. Beyond the counter was an area separated by opaque glass sliding doors. A bouncer stood at the entrance letting only a select few inside. Tina had already warned her there was an inner sanctum where only gang members and their friends were allowed. The passport to that zone appeared to be something on the wrist or forearm—a bracelet or mark perhaps?

A man stumbled between them, a banknote clutched in his hand. 'Excuse me, ladies. Can I get you a drink?' He sounded foreign—German, Kate guessed. He had clearly already had more alcohol than was wise. He would probably end up stripped and wallet-less before the end of the night. Kate ignored him but Tina played along. She was supposed to look as if she had aspirations for joining the ayams. Turning away to let her work, Kate found a tall slim Indonesian man had taken the stool beside her. Dark hair, soulful expression, he was attractive in a lost poet way. Their eyes met. Kate smiled in a friendly rather than flirty fashion.

'Hi.'

'Hello.' He sipped his drink. 'You want another one?'

Kate touched her sparkling water. 'No, thanks. I'm good for the moment.'

'Maybe later.'

'Maybe.'

'Are you from America?'

'No, England. You?'

'I'm from here.'

'You speak very good English.'

His face brightened. 'Thank you. I studied at college but I don't think I've ever spoken to an English girl. I'm glad the extra hours I worked were worth it.'

He was incredibly sweet, expression almost puppyish in its open pleasure at her compliment. 'I'm Kate, by the way.'

He held out his hand and gave hers a firm shake, holding on just a little longer than strictly necessary. 'Pleased to meet you, Kate. I'm Gani.'

Chapter 16

No longer allowed into headquarters while his suspension was in effect, Nathan met up with his team in a sandwich bar at nearby London Bridge station. The old station was a labyrinthine network of draughty tunnels and stairs taking passengers from the underground to the overground rail, which made it possible for them all to approach from different directions with next to no chance of anyone managing to follow them in the rush-hour crowds.

'So, Key, what did you find?' Nathan asked, putting his juice down beside his friend on the sticky table at the back of the cafe. Earthen-brown and green signs declared that everything here was freshly picked and organic; unfortunately the staff appeared to be trying to grown their own fungus on the dirty surfaces.

Kieran moved up closer to Raven to make room for him on the bench. 'Nothing. Absolutely nothing. I would swear to the system being secure.' Kieran tapped on his tablet computer and showed Nathan a series of diagrams that made absolutely no sense to him.

'What am I looking at? Spaghetti carbonara?'

'My diagnostics. The data is coming up reliably clean. No echo or bounce.'

Nathan massaged the back of his neck in weary resignation. 'So much for that idea. It's going to be human then.'

'That's the logical deduction.'

Raven offered Nathan a wafer biscuit in silent commiseration. 'How far has Isaac got with vetting—anyone know?'

Damien reached over the table and took two wafers. 'He was out all afternoon so we didn't get a chance to talk to him.'

'He met up with Kate and me in Covent Garden. I guess he is going to pursue this as much as possible away from his desk.'

'Doesn't stop us trying to find answers ourselves.'

'No, I guess not. Let's do a table round—see who we think we should look into first. Damien?'

His best friend pulled a face. 'Sergeant Rivers is out of the running as far as you're concerned? If he wasn't like, you know, *your dad*, I'd think it was him just because he is the only one who hates us all.'

Nathan knew it was only right that Damien should ask difficult questions, but still it was hard to have to query someone he loved. 'Yes, I'd stake my life on it—but that's because I live with the guy. If Dad is hiding a secret like this, then he is doing it twenty-four seven. He doesn't have it in him to live a double life: what you see is what you get.'

Kieran nodded, clicking over a flow chart of the leadership team within the YDA. 'I agree: he is low down on my list of possibles.'

'Thanks, Key.' Nathan felt warmed by his friend's support for his difficult-to-like parent.

'Not that he doesn't have it in him to be ruthless and uncaring,' continued Kieran blithely, 'and a marked propensity for violence; but he has the bullish character of someone who would tackle a problem head on, not a scheming mind playing a long game of double-cross.'

Raven nudged him.

'What?' Kieran blinked owlishly.

Nathan sighed. 'OK, Key, I think we've got the picture.

We'll come back to you in a moment.' Nathan was leaving Kieran until last, knowing his friend would have already started putting the data together. He wanted to hear about gut before logic. 'Raven, as someone new to the YDA, you might be able to sense more than the rest of us. Is there anyone who has made you feel uneasy, anyone who—I don't know—seems to be marching to a different tune?'

Raven tugged a spiral of hair and let it spring back while she gathered her thoughts. She tapped on the second of the mentors for the four student streams, A to D. The Cobra box opened on the tablet screen. 'Taylor Flint is the coldest and the one I know least about. Only for that reason, I suppose I would consider him first. What's his background?'

'He's ex-SIS—MI6 in layman's terms,' supplied Kieran, reading the information. 'Transferred out eight years ago, around the same time as Isaac was setting up the YDA. I think they knew each other professionally and Isaac persuaded him to come over and be in on the beginning of a new venture. He's married to a foreign languages teacher and has two children under ten who both attend a primary school in West London.'

Damien frowned. 'He's my mentor and I didn't know he had kids. How did I not know that?'

'As I said, Taylor keeps his cards close to his chest,' said Raven.

'Still, all sounds very conventional,' conceded Nathan.

'Not when you dig deeper and find out that the wife is Russian and one of the reasons why it was thought a good time for Flint to leave SIS,' said Kieran, enjoying springing his surprise.

'She was judged a security risk?' asked Nathan. How did this fit?

'Yes, she worked for the Russian secret intelligence service before the marriage—they met in Moscow—but I can find no sign that she kept up those links. They met socially at a party—Flint was working openly as intelligence liaison with the Russians, not spying, so it was all above board. She was a very junior official when she resigned and moved to England with him.'

Nathan scanned his mental map of international relations. This wasn't making much sense. 'Are the Scorpions entangled with the Russian SIS?'

'Not in any meaningful way. Naturally, the Russians are interested like we are. They also have a problem with trafficking. Nothing unusual there.'

'OK, let's put that aside for the moment. How about your mentor, Key: Dr Waterburn?'

Kieran opened up the biography he had put together on his boss. 'Clarice Waterburn.'

'Clarice?'

'Yes: her parents were admirers of the art deco ceramic artist, Clarice Cliff. They were both bohemian types, now living in retirement in St Ives. Her background is GCHQ—the government listening post in Cheltenham. Her CV is all very technical so I'll spare you the nitty-gritty, just take my word she knows her stuff. The information I could find is very light on personal issues. She lives close to HQ and has a cat—that's about it for detail.'

The hair on the back of Nathan's neck pricked. 'Is that a sign that she's hiding something, do you think?'

Kieran smiled. 'No, I think it's a sign that she needs a partner.' He grinned at Raven. 'She spends far too much time with her head buried in her work.'

OK, so maybe not her. Nathan couldn't really imagine Dr Waterburn having the temperament for betrayal. 'Last but not least: Jan Hardy, Kate's mentor.'

Kieran nodded. 'Yes, I looked deep into her background as she was the one best placed to betray Kate during that

192

mission.' Nathan noted that Kate had mentioned that too. 'I believe that she was the contact point with her Indonesian counterpart and the one who decided the nature of the mission as far as it involved Kate.'

'Which was?' asked Raven.

'The aim was ambitious: to infiltrate and obtain information to take apart the network Alfin and Yandi Gatra had put together in Jakarta. The law enforcement agencies had been able to clip off little pieces of the operation but they wanted to get something on those two so they could bring the whole thing down. It had been decided the job had to be done from the inside. Kate and Tina were to get recruited at a low level, work out which of the people close to the leaders were ripe for turning. Kate was encouraged to believe that Gani Meosido was the guy who could deliver on the goods on the Gatras—and the rest you know.'

'That sounds off. I mean, the YDA doesn't normally get involved with such risky missions.'

'Yes, it was unusual,' agreed Nathan, 'but the opportunity was too good to be passed over and had to be done by someone of the right age, or the Scorpions would never take the bait. Youth was thought to save them from being suspected and offer a basic level of protection. Strictly voluntary, Jan said, but we all knew who she wanted to take the mission. She had been putting Kate and Tina together for many of the training exercises and they had worked well as a pair. Kate said she was up for it and she'd just turned seventeen, so just over the minimum age for an overseas job. Both she and Tina were really eager to take down the traffickers—strike a blow for the victims.'

'At least, one of them was eager,' said Damien sourly.

'Yes, you're right. It's so easy to forget Tina wasn't what she seemed—she was so good at her cover.'

* * *

Greenwich library had grown a little noisier as the schools were out and some students had come in to do homework, or at least moan to their friends about having to do it. Kate chewed the end of her pen to distract herself from the next unpleasant chapter of her disaster. Looking at the end she saw a little pattern of toothmarks. The taste in her mouth was of ink.

A week into their mission and they had become regulars at Bar Z, waved through to the other side of the opaque glass without anyone asking for ID. Kate had been a little disappointed to find that the hidden room was just the same as the one open to the public—loud music, a bar, more locals than tourists but the same proportion of ayams trying their luck with the clientele. Tina had found out from one of the bartenders that this was just the ante-room to the real nerve centre. That was upstairs, out of sight. Of course it was: it was too dangerous to have secret operations only a glass panel away from casual visitors. Jan's orders to Kate were not to push things. The gang contacts they met would grow suspicious if they seemed too eager to penetrate deeper into the organization.

Preparing to go out for another evening of acting like the most stupid backpacker in Indonesia, Kate opted for drainpipe jeans and a sparkly top with red sequin lips. Tina was winding her hair into a complicated style held together with butterfly pins.

'What do you think of Gani?' Tina asked.

'I think he's promising.' Kate slicked on some lipstick to match her shirt.

'You're right about him being in the Scorpions—my bartender confirmed it.'

'I thought he might be when he got us through the glass door, but he doesn't seem the type, you know?'

'What type?' Tina arched a brow.

'Well, he's sweet and funny, for one thing. He's really a college student—wants to go into IT in a big international firm. He's dropped hints that he regrets the crowd he got mixed up with—hates what they do.'

'You think that's for real?'

'I don't know. What do you think?'

Tina skewered one of the hairpins into her bun. 'I think you like him.' Her calm, pretty face was for once wrinkled in a cheeky smile, dark brown eyes twinkling.

'Do not!' Kate felt herself blush.

'He's a nice guy. I don't blame you.'

'OK, I like him. I feel sorry for him.'

'He might be exactly the right one for our purposes.' Tina checked the contents of her purse.

'I don't want him to get hurt.'

'He could save lots of others if he is willing to turn. Why not ask him what his price is for getting out?'

'It's too soon to hint what I'm really doing here.'

'Maybe—but you could offer to help, couldn't you? Keep it vague and see what he says.'

'Do you think I should?' Kate felt relieved to have a partner to consult. She had been revolving the same idea in her own mind and not been able to make a decision. Her calls today to Jan kept missing her, probably thanks to the awkward time zone difference. Sometimes the texts and emails she received appeared to answering questions she hadn't asked. Long distance communication wasn't working as well as she had imagined.

Tina shrugged. 'You know him better than me but if you think he would be open to the suggestion, go for it. I don't want to spin this out too long or they'll wonder why I don't pick up any clients or ask for a job with them.'

'God, yes, of course.' Tina's role was a tricky one: she had to send out signals to interest the guys who ran the ayams without crossing the line to participation in that scene. 'I'll see what frame of mind Gani is in tonight. His bosses will be expecting him to reel me in as a patsy for their courier schemes; it's fun to think we can turn the tables on them.'

Tina tapped Kate's wrist. 'Exactly.'

Crouched disconsolately over a beer, Gani immediately perked up when Kate arrived at the bar. She felt a little flip in her stomach to see the most handsome guy in the place waiting for her.

195

'Here's my favourite girl!' he exclaimed, surprising her with a kiss on the mouth and a squeeze of her waist. He slung his arm around her shoulders and steered her towards a sofa at the back of the private zone. Tina flashed her a smile and disappeared to mingle at the bar.

'So tell me more about England,' said Gani, picking up where they had left their conversation the night before. He signalled to the waitress to bring them their usual drinks. 'It sounds so exotic. You really travelled with a circus?'

'Not a circus—a fair. You know, rides and things?'

He frowned, looking sweetly puzzled. 'Sorry, I don't. You'll have to explain.'

Despite her intentions to not give too much away about her background, Kate found herself telling him all about her upbringing, the fairgrounds across England, the characters who travelled the circuit. His laughter and appreciation egged her on. She missed out the mud and cold, wet weekends, making it sound more glamorous than it was.

Gani sighed and sipped his beer. 'I envy you. I hate my life here. I'd love that freedom.'

Here was her opening. 'You often say you feel trapped. Why is that, Gani?'

His hand played with a stray curl of her hair, sending delicious little shivers down her spine. 'It's difficult to explain.'

She rubbed the knee of his jeans. 'Try. I care—I really do.'

He turned towards her. 'You know something, Kate: you're lovely—a lovely girl inside and out. And I believe you do care but I've decided not to get you mixed up in my business. This must be the last night you come here: my . . . my people are getting too interested in you.'

'In me?' Kate touched her chest, her pulse leaping. Did they suspect?

'They have ways of using people—ways I hate.'

He meant the drug smuggling—good. 'You won't let them do that, will you?'

He brushed her jaw. 'I wouldn't let them hurt you, Kate. You're too special to me.' He leaned forward and kissed her.

Thoughts, ideas, plans faded. All Kate could think about was his confident, demanding kiss—not at all what she had expected from the shy college student. She let him lead, finding herself wrapped in an embrace, half reclined beneath him on the sofa.

196

He pressed a kiss to the hollow of her throat. 'Kate, you are perfect. I've been thinking about kissing you ever since we first met.'

'Gani . . . I . . . ' Kate began to feel guilty she had let this go so far—and in public for heaven's sake! She sat up, thankful that at least that no one appeared to be watching them make out in their dark corner.

Gani looked as flustered as her, ruffling his hair straight. 'I'm sorry. That was my fault. We can't do this here.'

She shouldn't do this anywhere, but neither could she walk away from him. She took his hand and gave it a gentle press. 'Let me help you. Please: I have connections, people who will sort out your problems.'

Gani glanced over his shoulder to the bar, his gaze falling on a big man with too much gold jewellery. With a throb of alarm, Kate recognized one of the two heads of the Scorpions: Yandi Gatra, the financial brains behind the gang. It was the first time she had seen him in the flesh. His skin shone under the light like fish at the market, oily and repellent. Oh my God, and Tina was sitting with him! That was way beyond what they expected to achieve tonight.

'We can't talk here. Let's go somewhere else,' whispered Gani.

This was outside mission protocol. She was supposed to stay with her partner at all times, where the Indonesian intelligence agents could keep them under surveillance. But Gani was about to break, she could tell.

'I'll just let my friend know. Where are we going?'

Gani was shifting nervously, wanting to escape now he had made the suggestion. 'Your place?'

Kate swallowed. The flat was Tina's and she might not approve; added to that, there was a danger that Gani might spot something. They locked away anything connected to the mission in a safe in the wardrobe but had she checked before they left that they'd done so tonight?

'No, not mine. I'd prefer somewhere public.'

'Fine. Maybe tomorrow.' Gain let go of her hand, subtly withdrawing. She was losing her chance!

'Do you have a safe place?' Had she really just said that against all her training? But this was Gani: gentle, kind Gani.

'I've got a room those guys don't know about.' He flicked his gaze to the bar.

'It's in a university accommodation block. It's where I do my studies when they let me have time to myself.'

'Is it far?'

'Not far.'

Knowing Tina might object to her departure, Kate decided to text her rather than speak. Tina was busy at that moment; she'd not be grateful if Kate interrupted her in a crucial conversation. Kate was aware she could lose Gani's trust during any delay getting the message to her. She watched Tina glance at the text and put the phone down. Tina would tell their Indonesian contact as soon as she could. 'All done. How do we get there?'

Relieved to be escaping, Gani jumped up, pulling her with him. 'We walk.'

On the journey to Gani's room, he began to confide in her just as she had hoped. He had been taking a course in computer science but run out of money to pay the next term's fee. The Gatras had stepped in and offered to give him the money in exchange for a few simple services. They needed someone to give their system an overhaul, update their computers worldwide.

Gani swung her hand in his. 'I thought it was just that, you understand: straight business proposition but, Kate, these guys aren't nice people. I found out too much and once you're in they find ways of keeping you. I'm trapped.'

'Oh Gani. I'm so sorry.'

He gave her a brave smile. 'You get back on your plane and head out of this mess—don't worry about me. I know you're having a year of adventure—think it's all a game this travel—but you don't see that you're vulnerable. You do realize that now, don't you? You should be more sensible: travel with others. You shouldn't be on your own. The world isn't like your England of green fields and fun fairs.'

He led her into a smart apartment complex. In the heat of the night, many of the flats had their balcony doors open and she was reassured to see students chatting or drinking in the sultry air. A few illuminated windows showed guys sitting at computers, working on assignments, oblivious to the noise outside. It only cooled off after midnight, so no one was ready to sleep. She felt reassured by the familiarity of the scene: though this was the other side of the world, students were a recognizable crowd anywhere on the planet. Gani led her up to the top floor and opened the door to a neat room. He lived like a hermit—no personal possessions lying about, no photos. Only his top-of-the-range computer sat on a desk by the window.

'Want a drink?' He opened up the mini fridge which was stocked with water.

'Thanks.' She unscrewed the cap, shivering with anticipation. The atmosphere was charged between them—so much at stake. 'Look, Gani, I can do more for you than you think. It's really safe to talk here?'

He nodded and pulled the blinds down, shutting them in to their private space. 'This is my den. Even my family doesn't know about this.'

'Gani, I've got connections to people—useful people—the sort that would be after the Scorpions.'

He raised his water in a mocking toast. 'Good luck to them, but it's impossible. What connections?'

Kate didn't want to give too much away so offered her cover story. 'My uncle—he's in the British government. He knows about these things. Let me contact him—ask what it would take to get you out.'

'Out of the country?'

'I don't know.' She hadn't been told to offer asylum but it sounded a reasonable request. 'Perhaps.'

'That's my price. Not because I want to leave—I love my country—but I'm not safe here. If I leave the Scorpions, they'll find a way of stinging me to death: that's their motto. Nowhere in Indonesia is beyond their reach.'

'That's your price, but my uncle might need something in exchange, something to bargain with as he straightens it out with the authorities.'

Gani put down his drink and moved next to where she was sitting on the edge of his bed. He brushed his thumb over her lips, damp from the drink. 'What kind of thing?' His dark eyes seemed so sad, so earnest.

Rational thought was difficult. 'Um . . . I don't know. Maybe something that can be used to prosecute the leaders of the Scorpions? Information on their bases, like the ones in London? You have access to their computer network—it shouldn't be too dangerous to dig some stuff out and pass it on. They need not even realize it was you who did it.'

He cradled her jaw, tilting her head for a kiss. 'Oh, they'll know. But maybe the risk would be worth it if I can be with you.'

Kate put down her pen, sickened by her memories. Looking back, should she have realized he was saying only what he calculated she wanted to hear, offering little crumbs to lure her along the path to destruction? She had left that night thinking he had fallen in love with her and genuinely needed her to help him escape the trap into which he had thrust his head. Instead it had been her he was snaring, using her unfamiliarity with flattery and the pretence of love to blind her to the danger. And Tina had encouraged her, telling her she was right to have taken the risk.

Gani had been so grateful when she returned with an offer to help him escape. He had promised to put everything she needed onto a special tiny memory stick, but only on the night she introduced him to the first in the chain of people who would smuggle him out. She had protested, saying she had to have it beforehand, but he explained that though he trusted her to keep her word, he didn't know her 'uncle' so he couldn't take the risk he would be left high and dry.

He had sounded so reasonable, so apologetic. Then again, she had been in bed with him at the time so hadn't been thinking straight, mistaking what she felt for love. She had thought him tender, open and honest, the best lover a girl could hope for in her first serious relationship, when all the time he had been laughing at the naive idiot he had seduced.

Trusting him more than her orders, she had taken the final step to betraying all she believed. To be fair to herself, she had let Tina know she was worried and that she was wondering if she was going about this the right way. Despite Tina's reassurances, she almost played it by the book, had been on the point of telling Jan Hardy that she was involved with a target but her calls had not gone through. So she had missed out on a chance to check her instincts were sound and that the relationship was worth continuing, but events had got away from her.

The rap on the door at five in the morning woke her. Tina wasn't back yet, staying away for a meeting with her Indonesian handler to give a progress report. Not expecting anyone, Kate cracked open the door.

'Kate!' It was Gani on the doorstep. He looked terrible: unshaven, clothes stained, eyes desperate. 'Please let me in!'

She took off the chain and he hurried inside, locking it again behind him. 'Gani, what's the matter?'

His breaths were coming in hiccups and sobs. 'Oh God, oh God, it's all over. They're going to kill me.'

She sat him down on her bed and held his hands, willing him to calm down. 'It's OK. You're safe here.'

'No,' he cried, 'No! I'm not safe anywhere. I . . . I took the information—downloaded it—the finances—the safe houses—the names—but . . . but I was caught in the act. Mr Gatra came in and asked me what I was doing on his personal computer and . . . and I panicked.'

'Panicked?' Kate went cold.

'I ran. I jumped out of the window at Bar Z and ran. They're after me.'

She went to the window and looked out on the early morning street. The traffic was moving as usual; she could see no signs of anyone watching her building. 'Do they know you're here?'

'No, no, of course not! I couldn't bear to get you into trouble.' He came to her side and hugged her tightly. 'You are the best thing that ever happened to me. I want to protect you. I can't stay here. I've got to go. Please, please, you've got to get me out right now!'

Kate felt like she had just stepped too near to a cliff edge and found it give way beneath her—all her preparations were crumbling. This was so against protocol but what else could she do? 'You have the information on you?'

Gani looked hurt that she had asked. 'Yes, I do. So is that the only thing you care about?'

'No, of course not!' She reached up and kissed him. 'I care about you, but you have to have something to offer—a ticket to freedom—to satisfy my uncle.'

He moved sensuously against her, pulling her tightly against his chest. 'You are the only thing that satisfies me. Just you, Kate. I can't wait to have you somewhere when we are both safe and can start again.'

She couldn't let him suffer because of a process she had set in motion. 'Give me a moment; I need to make a call. I'll see if the people who have agreed to smuggle you out can bring that forward.'

Gani smiled with what she had thought was relief. 'Thank you, Kekasih.' He knew she loved it when he called her 'sweetheart' in his language. 'I owe you my life.'

So she had rushed through the arrangement for bringing him out, asking the woman who was the first link in that chain to take him without the usual precautions. Miss Tanni had agreed because she trusted Kate to know what she was doing. That brave young woman, a plant in one of Jakarta's seediest nightclubs, was the one who was later executed as an example to others.

Kate couldn't bear that memory. Oh God, she was going to be sick. Grabbing her things, she rushed to the Ladies and vomited in the toilet. She hung over the bowl, waiting for the spell to pass. It wasn't the first time, nor, she guessed, would it be the last. She welcomed these bouts as punishment for her sins. But they weren't enough: she deserved so much worse.

Chapter 17

Nathan headed home on the Northern Line, mentally reviewing the information his team had examined. After the four mentors, they had discussed other long-serving members of staff. Closest to Isaac was his PA, Tamsin MacDonald, so they had spent a while considering her case. Digging into her background, Kieran had only been able to confirm what they already knew: she was a divorcee, lost her only child in Iraq, and now lived quietly in Pimlico. The news clipping of the death of Lance Corporal Joe MacDonald had made grim reading. One of the red caps, as the military police were known, Joe had been part of the invasion by the 16th Air Assault Brigade. Injured by small arms fire on patrol, carried back to an evacuation point by his commanding officer, Captain Hampton, Joe died in the helicopter on the way to hospital. Captain Hampton—Isaac—had been decorated for bravery. Mrs MacDonald had gone with him to the medal ceremony. Kieran had found a touching picture of her clinging to Isaac's arm as he reluctantly held up the award for the camera, blue eyes fierce under his red peaked cap. Isaac continued with his career, a first class officer regularly promoted up the ranks until he reached lieutenant colonel, at which point he left to establish the YDA. Clearly he had kept in touch with the mother of his old comrade, and had thought of her when he was looking for a reliable assistant.

As a red cap, the ones charged with internal investigations into the military, Isaac would have made lots of enemies. Damien even raised the possibility that Sergeant Rivers might have had a run-in with Isaac in an official capacity and be bearing a grudge. Kieran had shot that suggestion down by showing that Jim had a flawless record and no disciplinary infractions.

Moving on from the military connections, they had reviewed other members of staff, regular visitors, cleaning crew. Kieran had even briefly suggested Mr Bates, Raven's grandfather and caretaker for the premises, but that ended with a frosty look from his girlfriend and the others filling the awkward pause with a change of subject.

Kieran still had a lot to learn about not sharing every single step in his deductions, even when he knew he was going to dismiss the individual as a suspect.

Alighting at Clapham Junction, Nathan stopped in a shop doorway to text Kate. He was well aware she was planning to work on her report this afternoon and that would not be easy. She had insisted she do it alone as she couldn't face him reading it.

Everything OK?

There was a pause and then her reply arrived.

Will be. Almost done. xx

As he thought, she was having a horrible time, raking up the past. He wished she would let him be with her. He had been serious when he said nothing she could write would change his mind about her. She had been quite clear, though, that this was something she felt she had to do on her own.

Good luck with it. See you tomorrow. Love you. xxx

Words weren't enough. He almost turned round and got back on the Tube to go to her. Her reply arrived.

Looking forward to that. Have a good evening. xxxx

A very cool answer—almost like a polite stranger. His impulse to rush to her side faded. She had asked for space and he could at least give her that. He had hardly given her a moment to think about their relationship since he had handcuffed them together. Was she getting cold feet?

Still worrying, he tucked the phone in his pocket and headed for home. A new text pinged and he pulled it out.

Love you too. xxxxx

He grinned. He was getting jittery about nothing. That said more about his self-doubt than hers. He now noticed she had been increasing the 'x's by one every message, which meant she now owed him eleven. A very intriguing thought.

Turning into his street, he jogged to his door and got out his keys. As he fitted the Yale into the lock, a black cab drew up alongside him and rolled down the window.

'Hey, mate, are you Nathan Hunter?'

'I didn't order a cab.'

'Yeah, I know. I got a booking to pick up this package for you and wait until you read it. You won't believe how much is on the meter waiting for you to show up.' He held out a blue envelope, YDA stationery. Cautiously, Nathan took the letter and opened it.

Nathan, sorry for the cloak and dagger approach but I prefer not to ring your home or your mobile in case these are insecure. Please join me at the Fresh Bean cafe on Vauxhall Bridge Road. I have made a break-through this afternoon and we must now move quickly.

    Isaac

Nathan reread the message. The handwriting was Isaac's but he would have expected him to use Raven to pass the news, as this had worked successfully earlier in the day.

'You getting in, mate?' asked the cabbie. 'I was told to take you to some place in Vauxhall.'

Nathan examined the vehicle, checking for clues. The man's ID was swinging from the driver's mirror; the plate on the back showed the cab was registered with the local council. It all looked above board. He could take the ride and then check out the meeting place before entering. He didn't know Fresh Bean, but Vauxhall Bridge Road was a busy thoroughfare right by the MI6 building, and one of the most public places in the capital thanks to the CCTV on every corner. He climbed in the back and texted Damien.

Late meeting with Isaac near Lego house. Tell the team to stand by and I'll let you know what he says.

Damien would understand what he meant, as they had joked before now that the MI6 building looked like it had been pieced together by an eight-year-old from cream plastic bricks.

Remembering the warning about the meter, Nathan checked the contents of his wallet. He was still carrying around the money he had withdrawn for Kate back in Suffolk. 'You do receipts, right?'

'Sure, mate.' The cabbie tapped the gauge, which was showing over fifty pounds. 'Must be a millionaire, the guy who sent me. Wish I had that kind of money. Now I once had that actor who played King George in my cab—there was a guy who knew how to tip royally.'

Half listening to the driver's chatter, Nathan sat back to puzzle over what Isaac could have found.

Library on the point of closing, Kate decided to finish her account back at the flat. Letting herself in with the spare key, she found Julian in the hallway with his canvas satchel slung over one shoulder, small case in hand.

'Oh, Kate, I'm so pleased you're back. I left a note but now I can tell you myself.' He beamed at her.

'Tell me what?'

'A lesser yellowlegs had been spotted in Hampshire!'

'Oh, um, great.'

'I'm just running down there now and will stay over for the dawn chorus. You make yourself at home—there's pasta in the fridge.' He jingled his car keys. 'Do you want me to tell Damien you're here alone? He'd come and stay, I'm sure, if you want the company?'

That was the last thing she wanted, not with her report to finish and her doubts about Damien's reliability still fresh.

'No, please, don't. I'll be fine, really I will.'

Julian was already in an obscure field in Hampshire in spirit, even if bodily he was in London. 'Well then, good. I'll see you tomorrow evening then. Bye!' With a slam of the door, he was out and hurrying towards his car parked further down the street.

Lesser yellowlegs? Kate had to smile. Would he be as excited if it were a greater yellowlegs? She'd have to google the breed later to prepare for his return. She had the feeling she was about to find out much more about the bird than she ever imagined she would need to know.

Taking his hint about supper, Kate boiled up some of the fresh pasta in the cheerful yellow kitchen and forced herself to eat a whole plateful with a green salad and a sprinkle of parmesan. Nathan and her gran were right: she had lost too much weight over the last year and it was time she started looking after herself properly.

Finally, she could put things off no longer: she owed Isaac the end of her report. She promised herself she wouldn't get sick again. It was only her ordeal she had to write about, not someone else's, and in a way she deserved what had happened as she had committed the sin of being reckless and over-confident. She cleared the table, made herself a cup of mint tea, and took out her pad and pen to finish her account.

Tina didn't come back that day after Kate had sent Gani off down the chain of smugglers. She passed him over to Miss Tanni, promising to find him again when he was safe. Kate spent the day worrying about Gani and her partner. She filed a report for Jan to read, saying briefly what she had done and asking for more instructions but no one replied from London. She tried the Indonesian contact numbers she had been given, but these also rang out without anyone answering. It felt as though all her routes of communication were cut off. Even Jan's phone went to voicemail each time she tried.

At eight in the evening, Tina finally turned up, her key scraping in the door.

'Where have you been?' snapped Kate once she saw her friend was OK.

'At the briefing. I told you last night.' Tina seemed completely oblivious to Kate's distress. She stripped off her shirt and put on a fresh one.

'You could've replied to one of my texts.'

'Sorry—didn't get them. What's happened to get you so upset?'

'Gani's out.'

'Already?' Tina's eyes widened. 'But I thought that was going to happen next week?'

'He was caught getting the information—it almost cost him his life but he ran.'

'Ran here?' Tina crossed to the window and checked the street. 'To you?'

'Yes.'

Tina spun round, manner completely changed. 'Then what are you doing sitting there? We need to go.'

'You think they'll come looking for him at ours?'

'Don't be an idiot: of course they will! They know you're friends with him.' Tina grabbed a case and stuffed her belongings inside. Kate's bag was already packed as she had never taken things out of her rucksack in case she had to run at short notice. Tina emptied the safe and slipped the contents into her handbag. 'Here: don't forget your coat.' She bundled the thick black jacket into Kate's arms.

Picking up Tina's urgency, Kate tidied away the last few things she had out—a novel, her phone. 'Where are we going?'

'A safe house. Come on. If Gani's passed on the information, our part in this operation is over.'

They hurried out onto the street. Kate sweated under the load of her rucksack and puffa jacket. She was in half a mind to dump the coat but Tina grabbed her wrist.

'No, don't: they mustn't find any trace of either of us. We've got to disappear completely.'

Tina led Kate without hesitation through some unfamiliar streets, past street sellers and rickshaw stands, across streams of slow-moving traffic. Kate checked the position of the landmark flyover she used to keep track of her whereabouts. They seemed to be heading in the general direction of Bar Z but by another route a couple of streets further north.

'Shouldn't we be getting out of the area?' Kate asked.

'The closest safe house is the one we've been using for the operation,' Tina explained. 'My contact will help us get out without anyone knowing where we've gone. Don't worry: no one will look for us there.'

Some warning instinct niggled in the back of Kate's mind. But no, this was her partner. She had been told to listen to Tina for local knowledge.

Tina stopped at the rear of a building covered in fire escapes. The windows were barred on every level. As she had said, it looked secure, the kind of place the Indonesian police might use. Kate still couldn't shake her unease but what choice did she have? Tina rapped on a door and entered immediately, like she had done this many times before. This was probably where she came for her meetings, Kate guessed. Tina pointed to a small room just off the back door where an elderly man sat watching them curiously, tufts of white hair surrounding a bald crown.

'Leave your bag there. It'll be safe with him.'

Gratefully, Kate slid out of the rucksack straps. She tucked her wallet and passport in her jacket and carried that up the stairs with her.

Pausing outside a second door on the first floor, Tina knocked in a strange one-two, one-two pattern—a bit like Kate's heart was beating just then. The door opened and Tina ushered her to go ahead.

'Oh my God: Gani!' Kate couldn't stop her cry of distress. Gani was chained up by the wrists, hanging from a beam in the ceiling, head slumped forward.

'What is this?' Kate gripped Tina by the elbow, looking frantically round for the police, but she knew. She knew.

Music thumped through the floor. They were in the upper room of Bar Z, having arrived from the back entrance. Tina had brought her into the inner sanctum and Gani was going to die if Kate couldn't think of a way of saving him.

Yandi Gatra ambled forward. He said something rapid in Indonesian to Tina, who nodded. He then gave Kate a mocking bow. 'I am pleased to meet you, Miss Pearl. Thank you for helping with our little problem.'

Did he mean Gani? What did she have to bargain with?'

'Please, Mr Gatra, let him go. It's my fault. I persuaded him to . . . to . . . ' She couldn't admit what he had done in case Yandi didn't realize. 'To run away with me.'

Then Gani lifted his head and grinned. He slipped his hands free of the loose manacles. 'Still so sweet. You didn't persuade me to do anything, Kekasih: it was the other way round. And you did everything I asked, didn't you? Everything.' His gaze felt like the touch of grubby fingers as it swept over her.

'Tina?' Kate reached out to her last hope.

'Oh, yes, Tina. I don't think you've been properly introduced, have you?' Gani put his arm around Kate's waist and propelled her to face her partner. 'Meet my sister, Agustina. I'm Gani Meosido. And this is my cousin, Yandi Gatra. Alfin will be along as soon as he's disposed of the men monitoring you both tonight.'

'Your sister?' Kate's thoughts tumbled in an avalanche of confusion.

Tina shrugged, slim hands smoothing down her black silk skirt. 'Sorry, Kate. It was nothing personal. I had a job to do—just like you.'

Yandi patted Tina's shoulder and said something to her in their native tongue, too fast for Kate to follow.

Tina went up on tiptoes and kissed his cheek. 'Goodbye, Kate.' With a last look at her brother, Tina exited through the door leading to the club.

Kate put her pen down and took a determined sip of her tea. She could face this. It was over—many of the people involved were dead—she had to give the details in case they helped Isaac. It would be in the timings, he said.

Gani led her over to a leather sofa and pushed her down. Frozen, Kate did as he demanded, hands gripped in her lap. He sat beside her and pulled her against him, expecting her to curl up with him as she would once willingly have done. His touch on her neck now read as a threat rather than tenderness, the tug on her hair painful not playful. How could she have been so wrong about him?

'I suppose you would like to know what has been going on?'

She nodded.

'Ah, my so serious Kate, lost your tongue?' He rubbed her cheek with his thumb. 'I hope it's temporary as you'll want to find it later.'

The other leader of the Scorpions, Alfin Gatra, came in. A handsome man dressed in a sharply tailored suit, he threw Kate a shrewd look, nodded once, then went over to join his brother. Heads together over a small table set for supper, the Gatras left the foreign agent to their cousin.

Gani tapped Kate's nose. 'I am sorry to be the bearer of bad news, but you have betrayed your allies at the YDA and in the Indonesian security services. Even as we sit here, the weak links in the smuggling operation are being removed. As for your friend, Miss Tanni: well, she has had an unfortunate accident with scorpions.' He reached down into his sports bag and took a glass jar. Six scorpions scuttled over each other inside. 'These ones. The footage is online if you care to see?'

211

Kate shook her head, bile rising in her throat.

'So, you understand, Kekasih, that you are not popular with your allies at the moment. They will be very, very angry with you.' He traced the outline of her ear, nipping the lobe in warning as she tried to pull away. 'In fact, I am the only person in the entire world who is on your side.'

'On my side?' Her voice sounded wobbly but she was holding herself together by a thread.

'Of course, Kekasih. You're still my girl, aren't you? But there's been a change of plan: rather than me come over to your people, you have to come over to mine. We'll look after you.' He nudged her to sit up and framed her face with his hands, staring deep into her eyes. 'Oh, you poor baby. I do love you, you know. You are so brave, trying to do the right thing but failing so badly. That takes courage—far more than success.'

Kate wanted to protest that she wasn't his—wouldn't go over to his side—but she knew that any disagreement would end violently for her. She was trapped. And from the glee in his eyes, he knew it.

'I feel sorry for you. It was so easy to set up. Your boss doesn't know what's going on right under his nose.'

Was Gani really saying that the double-cross started in the YDA? It was one more blow on top of the numbing shock she was already feeling. That would explain so much—the calls that hadn't been returned, Tina's infiltration.

'As I see it, you've nowhere else to go. That leaves me.'

Kate felt the last shreds of hope shrivel and die.

'So, let's make sure you understand your position. You're my girl: say it.'

'I . . .' Kate couldn't turn her head as he held her face too firmly, but she sensed the room had gone quiet. Others were waiting for her answer. 'I'm your girl.'

'See: that wasn't too hard, was it?' He kissed her and let her chin go. Kate turned her head just in time to see one of the Gatra's bodyguards holstering his weapon. It did not come as a shock to know that he had been prepared to shoot her if she had given the wrong answer.

Gani got up and pulled her to her feet. 'Now let's make this official.' He pocketed the handcuffs he had pretended to wear and towed her past the Gatras.

Alfin said something curt.

Gani's demeanour changed to cringing respect. His reply could be understood from his gesture to the stairs.

Alfin changed to English. 'I gave my word that she would not be killed.'

Word to whom? Kate wondered, pen hovering over the paper. She hadn't remembered that detail until now. Someone had been prepared to use her but stopped short of murdering her: that suggested they knew her well enough to care a little for her survival.

Alfin dropped his hand to let them proceed up the stairs. 'At the moment, I cannot see any reason to change that.'

Kate gulped and tried to look harmless. Tried? Who was she kidding? She was harmless—worse, useless.

'Come along, baby. You won't be any trouble, will you?' Gani steered her up the narrow steps. 'We're just going to pay a visit to Old Teguh.' He opened the door to a little room where a man sat watching a portable TV, wizen features bathed in a cold blue light. 'Teguh, another customer.'

Kate now noticed that the equipment belonging to the tattoo artist lay on the low bench in front of him. 'No, please!'

Gani smiled. 'You're my girl, remember? This is nothing.' He made a dismissive gesture at the tools. 'If you refuse the gang sign, then I'll have to think you weren't telling me the truth.' He pulled a long face. 'I don't think either of us would like what happens if I decide that.' He took the handcuffs and snapped one around her wrist. He chained the other end to an iron bar running along the edge of the bench. Clearly, she was not the first customer to be unhappy at having the gang mark forced on her. Gani rattled off something in Indonesian and the old man laughed. Taking a final regretful glance at his programme, Old Teguh switched off and plugged in his lamp. He turned Kate's arm over to expose the pale inner skin, rubbing the surface lightly. He said something and smiled up at Gani.

Gani sat down on a stool and pulled Kate onto his lap. 'He says you're a good canvas for his art.'

She turned her head away from the whirr of the ink injector. Gani took her chin and firmly steered her back.

'No, no, Kekasih: watch. Teguh is a master. You'll find this instructive.'

Through eyes wet with tears, she watched the insect form on her wrist. The pain of the application was nothing to the emotions raging inside her. Her sanity was saved by the welcome arrival of numbness that dulled her perceptions. She felt as if she was no longer present, floating somewhere safe above her body. Days could have passed, but it was probably more like an hour—and then Teguh finished. He wiped off his handiwork and gave a pleased nod. Gani unfastened the handcuffs, leaving them on the bench. He wound his fingers through Kate's, raised her arm and kissed the tattoo.

'Well done: not a flinch or a whimper. I'm proud of you.' His poet's eyes that she had once thought beautiful shone with admiration. 'We've a room ready for you upstairs. You must be very tired—you need to sleep.'

Kate stared out the window at the trees in the park, a pearlescent moon netted in the branches. Something had died inside her that night—her sense of self-worth as she realized she had betrayed her training and the YDA. It had only started to come alive again thanks to Nathan, but the rebirth was painful. She wanted to both look and not look, like the feeling when passing an accident on the other carriageway of a motorway. Thinking back to the person she had been that night, she was able to find some pity as well as her more usual feeling of self-loathing at her mistakes.

Kate woke next morning feeling a sharp sting on the back of her neck. Having had nightmares about scorpions she jerked up with a scream, only to find Gani sitting on the side of her mattress, laughing at her. Her eyes sought out the jar of scorpions that he had put on his bedside table. The lid was still on; all six were inside, trying to use each other to climb out.

'Morning, sleepy head.' Gani seemed euphoric—but then he would be, as from his perspective the operation had gone brilliantly. 'I've got to go to lectures

214

but I'll be back later. Tina might call in on you but I've left you water and something to eat. I don't suppose I need to tell you that you have to stay here?'

Kate fumbled for the sore patch on her neck.

He pulled her hand down. 'Leave it alone. From the looks of it, you've got a bite there—nothing to worry about.' He picked up the jar from his bedside table. 'See you later.'

When the door closed behind him, Kate took her first proper breath. Oh God, oh God. Curling up, she screamed, muffling the noise in the sheet. The numbness that had come over her in the tattooist's room was ebbing like flood waters receding, leaving a wrecked landscape behind.

Miss Tanni had died because of her.

She had crashed the mission—totally—spectacularly.

The Gatras had turned all their clever plans back on the YDA and the Indonesian investigators, using Kate to root out the disloyal elements.

She didn't know who to trust or how to get out. Tina had been the local link but she was one of them. If Kate escaped and appealed to the police, she'd probably be turning herself over to the same ones who had helped compromise the mission. Her phone was gone.

Come on, Kate: there are always other options.

Forcing herself to get up and explore her prison, she discovered her backpack and coat in the corner. She dressed in clean clothes, trying to ignore her shaking hands, but the buttons kept getting away from her. Digging to the bottom of the bag, she chose one of her few long sleeved tops to hide the tattoo. She couldn't bear to see her wrist. Going to the window, she pulled back the thin green curtain. The room looked out on one of the fire escapes but the window was barred. Testing the struts, she discovered they were new and very strong, held in place by a padlock to an iron frame. No sign of the key. That put the option of setting fire to the place off the agenda, as she would be trapped inside.

She paced the room, rubbing her arms. She only stopped when she realized that her ragged nails had drawn blood at her wrists.

Kate stared at the words she had written. That was the beginning of being alone, a period that had lasted a year, until she met Nathan. She wasn't sure how long they had kept her in that room—days, maybe. Tina had come by, at first wary, but finding Kate too afraid to attack her, she chatted away as if nothing had happened. Kate spent those visits on automatic pilot, not daring to release the furious words dammed up inside. Tina had even had the gall to say that Kate was lucky.

Lucky? Kate had given a hollow laugh.

No, no, Tina had said, Kate was lucky for attracting genuine affection from her brother. Gani was apparently serious that he wanted to keep her. He was planning to travel with her once she could be trusted, as he believed her feelings for him would persuade her that he was her best and only choice. Her passport would be very useful to him in his role as lieutenant to his cousins.

'They're all after you, you know,' Tina had informed her cheerfully one afternoon when she dropped round with some magazines.

'Who's after me?' Kate didn't move away from the window. She spent many hours gazing out, hoping for rescue, but none came. The view stayed the same: shuttered windows on the apartments opposite, cranes moving on the building site beyond, blue skies scored with jet trails.

'Isaac, Jan Hardy, everyone at the YDA. They think you ran when things went wrong—or turned traitor. The agency is likely to be shut down to avoid more embarrassment.'

'How do you know this?' Kate bit her nail. The news was no more than she expected; it was what she would have thought in Isaac's place.

'Oh, we have our sources. Always have. Enjoy the magazines. I don't want them back; I've already read them.'

Tina's words were confirmation that the YDA was not secure. When—if—Kate got out, she knew she would be on her own.

Her chance came a day later. It had been a sweltering afternoon and Gani had opened the bars so he could sit out on the fire escape and smoke in the cool of the evening. Trying not to look too obvious, Kate watched carefully for where he put the key: inside pocket of his computer case. After that, she had been particularly attentive to him, pretending that she was getting used to her new role in his life. She hated this subservient Kate, but if that was what it would take to disarm him, then she'd pretend he had won.

That night, when Gani fell asleep, snoring lightly as he lay on his back, she got up off her mattress and retrieved the key. Picking up the small bag she had already packed and her puffa jacket, a useful second carrier as it held her passport and money, she eased the bars open, thankful that the hand lotion she had smeared on the hinges earlier worked to stop any squeaks. She hesitated. Gani continued sleeping. Knowing there was unlikely to be a better opportunity, she quietly slid the bars back in place and walked softly down the fire escape, quelling the urge to make a less cautious run for it. Faint night noises carried on the breeze: music, traffic, the occasional voice raised in anger, a baby crying. No one raised the alarm that the prisoner had escaped.

Arriving safely on the ground in the deserted back street, Kate slid into the shadows and disappeared.

Chapter 18

Nathan woke up with a crashing headache. Reaching for his bedside light, his hand found nothing. He wasn't in his own room. The smell—the temperature—the feeling wasn't right. Rolling on his back, he looked up at the unfamiliar ceiling: grey concrete and a bare bulb. Light came in from a high window glazed with thick frosted glass. His bed was a mattress on the floor. No blanket. From the chill in the air and the sound of a whistling wind, he guessed that the room was an attic.

Whatever the reason he was here, it could not be good news.

Ignoring the pain in his temples, he tried to piece together the last things he could remember. He had got out at the Fresh Bean cafe as instructed and paid the taxi. Rather than go in directly, he had lingered outside checking to see if Isaac had arrived. He had not shown up and Nathan was beginning to have serious misgivings about entering. Caution won out. This meeting had been set up against usual protocols. Pausing in a shop doorway he had taken his eyes off the street for a second to text Damien to say he was giving up and heading home. Then his world had gone black.

He must have been knocked unconscious.

Nathan sat up woozily and massaged his temples, too alarmed to lie still. But the note had been Isaac's handwriting.

Did that mean Isaac had also been abducted—was that why he hadn't shown up? Or, Nathan took a deep breath, had they been wrong about their boss all along? Had Isaac been the one sabotaging his own organization?

They were facing extinction if that was the case. Thank God he had never told Isaac where Kate was.

Pain easing a fraction, Nathan forced himself to stand, gaining his balance by holding on to the wall. *Gather the available information and make a plan*: his training came rushing back.

The traffic noise outside suggested he was still in London.

The building felt industrial rather than domestic—rough concrete showing signs of age. He ran his fingers over the surface feeling for cracks or weaknesses. It crumbled to show a steel network under the concrete. No way through that. He would make a guess that he was in some scruffy part of south London not too far from where he had been taken, otherwise why bring him in from Battersea?

The door was sturdy. Glass inset with wire, so impossible to smash without a tool. The room was bare apart from the mattress. Getting out under his own power was not likely. He would have to wait until his captors showed up and he found out what they wanted.

Know your enemy.

So who were they? Most likely this was connected with Kate. He had no other ongoing missions and no enemies. That meant when the Scorpions had failed to capture her, they had turned to someone to whom they knew she was close. He had been sold out by the same source in the YDA; how else would they have got news of such a new relationship?

And why take the risk of abducting him off a busy thoroughfare and lock him up here? He swore under his breath as the answer became obvious. The Scorpions wanted him as their hostage. They were going to use him to do what they hadn't achieved in the last twelve months: they were making Kate come to them.

Kate woke up at ten, having found it difficult to fall asleep after putting the finishing touches to her report. It sat now in an envelope tucked in a book under her bed, waiting for Nathan to deliver it for her. Horrible to relive, but somehow putting it all down on paper had made it more distant, the horror of it more like a story than ever-present reality. Yawning, enjoying that feeling of being able to look a wreck with no one to see the rumpled hair and make-up-less face, she wandered to the window and cracked open the curtain. The day was cloudy, spits of rain not quite enough to require an umbrella. She hoped Julian was enjoying better weather for his bird-watching. She texted a quick 'good morning' to Nathan, something nagging at the back of her mind.

It wasn't until she reached the kettle in the kitchen that she remembered: her appointment at the doctor's. Blast! She barely had time to get dressed, slick on a quick brush of mascara and get there, let alone have breakfast. Hurriedly throwing on some clothes and brushing her teeth, she grabbed her purse and keys and jogged down the stairs. At least she had spotted the surgery the day before so didn't waste time finding it. She gave her name to the receptionist and took the bundle of forms to fill out, then sat on one of the bright orange plastic chairs in the busy waiting room and began the tedious task of completing the boxes. Every few moments she checked her phone to see if Nathan had replied to her text yet. No answer. He was probably on the Underground, travelling over to see her. She cheered up at that thought, imagining them having brunch together in Julian's lovely kitchen.

'Katherine Pearl?' Dr Chaudri appeared in the doorway leading to the consulting rooms.

Kate leapt up. 'That's me.'

'This way, please.' With a friendly smile, the doctor led her through to his room and gestured her to take a seat alongside his desk. 'Now, what seems to be the matter?' he glanced over her forms then put them in his in-tray.

'I've got an infected bite on the back of my neck.' Kate lifted her hair and twisted to indicate the area.

'I see. Do you know what kind of bite?' The doctor selected a little torch tool from his drawer.

'I was in Indonesia when I first got it. It seemed to clear up but then started hurting again. I might have scratched it or something.'

'When was this?'

'Nearly a year back when I first noticed it, but it really started hurting badly about a month ago.'

He tutted. 'You really shouldn't have left it that long. But better late than never. Let's have a look.'

Holding her hair up for him, she waited while he probed the spot. He seemed to be taking a very long time about it.

'That's . . . very odd,' he said finally.

Remembering Damien's warning about weird skin burrowing creatures, Kate shivered. 'In what way odd?'

'It's not a bite, Miss Pearl. You appear to have a foreign object lodged under your skin. I can just see the edge of it. It's been working its way to the surface. I think we should get it out and then I'll write you a prescription for some antiseptic cream. Once the splinter is gone, it should heal up rapidly.'

'So it's not alive? Not a maggot or something?'

Dr Chaudri chuckled. 'Now who has been filling your head with such horrors? No, it is likely to be something that caught on your neck—a thorn most probably. I'll need you to lie down so I can get to it with my tweezers.'

Kicking off her shoes, Kate lay on the paper cover on the doctor's couch. She felt a swipe of cool ointment.

'That's just to clean and numb the area,' Dr Chaudri explained.

There was a probe then a sharp tug. Something dropped into the kidney shaped tray beside her. The doctor cleaned the area a second time.

'All gone. You should be fine now. It will be sore for a few days but now the splinter is out, I can't imagine it will cause you any more difficulty.'

'What was it?'

The doctor peered into the tray. 'Very peculiar. Not a thorn after all. I'd say it looks like one of those tags vets use on domestic pets—a subdermal microchip. Has one of your friends played a joke on you? If so, I'd say it was very dangerous.'

Kate remembered Gani and the sting on her neck. Had he tagged her? But no, that didn't make sense: he would have known that a tracker had already been sewn into the jacket. A veterinary tag didn't broadcast positions, just carried the pet's identification, so it wasn't useful to him in locating her if she escaped. So what had he put under her skin?

'I . . . I think it was an accident.' Kate tried to make light of it. 'Can I take it?'

'Strange kind of accident.' Dr Chaudri slipped off the latex gloves he had been wearing. 'Of course you can take it. It's yours after all. I'll give you a little medicine pot to keep it in.'

After thanking the doctor for his help and taking the prescription, Kate walked home, deep in thought, fingering the container in her pocket. A microchip. What kind of information could be on it?

There had been something that had been puzzling her ever since Nathan had told her that Gani and Tina were dead. Gani had been executed even though he had successfully dismantled the agent network within the Scorpions' ranks. That should have brought him rewards and promotion. He must have done something extreme to annoy his cousins—so bad that they had killed Tina too. Had he been playing yet another game, a further double-cross? Had he really downloaded the information as she had suggested, waiting to see which way the wind blew? That would be like him.

But why plant it on her?

The pieces began to fall in place. Her British passport—his surprising desire to travel with her. Despite his empty words of love, he had not cared about her; he had only ever cared about himself. He had been planning to take the information out of the country and she had been a useful mule—just of data rather than drugs—that's what she had missed. If she had been caught by the Gatras, he could have denied all knowledge of it. But what had he planned to do with the microchip if and when he met up with her? It would have been data dynamite. Perhaps he would have bargained for a greater share of the Scorpions' profits by planning to use it as blackmail? Sold it to the highest bidder if his cousins hadn't given in to his demands?

So that was why Gani had let her escape. She had congratulated herself on seizing her single opportunity but she had always been aware in one part of her brain that it had gone too easily. She had been in a very effective prison, subdued, scared, but they had never taken away her money and passport—the first step to keeping someone close. Looking back, it had been unlike Gani to let her see the key, make it so simple for her to slip away. A more plausible explanation for that evening was that he had meant her to go and probably intended to follow, thanks to the tracker his sister had planted. It was easier to let her leave the country willingly before catching up, rather than risking taking her through airport security checkpoints himself in case she panicked and appealed for help from the authorities. He had succeeded in making her think she had to do it totally on her own and keep away from all sources of aid.

But he had miscalculated. Like so many clever people, he had assumed everyone else were fools. His deception must have been discovered and he paid the ultimate price. He had had no time to catch up with her—just time to tell his murderers what she was carrying. That was why the hunt for her had been so intense: she was a walking cache of incriminating evidence.

Gani had left her a legacy of amazing power—she could bring down the Scorpions if she got this into the right hands.

With a renewed spring in her step, Kate jogged home, hoping to find Nathan waiting for her. She couldn't wait to share her good news.

But Kate didn't find Nathan waiting on the step; instead she found Damien already inside.

'Damien?' Kate didn't even have time to hang up her jacket before he was on to her, trying to bundle her out of the door.

'They've got Nathan—come on: we've got to save him. I've already wasted an hour waiting for you and they gave me until midday to respond.' He looked quite wild, blond hair spiked up in frustration.

She yanked her arm free. 'What?'

'The Scorpions. They abducted Nathan last night. They want you in exchange.'

'You're joking!'

He swept his hand through his hair again, annoyed that he had to take the time to explain. 'They promised not to hurt you, but you've got something they need. The deal is I take you and they hand over Nathan unharmed. If I don't do that, they'll start slicing bits off him until we agree to their terms.'

Nathan! Kate backed away from him. 'Hang on, hang on: we can't just go rushing into this!'

Damien uttered a harsh swear word. 'I'm not giving you a choice—*I* was given no choice. They're watching me. I'm not to contact anyone—not to do anything other than fetch you and bring you to the rendezvous.' He was shaking with fury. 'I thought you cared for Nathan?'

'I do.'

'Then why the hell are you stalling?'

'Because I'm trying to think how to come out of this alive!'

Panting hard from the shouting, they glared at each other. Damien crumpled first, sliding down the wall to sit on the floor.

'I'm sorry—sorry. I'm just desperate. I don't know what to do.'

A key scraped in the lock. Damien shot to his feet just in time to greet his uncle.

'Hello, one and all!' called Julian cheerfully, satchel swinging on his shoulder, Thermos flask banging at his hip. 'Damien— lovely to see you. Kate, you're looking better. Nathan here?'

'No,' said Damien hoarsely.

Julian bustled past them and dumped his bird-watching gear in the front room. 'I've had such a marvellous time—I simply must tell you all about it—but after I've attended to the call of nature.' Whistling, he headed for the bathroom.

Kate found she was digging her nails into her palms. With careful deliberation, she uncurled her fists. She didn't trust Damien but she obviously couldn't leave Nathan to be tortured. She needed a better set of choices.

'Give me a moment, Damien. You make our excuses to your uncle while I just . . . just grab my travel card.'

Taking a detour via the living room, she closed the door to the hallway and burrowed through Uncle Julian's satchel.

Thankfully the item she needed was still there. Once in her bedroom, she put the bottle containing the chip the doctor removed in an envelope along with her report for Isaac. Sealing it, she quickly texted Raven.

Urgent: please pick up report from Julian's house and show Kieran the contents. Nathan abducted. Damien taking me to him. I'll try to talk him free but you'll need this to find us.

She hoped the chip contained information on the London bases used by the gang—Nathan had to be in one of them. Knowing the gang too well, she was aware that they would likely kill the hostages once they had the data, even if she made a bargain. Delay was the best policy. No way was she walking into this carrying the goods; better to have the information somewhere else, so the gang had to keep them alive in the hope of fetching it. There was no time for more. Sending the text, she quickly deleted it from the messages in case anyone checked. She left the envelope lying in the middle of her bed addressed to Raven with a similar message tucked inside.

'Kate—hurry up!' shouted Damien.

Standing with her back to the door so Damien couldn't barge in, she opened the little box of syringes. Was this a totally stupid idea? Probably. With a gulp, she injected one of the bird tags in the middle of the scorpion's belly on her inner arm. She had to hope Gani had not been specific about where he had put his data. She wasn't supposed to know, was she? But she couldn't risk them seeing her neck in case they guessed that she had removed it already. The tattoo made sense, because on the night in question it had been sore and that would have hidden what he had done.

'Kate!' The door rattled as he thumped on it.

'Really, Damien,' complained Julian, 'I thought I taught

you manners. Young ladies have to do young lady things that can't be hurried.'

Kate came into the hallway in time to see Damien on the point of invading her room. 'Thanks, Julian. I look forward to hearing about your trip when we get back.' She was amazed she sounded so cool.

Julian patted her shoulder. 'I've got photos.'

'Excellent. See you later.'

Damien and Kate emerged on to the street. Looking up, Kate saw Julian was watching them from the window.

'What did you tell him?'

'That we were going to meet up with Nathan.' Damien's tone was terse but he seemed less frantic now they were on their way. 'We need a plan.'

'I agree.'

'My phone's not secure but I left a message for Kieran in his room. He should have got it by now.'

'Saying?'

'Everything I know: they've got Nathan, and if we tell anyone—police, Isaac, another member of staff—they'll kill him. I said I was fetching you and heading for the rendezvous point at the Nine Elms supermarket in Vauxhall.'

'This isn't a plan: this is a suicide mission.' Kate tried not to touch the new bump she had made in the centre of her tattoo. She hoped she had calculated this correctly. She had to build in as much delay as possible so Kieran could get to work.

'That's not what I meant by a plan—that's me doing what I was instructed so they didn't start in on him. Now they can see we are on our way,' Damien's gaze flicked over everyone else walking towards the river shuttle bus, 'we can come up with a way of getting out of this alive.'

Kate took a quick survey of her companion, weighing up his trustworthiness. His eyes were burning with a fierce

227

warrior light. He was not so much scared as furious. That still didn't clear up the rather pressing matter of whether or not he was in on this. He could be being blackmailed as she had first suspected—an unwilling accomplice.

'They might let you two go but I doubt they'll keep their word about not harming me,' she said quietly.

Damien shook his head in denial. 'I won't let them hurt you, I promise.'

That was not a promise he was sure he could keep.

Kate wished she had more time to think. 'Let me do the talking. I know these people better than you.' They joined the queue filing onto the boat to take them upriver.

'What do you plan to say?'

'That I'll make a trade. Get Nathan free and I'll give them what they want.'

'I thought you didn't know what they want.'

'Then I'll have to ask them, won't I?'

Damien waited until the boat cast off, then moved them to a spot on deck where he could be sure no one was listening. 'Let's contact Raven—check Kieran's found the note I left him at HQ. Your phone is secure, right?'

'I think so—only bought it yesterday.'

Damien took it from her and began typing the message. He then swore and deleted it. 'Can't.'

'What do you mean?'

'I've just realized: they've got Nathan—which means they have his phone.'

She caught up with his thought. 'And that gives them my number.' And she'd already contacted Raven on it!

Damien opened the back and took out the SIM card. Efficiently snapping it in two, he threw the pieces into the Thames. 'They'll have trouble triangulating a signal from that. We'll get off at the Tower and go the rest of the way by taxi. The Underground is too easy to watch.' He steered her towards the disembarkation point as they neared the landmark bridge. 'We'll buy a new SIM card if we see a shop on the way.'

Kate felt a little safer with him at this suggestion. Maybe he wasn't bluffing when he said he wanted to contact Raven?

They reached the Nine Elms supermarket a few minutes after the midday deadline Damien had been given. There just had been no way to cross Central London any faster—she hoped the kidnappers understood that. A busy Saturday morning, it was bizarre to find themselves suddenly surrounded by people going about their ordinary business.

'What now?' Kate checked her phone. The new SIM was inside but as yet she had no response from Raven. She may not know to check this new unknown number. Kate had a sickening sense of deja vu. Calls and messages not getting through: she'd been there before in Jakarta. There was a clue in this if only she could follow the links.

'Let's message Kieran.' Kate pulled Damien into the aisle by baby foods.

'But...'

'I don't have time to explain.' She tapped quickly and pressed send.

Damien put his hand over hers. 'No, you really do have time.'

'OK, look, when things went wrong in Jakarta, none of my messages got through.'

'That's because you didn't send any messages. I've seen the file.'

'Not true—I sent loads. It's like today. No response. The person on the inside is jamming communication. That made me think: no one would dare tamper with Kieran's phone. He would be on to it like a shot and I bet his isn't standard issue.'

'No, he customizes all his tech. But how would they do that to the rest of us?'

Kate rubbed her forehead. 'I'm guessing denying access to the network to YDA phones. Reception dips from time to time—people might just dismiss it as one of those things, but not Kieran. If you don't do it too frequently then . . . ' She finished the sentence with a shrug. 'I'd bet the wifi in the YDA is mysteriously down as well. I'm hoping Kieran will have his ways round that once he twigs there's an emergency.'

Her phone pinged.

Got D's note. We're on it. K&R

Proof that Damien hadn't lied to her: that made her feel a hundred times better. Kate showed him the message. 'See: what did I tell you?'

'And if we think about it, I'm sure this will tell us who the double agent is. The best bet is the person who sets up the phones, pays the bills and so on.' Damien frowned as an idea formed. 'Surely not?'

'What?'

Damien's face was ashen. 'I can't believe it but I think it's . . . '

'Damien!' A shopping trolley stopped short of the small of Damien's back. Over a generous supply of kitchen towels and cauliflowers, Tamsin MacDonald smiled pleasantly at them both. 'Oh my word, and Kate! I'm surprised to see you two together—amazed, in fact. Does Isaac know you found Kate?'

Damien moved Kate a little behind him. That told Kate everything she needed to know. 'Kate? No, this is Julie—an old friend from school. Can see how you confused them—they do look alike. Nice seeing you, Julie. Catch up some time later, all right?'

Mrs MacDonald gave a funny little laugh. 'Don't be silly, Damien. I know Kate too well to fall for that one.' Kate tried to retreat but found a second shopping trolley blocked the aisle. Whereas Mrs MacDonald looked an entirely plausible Saturday shopper, this one was empty and was being pushed by the duo who almost caught her at the Willows. Now she understood why they hadn't needed her alive. They just needed her body. 'How are you, dear?' continued Mrs MacDonald. 'I'm glad to see you're not looking too bad after your difficult experience. I never wished that on you.'

Kate guessed Mrs MacDonald knew far more about just how difficult the experience had been. She had engineered it.

Mrs MacDonald checked her watch. 'We can have a chat later, but we'd better get back before our friends lose patience and hurt dear Nathan. He's such a lovely boy—so like my Joe.'

Kate's mind was whirling. They had one advantage—Kieran and Raven knew part of what was happening. She must keep that a secret, let Mrs MacDonald think that her communications blackout had worked. Kate backed into the shelf of nappies and dropped the phone down behind the front row.

'I . . . don't want to go with you.'

Mrs MacDonald shook her head sadly. 'Please, Kate, don't over-react. They won't hurt you. They just need to search you. They've given me their word and so far they've always kept it. You won't be harmed.'

'Why should we believe you?' asked Damien, clearly eyeing up the many opportunities to appeal for help from staff and customers in a busy shop.

'Because you aren't the target. This isn't about you at all—it's about Isaac Hampton. Do come along.'

Sounding disturbingly like a mad Mary Poppins, Mrs MacDonald abandoned her trolley and led the way out of the shop.

Kate looked to Damien. Their eyes met and silently they agreed to follow. If they wanted to save Nathan, they had no choice.

Nathan looked up as the bolt on the outside of his door scraped open. Two guards stood outside, assault rifles held low, pointing at his head. One gestured for him to come out. Getting slowly to his feet, he walked, hands spread to show he wasn't intending to make any sudden moves. He stepped into a high-ceilinged warehouse, empty apart from square concrete pillars supporting the roof. Water dripped through a gap in the corrugated iron forming a dank pool on the dirty grey floor. Pigeons cooed at the far end. He could just spot them roosting in the eaves, white droppings marking the spot below their favoured perch. A train rumbled by, close but unseen.

The guard who had ordered him to move now held up his gun to stop him. Nathan tried to get some clues from his two captors' faces but they were inscrutable: the balding one had a square, reddened face of someone who had been in the sun too long, fingers swollen, rings too tight; the second was younger, fitter, with dark hair and stubble. That would be the one who would be up to catching him if Nathan made a run for it. His brain ran through the opportunities: the door over on the far right? But that was the obvious route, most likely to be guarded. Up to the rafters then out through the roof? That was a little better as it had the element of surprise. OK, now he had decided he just had to wait for his chance. Best not to try anything while he had two guns on him.

Nathan heard footsteps on the stairs and watched as a small group of men entered. The famous Gatra brothers were among them: that was a surprise. He would have thought they would keep far away from the dirty work. Two aides and four bodyguards accompanied them, fanning out to make a protective entourage. The aides carried folding chairs which they erected for the Gatras. The two gang bosses took their seats and ignored Nathan, not interrupting the conversation they had been having on their way into the room. One aide passed Yandi his phone. He read the message, nodded and then continued talking.

Nathan was getting the idea that he really wasn't important in this scene. There was going to be no gloating evil guy explanation of why he had been brought here, like in the movies. He would just have to go with his own guesses.

And they were not pleasant. If he had been brought out and made to wait with the Gatras, that meant they had their reason. Kate was on her way.

Chapter 19

Expecting cars with blacked-out windows, Kate was surprised when Mrs MacDonald led them on foot behind the supermarket to the industrial area of New Covent Garden; this was where fruit and vegetables were delivered for wholesale to the capital. Deliveries were made early in the morning so by now it was quiet, not even a security guard patrolling. Mrs MacDonald had a swipe card and code to get into the complex, though she had to put on her glasses to read the numbers off, giving Kate and Damien time to memorize the number. Taking a step, Mrs MacDonald paused in the gateway and turned to face them. Kate had a sickening sense that the woman had completely misjudged the trouble into which she had plunged them all.

'We are just popping into that building over there.' She pointed to one of the older storage warehouses on the edge facing the railway, one that looked derelict. 'I'm sure I don't need to warn you to behave, do I?'

Her school-teacherly manner was getting on Kate's nerves. 'You've got to be crazy, Mrs MacDonald. You are suggesting we walk into a Scorpion trap and "behave"?'

'Yes, I am.' She patted Kate's arm. 'There's no need to worry.'

'So you said.' Damien glanced at the men shadowing them. 'But I don't think you quite get what's going on here. These guys have already tried to kill Kate once.'

'Nonsense!' Mrs MacDonald waved away the suggestion and headed towards the building 'Kate has information they need, so of course they won't kill her.'

So Mrs MacDonald had no idea what form that data was in; she probably did think they were all going to emerge from this alive. She was involved with matters way above her pay grade. But why was she even doing this?

'You said this is about Colonel Hampton and not us.' Kate asked, catching up with Mrs MacDonald. 'What did you mean?'

'Simple really. Isaac took my baby from me so I'm taking his—the YDA. He has poured himself into it, heart and soul. I meant it to unravel when you first disappeared but unfortunately Isaac talked himself out of trouble. Not this time, though.' Her lips pressed in a satisfied line, not quite a smile, more a gloat.

That was a perverse twisting of the truth. Mrs MacDonald was so set on her revenge she was blind to the quagmire in which she had sunk them all. Kate felt so angry with her she wanted to scream; instead she had to settle for argument. 'But Isaac tried to save your son. You can't blame Isaac for the war. Your son chose to be a soldier.'

'Oh, not that.' Mrs MacDonald dismissed Isaac's bravery under fire with a shrug. She tucked her glasses back into her handbag. 'No, it was what he was doing to Joe that caused my son to die. Joe was bullied by that man to breaking point and intended to get killed that day. His comrades said he purposely walked out from his cover and took the bullet.'

'Why would he do that?'

'The investigation, of course.'

'What investigation?'

There was no time for an answer to Kate's question as they had reached the building.

'Quiet now. I'll tell you about it later. It's only fair that you understand exactly why you've been inconvenienced by all this.'

Inconvenienced? This wasn't some leaves-on-the-line train delay, but total life collapse. Her palm itched to slap the woman's complacent face, force her to wake up and see what was really happening.

Damien took Kate's hand and pulled her back. 'Don't,' he whispered. 'No use. I think she's so screwed up she won't see reason.'

Kate reached for her hard-learned control. She had passed through the fires of hell to get back here; she was not going to forget this was about saving Nathan. She gave Damien a terse nod.

Prompted by a shove from their two minders, they followed Mrs MacDonald inside the building and up the concrete staircase. Damien hadn't let go of her hand and Kate realized he was signing to her, finger tickling her palm.

P. L. A. N. ?

She squeezed a 'yes'.

?

D.A.T.A.4.U.S.

He released her palm, wanting to have both hands free for what came next. Kate regretted that she hadn't had a chance to explain the microchip she was now carrying was fake, or that she had left a written message for Kieran and Raven at Julian's. They really should not have run headlong into this.

On the other hand, it might play better if Damien didn't know. That way she could control the steps in the bargaining.

Come on, Kate: don't start doubting yourself. You can do this. You've survived these guys a year so you can get through another day.

Mrs MacDonald was out of breath by the time they reached the top floor. She took a tissue out of her pocket and pressed it delicately to her forehead. 'My goodness, I really should do more exercise. Now, don't forget, once we get in there, I'll make sure I get you all out alive. Just do as I say.' With a last smile at Kate and Damien, she pushed the door open and walked out into the attic room.

A small group of people waited for her in the centre. Kate's spirits leapt when she saw Nathan standing between two guards. First worry put to rest: he was alive. He had no visible injuries, but from the way he was swaying on his feet he wasn't in his best form. Neither did he look happy to see her. She gave him a reassuring smile but that only seemed to make him glower even harder.

Alfin Gatra stood up and held out a hand to Mrs MacDonald. Kate hadn't seen him since Bar Z and some of her old paralysis crept back. He made her feel numb inside, partly because he reminded her so strongly of Gani, sharing the same family features of sculpted cheekbones and liquid brown eyes. Yet Alfin was older and his eyes already showed the damage done by years of violence: no one would mistake him for a poet; his cold gaze was that of a killer.

'Delighted to meet you at long last, Mrs MacDonald. And you've delivered her as you promised.' Alfin's attention turned to Kate. 'You are one elusive lady, Miss Pearl.'

Kate pressed her lips together, eyes fixed on Nathan. *I had to come. Please understand that.*

'Please, take my seat.' Alfin stepped away from his chair.

'Thank you, young man.' Mrs MacDonald put her handbag down beside her and folded her hands neatly in her lap. She could have been sitting at a WI meeting.

'I'd like to thank you for reaching out to us two years ago.'

'No need to thank me. You seemed the most promising of my alternatives. When this mission was first mooted in the minutes, I thought it worth taking the risk.'

'It was a pleasant surprise to us too, making everything so much easier. Thank you also for writing that note yesterday to bring us our most useful bait.'

'Oh, I learned to forge Isaac's handwriting years ago—part of running the office my way. That was no trouble.'

Alfin clicked his fingers. 'Search our guests.'

Two of the bodyguards quickly patted down Damien and Kate, removing Damien's phone and checking his call register.

'That won't be working,' said Mrs MacDonald. 'I did as I promised—the YDA mobile phone contracts are temporarily suspended due to billing difficulties. Only the landlines are working. You should be getting an "emergency calls only" message.'

The guard nodded and stamped on Damien's mobile.

'And the girl?' asked Alfin.

'No phone,' said her searcher.

Damien didn't give her away by the least twitch of surprise.

Alfin waved the bodyguards back to their original positions. 'So, do you agree, Mrs MacDonald, that we have kept our side of the bargain? That we have struck the final blow to Hampton's brainchild?'

She nodded. 'Yes, yes, the YDA will never recover from this.'

'Recover from what?' asked Damien.

'Well, I may not have been entirely truthful with you.' She dabbed her mouth with her tissue, collecting beads of sweat that had gathered there, a sign that she was more nervous than she let on. 'I said you wouldn't be harmed, but Kate might have to spend some time in an Indonesian jail for shooting the Meosidos. Isn't that correct, Mr Gatra?'

Alfin nodded, toying with a hotel keycard between finger and thumb. 'Yes, the evidence is overwhelming.'

Nathan swore.

'You bitch!' shouted Damien, lurching towards her. He took a gun butt to his stomach for his outburst. He went down on his knees, eyes bright with rage.

Mrs MacDonald flinched at the violence. 'Now, now, Damien, manners! I'm not expecting you to be pleased but it is the neatest solution. If Kate serves the sentence, it means she stays alive—you have to see that is the best way of ensuring our friends here don't do anything rash. The government will negotiate for her to serve the remainder of her sentence here and then quietly let her out. I'm sure it will be only a few years—five at the most.'

'And what about us?' asked Nathan. 'Damien and me? Did you ask about us?'

She creased her brow. 'Well, no, no. But I'm sure we could come to some similar beneficial decision on that, can't we? I've always found Mr Gatra very reasonable. Perhaps the boys can be relocated for a year or two? I'll vouch for them not contacting anyone if they know it would endanger Kate.' She looked up hopefully to Alfin. Behind her back, Yandi flicked a glance at his nearest bodyguard.

Kate knew what was going to happen. She'd seen this manoeuvre back in Jakarta. One of Nathan's guards—the young one with heavy stubble—stepped in front of Mrs MacDonald. She tried to intervene but she was too far away. 'No, please!'

A shot rang out, throwing Mrs MacDonald back in her chair.

Kate sat on the floor before she fainted, head on her knees.

'Kate!' Nathan tried to reach her but the older guard held him back.

Alfin gave a mocking bow to the body. 'Thank you, Mrs MacDonald. We kept our bargain. You'll be pleased that the YDA certainly won't survive the death of its loyal administrator. That was your life's ambition, after all.'

Yandi gave another flick of a finger and two guards took hold of the chair and dragged it behind a pillar, a trail of blood marking their passage.

Alfin turned back to the three remaining hostages. 'I do not need to tell you that we are deadly serious, do I?'

'Not after that,' agreed Nathan bitterly.

Two polished toecaps on expensive Italian shoes stopped by her feet. 'Now, Miss Pearl, the rest is down to you. You have information that we need. Do you know what I mean by that?'

Kate swallowed, not quite sure how to play this now the moment had come. Mrs MacDonald's death had thrown her.

Alfin put a finger under her chin and lifted her eyes to his. Kate could hear Nathan's sharp intake of breath. 'Where did Gani put it?'

What had her plan been? *Pretend ignorance to buy time.* 'Put what?'

'He told us that he planted some information on you.'

'He . . . he did?' Her voice was shaking, which probably was a good thing for her innocent act. 'But the only thing he put on me was this.' She raised her wrist and drew back the cuff to show the tattoo.

Alfin gripped her wrist and brushed his thumb over her pulse. He had to feel the lump just under the skin.

'It's been sore for a while now,' Kate added.

Alfin pulled her to her feet and led her over to Yandi, who was still seated in his chair as if nothing extraordinary was happening. He could have been watching a test match at the Oval, legs crossed at the ankles, death and mayhem unfolding in front of him. And to him, maybe this was all very ordinary; murder was his daily routine.

Alfin asked him a question in their native language, thrusting Kate's wrist forward.

Heaving himself upright, Yandi took out a little LED torch from his breast pocket and shone it on the area. Kate wished now she had thought to put it somewhere further from major veins. His reply was also in Indonesian but Kate caught the words for agreement.

'What's going on?' asked Nathan. 'What are you doing with Kate?'

Alfin let Kate go and laced his fingers together, cracking the knuckles. 'Information, Mr Hunter. They used to say that angels danced on pinheads. Now you can store an entire government database on one and make everyone dance to your tune.'

Kate rubbed her wrist, bruised after being yanked about. 'Is that what I've got here? A government database?'

Alfin shook his head but didn't explain that it was data on his organization.

The best way to play this was innocent—for the moment. 'Take it—I don't want it on me!'

'We will, but I need to check that this is what we are looking for.' He gestured to one of his aides to fetch a briefcase. 'My cousin was full of tricks and jokes; I'm sure you remember, Kate. You and he were, after all, very close.'

She dropped her gaze to the floor, feeling a hot rush of fury. Not shame this time—she was past that, and certainly not stirred up by anything these killers could say. These men had used her and were now trying to make her feel guilty. Finally she allowed herself to be angry—it was a cleansing, mind-focusing experience. 'Yes, he was, wasn't he? Was that why you had him executed?'

'Yes, exactly.' Alfin clicked open the case and took out a scanner. He scrutinized the readout then approached Kate. 'This will give us the chip identification number. Gani was persuaded to divulge that to us before he left us.'

241

Kate had only the pretence of cooperation in her favour so she held up her arm. Nathan was watching her closely. He knew her well enough to realize she hadn't had any lump on her arm when he had last touched her. His eyes went to her nape. Did he remember she had gone to the doctor's today? Was he able to guess where this was going? The last thing she needed was for him to give her careful bluff away too soon. She wanted to spin out the delay to its full extent, hoping for the cavalry to arrive.

Alfin ran the device over her arm and read the long serial number out to Yandi, who entered it into his tablet. There was silence as he waited for the confirmation it was the same. The frown on Yandi's puffy face deepened.

'What is this . . . this Essex Marsh black-tailed godwit?' he asked.

Damien's gaze leapt to Kate's face, joining the dots with lightning speed. Nathan, who didn't know the contents of Julian's satchel, looked bewildered.

'Is it a code?' snapped Alfin. 'Has the chip corrupted?'

Yandi followed a few more links on his screen. 'No, the chip is registered as part of a conservation scheme. It's real.'

Alfin loomed over Kate, gripping her wrist tightly in his fist. He pulled her up on her toes. 'Why is this in your wrist?'

She stared at the second button of his shirt.

'Where is the real microchip?' He shook her, making her teeth rattle.

'Leave her! I've got it!' shouted Nathan.

No, Nathan, don't do that! Kate groaned silently. He had forgotten the appointment and thought she still had it in her neck.

'You?' Alfin released her and swung round to confront Nathan. 'Where?'

Nathan's eyes slid to Kate. Poor guy had no plan but to deflect violence away from her.

Kate slipped past Alfin, coming to stand between Nathan and the threat. 'It's OK, Nathan, you don't need to lie.' She lifted her hair to reveal the plaster on the back of her neck. 'The truth is, Mr Gatra, I found the chip this morning and had it removed. When I discovered that you had Nathan, I decided that the only way I could bargain for our release was to put it in a safe place.'

Alfin's handsome face took on an ugly expression, teeth bared. 'You did what?'

Kate's knees were shaking. 'If you don't release us, I have left instructions for it to be opened and used against you.'

Quick as a snake, Alfin unholstered a handgun hidden under his jacket and held it to her forehead. 'I'll kill you.'

Kate closed her eyes. 'No one else knows where it is,' she whispered.

She felt the waft of air as his aim moved away. Opening her eyes, she saw he had trained the gun on Nathan.

'I'll kill *him*.'

'If you do, then I don't care what you do to me—I'll die knowing that your organization is destroyed. I've . . . I've left a note to be opened on my death with a map and photograph to show a friend where it is.'

Yandi stood up and put his hand on his brother's arm to lower the gun. He was speaking rapidly in Indonesian. Alfin gave a tight nod and holstered his weapon. Kate felt the spring of tension unwind a fraction. She backed up until she stood directly in front of Nathan. His arms came up to encircle her, his head dipping to her crown for a light brush of his lips. Damien moved to stand at Nathan's right.

'This is interesting,' muttered Damien, expression bleak.

'You shouldn't have come.' Nathan squeezed her tightly against him.

She would have safely bet the entire sum of her college

fund on those being the first words he would say to them. 'We were given no choice.'

'Kate, what are you doing?' Damien asked.

'Buying time the only way I know how,' she admitted. She could not work out if her desperate game of high stakes had just saved or condemned them.

Damien nudged Nathan. 'You've got to admit the girl has balls to take on the Gatras at their own game.'

'She's amazing.' He pressed his cheek to her crown, body thrumming with tension.

The Gatras came to some agreement between them. Yandi took over as questioner.

He stood before her, arms folded. 'Where is this chip?'

Kate allowed herself to relish the warmth of Nathan at her back for a second before playing her final dangerous card. 'I'll take you to it, but only when you show me proof that the boys have been allowed to go. I want to see footage of them walking alone—unharmed—into the YDA headquarters, and then I'll give it to you.'

'No, not like this, Kate,' whispered Nathan, as the Gatras had another of their rapid conversations.

She turned to look up at him, trying to memorize every beloved line and curve of his face. She was far from certain she would ever see it again. 'Do you have a better suggestion?'

Damien squeezed Nathan's arm in warning, telling him not to throw away this opportunity. Thank goodness, thought Kate, that Damien was here with her; Nathan would never agree to separate from her if he wasn't also thinking of his friend. At least this way there was a slim chance they would get free, and the authorities could mount a rescue before the Gatras killed her. She had no illusions that the moment they realized she had no intention of handing over the chip she would be executed, and probably not as mercifully as Mrs MacDonald.

Even if she kept her side of the bargain they would kill her anyway, so there was no option she could negotiate that had 'Kate emerges alive' written on it.

'Agreed,' rapped Alfin. 'The two boys stay here and you come with us. They will be released when we are clear of the area. Later we will show you proof that they are safe and well.'

Kate dipped her head in acknowledgement. 'Don't misjudge me, Mr Gatra. I will tell you nothing if you don't keep your side of this deal.'

Yandi made a remark in Indonesian and laughed. Kate would bet that he had said something about her not being so brave after a few hours of one of their torturers. She just had to hope that being in London would cramp their style in the torture department. The Dorchester Hotel would surely frown on such behaviour, even from high-paying guests.

Picking up the same vibes, Nathan was getting desperate. 'Kate, please,' he whispered. 'Can't we stick together?'

Kate turned fully so she could hug him. 'It's the best I can come up with, Nathan. You know me: I'm an improvise-as-I-go-along kind of girl.'

He brushed her cheek, his expression torn. 'No, you're just my kind of girl.' He closed his eyes briefly, drawing on his deep reserves of steady courage that she knew saw him through crises. 'We'll get out, I promise, and come get you.' The last was whispered in her ear. 'Just you stay alive.'

She might regret much about the last few days, but meeting Nathan was one thing for which she would always be grateful. He was simply the best person she knew. 'I'll try. I don't trust these guys to keep their promises. You've got to be careful.'

Yandi signalled it was time to depart. An aide collected his chair and hurried out to summon their car.

'Come, Miss Pearl. I have had quite enough of this place.' Alfin looked over the pigeon-fouled warehouse with disgust.

He pushed her to walk ahead of him in the broad wake of his brother. 'You are going to be our guest until this is all sorted to our satisfaction.' As they reached the exit, he called over his shoulder to the two guards flanking Nathan. 'Deal with the boys.'

The men nodded, eyes implacable over their gunstocks. Kate had a chilling feeling she had just witnessed him order the boys' death.

'Nathan!' she shouted.

'I know, Kate: I love you too!' he replied, but his eyes were telling her that he had known that she meant to warn them. Surprise was the only advantage left to him and Damien so she could not spoil that.

There was nothing else she could do for him—the thought tore at her like tiger claws. 'I love you. Damien: look after him!'

'Will do,' said Damien, his expression reassuringly lethal.

Alfin paused in the doorway. 'Get rid of the body afterwards.' He pointed at Mrs MacDonald. 'A fire should do it. You are not to leave here until the scene has been destroyed.'

'Yes, sir,' replied the older of the two men.

Had she made the wrong choice again? Just like Jakarta, had her snap decision caused others to meet with disaster? Dazed with terror, Kate was powerless to stop herself being escorted roughly down the stairs. Two armed men against two boys. Nathan and Damien had no chance. They would die first, then she would be next and it would be her fault.

A black limousine waited for the Gatras at the bottom of the steps, a yellowed cabbage leaf incongruously plastered against the shining metal hub cap of the rear wheel.

A guard opened the passenger door. Yandi got in with as much elegance as a hippo on land. Alfin indicated that Kate was to enter next. He sat beside her on the rear seat so that she was wedged between him and his brother. Two bodyguards took the backwards-facing seats opposite them, their expressions harder than stone, a little bored if anything.

'Now, Miss Pearl,' said Alfin in his silky voice, 'I think it's time we negotiated the real deal, don't you?'

Chapter 20

Nathan was well aware that he needed full concentration on his own situation, but he couldn't stop a groan, only a hint of his anguished inner cry, as he saw Kate pushed through the swing doors and into the stairwell.

'Nat,' murmured Damien.

Focus. You've got to survive. Nathan tapped his left thigh, their signal that he was on the case. Kate had tried her hardest to negotiate an exit for them that left them alive but the Gatras would not want witnesses to murder to survive. These two thugs had been instructed to kill them.

Damien spread his fingers over his right ribs. That meant he was taking out the younger dark haired guard on their right, leaving the older, red-faced one to Nathan. Damien always picked the tougher targets.

Nathan scratched his nose, which Damien would understand as *Attack so that the guards were facing each other.* If they got off a shot from that position, they risked killing their own side.

Damien eased his collar away from his neck. *It's gonna be close.*

Nathan pressed his stomach. *Ya think?*

The guards were waiting to hear the sound of the Gatras' car depart from the forecourt. Sometimes the oldest tricks are the best ones. Nathan gave Damien the nod that he had something.

Damien shifted his foot—once, twice, three times.

'Oh my God, I swear she moved! Is she alive?' Nathan pointed to the very dead body of Mrs MacDonald with a quivering finger.

Shocked, the guards' eyes naturally arrowed to the corpse. Nathan's target got an elbow in the face, followed by a kick to the groin. Staggering as the pain registered, the guard tried to bring up his gun, but Nathan and Damien were fighting back to back, leaving no room to get off a clear shot. A bullet flew into the ceiling from Damien's attacker. Pigeons burst from all corners, swarming with panic, their wing flaps sounding a bizarre round of applause. Another sharp spray of ammunition—Damien must be wrestling for the gun but Nathan had to get his man down before he could assist. A second kick to the groin followed by one to the kneecap, Nathan's target went to the ground. Nathan grabbed the gun and turned it so that the end was now pointing at the man's stomach. Behind him, he heard a strangled cry and Damien's guy fell forward, clutching his throat. The gunstock had smashed into his larynx during the struggle. Breathing hard, Damien ripped the rifle from the guard's hands and turned it deftly to point at the man. For a split second, Nathan thought Damien was going to press the trigger—he could see that his friend was tempted. The man in his sights had been the one to shoot Mrs MacDonald.

'Damien,' he said softly. 'Law enforcement; not law in our own hands.' That was the first rule any Yoda learned: they were investigators policing society, not terrorizing it.

Damien shook himself, throwing off his rage with a huge mental effort. 'On your knees, scumbag, hands behind head.'

The two guards exchanged a look.

'Don't think about it,' added Nathan coolly, 'just do it.'

His implacable tone impressed the men that they were serious. Thugs-for-hire, they had thought they were dealing with amateurs, having no idea what it meant to be products of Isaac's tough training.

'What shall we do with them?' asked Damien.

'There is a prison cell just over there. It's impossible to get out of—believe me, I tried.' And there was a pleasing symmetry of the jailers becoming the jailed.

'OK, guys, you heard my friend. Walk slowly over to that room. Keep your hands where I can see them.' Never wavering in his aim, Damien escorted the men to the room where Nathan had passed the night. Nathan stood ready to slam the door the moment the men were inside. He felt a huge sense of relief once the bolts were pushed home. First major obstacle out of their way.

'Thank God that worked.' He flicked the safety on the gun and leaned back against the wall.

'Well done, mate.' Damien gave him a one-armed hug, both rather surprised to have come out of that alive. 'Right: let's get out of here and go get your girl.' Success had revived his optimism.

'What do we do with these?' Nathan hefted the rifle.

Damien ejected the magazine. 'We follow the rules.' He quirked his lips, silently acknowledging to his friend how tempted he had been the break the most serious of them all just a moment ago when he had held the gun on Mrs MacDonald's killer. 'With those guys locked up, we don't need them. Let's break them down and dump them with the body.'

'OK, but take the ammo—just in case someone else gets here first. The police can pick the guns up later when they deal with the body and the prisoners.'

'Adds a firearms offence to the many charges they're facing, and the police will need the gun to nail the killer.' Damien looked bleakly over at the body sitting slumped in the shadows. 'I don't understand it. Why would she do that to us?'

'No idea, but we'll find out.'

Leaving Damien to disassemble to rifles, Nathan went to the exit to check no one else was outside. He pushed on the swing door but it only moved a tiny amount. He then pulled— no good. Finally, he rattled it hard, getting a clearer sense of what was stopping it moving.

'Damien, they've barred the exit—some kind of chain and padlock I guess. It can only be removed from the outside.'

Damien piled the guns by Mrs MacDonald's feet. 'Brilliant. I bet the Gatras did that expecting their stooges to set fire to the place after killing us and die in the blaze. Tidy solution to two more witnesses.'

Nathan stamped down on the swell of desperation. No point giving in to emotion. He needed his professional head screwed on tight, feelings battened down. They had to get out to save Kate—she must have very little time before the Scorpions turned their most extreme interrogation techniques on her. Looking around the room, he remembered his earlier thought about going up rather than down. With Damien's help that would now be possible.

'Damien, you remember that circus training we did?'

Typically, Damien had picked card skills and magic tricks. Nathan had plumped for something more physical: high wire. The performer who had showed him the secrets had also taught him how to mount using a fellow performer.

Damien groaned. He had remembered very clearly because he had been the partner with whom Nathan had most often trained. 'Jeez, Nat, most acrobats are skinny little blokes.' Complain though he might, Damien was looking for the right spot. 'Here?'

'Yeah.' Nathan slipped off his shoes, eyeing the beam and its row of interested pigeon spectators. 'Ready?'

Damien went down on one knee forming a stirrup with his

hands. The idea was to turn him into a human spring board. As Nathan placed his foot in his hands, Damien would rise and throw Nathan upwards, adding to his lift. It was all in the timing, according to Manolo, his circus trainer. Damien gave him the nod. 'Go for it.'

Giving himself a decent run up, Nathan sprinted forward. His foot found Damien's cradled hands and he felt the extra surge upwards. He extended his body as far as could, finger tips reaching . . . reaching. His hands slapped into the beam and he curled his fingers, cursing as they slipped in pigeon droppings. Grimly he clung on, swinging gently from his fully stretched arms. Once he had inched his fingers to take a firmer grip, he began to increase his sway. Like an gymnast on the bars, the idea was to use body weight to help, not fight against gravity. That was the theory, but he had only ever practised on proper gym equipment, never on a rusty metal beam studded with iron bolts. He ignored the bite against his palms. Damien waited silently below, knowing this couldn't be rushed. Nathan got the right propulsion to swing legs up and round. He ended up straddling the beam a dizzying height over the floor.

'Great job!' called Damien. 'Now see if there's a way out.'

Nathan got to his feet and made his way along the beam. That part was easy: compared to a rope the beam was a walk in the park. He reached the spot where he had noticed the pigeons had got in. The corrugated iron had been dislodged in a storm and never repaired. Stretching up, Nathan was able to punch out the panel to reveal the sky above.

'Yeah, we can get out on the roof here,' he confirmed. Damien threw his shoes up to him. 'You next?'

Damien rubbed his palms together. 'Help me up.'

Even lying on his stomach, arms dangling, Nathan couldn't grab Damien's hands. His friend just could not get enough lift no matter how hard he jumped.

'Spider-Man, we need another solution,' said Damien.

That gave Nathan an idea. 'In the absence of handy webs, it'll have to be your jeans. Take them off. I'll use them as a rope.'

'Why mine?'

'Because you're on the floor and I'm balanced on a ceiling beam, duh.'

With muttered curses, Damien scrambled out of his jeans and chucked them up to Nathan, a few coins tumbling back on his head.

'I hope these designer threads of yours are well made.' Nathan took hold of the far end of one leg and let the jeans dangled. He braced himself as Damien ran up and jumped. This time Damien was able to get hold of the jeans-rope about mid-thigh. There was an ominous rip, he dropped a fraction but then the jeans held. He quickly climbed up, hand over hand until he was able to put a leg over the beam. With only boxers on his lower half, he was free with his swearing as the rusty metal grated against his skin.

'Best put these back on.' Nathan passed him the trousers. 'Can't have you scaring the pigeons.'

Using Nathan to steady himself, Damien quickly dressed. He grimaced when he saw the damage. 'Ripped in the crotch. Saved by the waistband.'

'OK, now give me a leg up to the roof.' Nathan pulled himself out through the gap he had made. The roof was a gentle incline, easy to stand on without sliding. He reached back through the gap and helped Damien up. Both crouched for a second under the cloudy London skies, relieved to have escaped the attic below. The viaduct of Vauxhall railway station was only a stone's throw away; beyond that lay the river and the buildings on the South Bank—the MI6 headquarters, the expensive riverside apartments, a little further on Lambeth

Palace, where the Archbishop of Canterbury had his London residence. Battersea Power Station lay over to their left, four white towers against the grey clouds.

'We'll have to be careful crossing this,' Nathan said, pointing at the acre of roof in front of them. 'If one section had slipped, there will be others.'

'As we came in, I noticed a fire escape on the outside wall at that end. Yeah, over there, level with the signal box on the viaduct.' Damien indicated the far side. 'It might go all the way to the roof if we're lucky.'

'Let's keep two metres apart so if one panel goes, we don't take the other with us.'

'Cheery thought. Thanks, mate.'

Smiling at his friend's black humour, Nathan started a careful progress across the corrugated iron.

'How are you doing?' called Damien. 'Head giving you any trouble?' Damien's foot slid as a loose panel see-sawed and fell into the room below. Damien stepped back. He gave Nathan a grim smile. 'So, not that way then.'

'I'm OK—trying not to think about the headache.' Nathan picked up his pace and crossed the last ten metres of roof. Reaching the edge where Damien had spotted the fire exit, he peered over the edge to locate it: a ladder bolted to the wall. 'Good call, Damien. It's here,' he shouted.

Damien reached the relative safety of the roof edge. 'I'm not ashamed to admit I'm pleased that's over.'

Nathan tested the ladder. It looked rusty but sound enough to chance. 'Nothing ventured . . . ' He began climbing down. Wisely, Damien waited until he was at the bottom before following.

'Where next?' Nathan asked when his friend reached him.

'Gate's that way. Let's get out of this compound—see if we can find someone with a working mobile out there.' Damien gestured to the street beyond. There were no pedestrians but cars were at a standstill in a traffic snarl-up—unusual for this area on a Saturday.

Nathan reached the barrier first and swore when he saw the locking mechanism. 'We need the code.'

'Don't worry—I know it.' As Damien punched in the combination to open the gate, a motorcycle screeched up the approach road to the market. A man in black leathers got off and removed his helmet.

'Isaac!' shouted Nathan. 'Over here!'

'Thank God you're alive!' Isaac strode over. 'Where's Kate?' He lifted his eyes fearfully to the building behind. 'Is she . . . ?'

Nathan cut him off. 'She's with the Gatras. She tried to bargain for our safety with some information she had—a subdermal chip. She only found it this morning.'

Isaac nodded; this came as no news to him. 'Thanks to her quick thinking, Kieran has the chip. He's just unscrambling the data—enough to find this place on the list of safe houses—but I also got him to shut down this part of London by messing with the traffic lights.'

Damien whistled. 'So it's his work—the jam. How did you know where to look?'

'Kate sent a message from the supermarket. Kieran traced it. We only had a general area so had to take out the whole road system round here to lock it down.' Isaac led them back to the bike. 'Hell to pay with the mayor when we've finished. The Gatras will still be here if they didn't leave on foot. I've got the Tube and overground rail watched.'

'It's not likely they'd choose to abandon a vehicle unless they suspect they're being chased,' said Nathan. 'Look for some kind of luxury car. I think they were heading back to their London base. Dorchester Hotel, wasn't it?'

Isaac got on the bike. 'That means the Vauxhall Bridge

junction—best route over the river from here. Let's go.' He picked up his helmet. 'Nathan, you get on behind me. Damien, you're going to have to hold on to him.'

Isaac barked a few orders into the shortwave radio attached to his collar. From the commands rapped out to Jim Rivers, Nathan guessed the YDA had abandoned phones, realizing they were compromised or not working. That reminded him: Isaac didn't know the worst.

'Isaac, Mrs MacDonald . . . '

'What?' Isaac kicked the starter motor.

'She was shot—in there. She died instantly.'

Isaac let the engine die. 'You're not joking.'

'No.'

His shoulders slumped forward as he rested his weight on his arms. He then kicked the starter pedal again. 'Right—deal with that later. Kate first.'

Kate felt sick. Sitting so close to the Gatras, she could smell Alfin's expensive aftershave and Yandi's mixture of soap and sweat. The car had been crawling along for a few minutes and now had stopped completely, prolonging her suffering. The two bodyguards stared blankly out of the window, both wearing shades so no trace of humanity could be seen. They could have been robots for all the warmth of their expression. She discounted them as having any conscience about what their bosses had planned for a few teenagers. Once more, she was on her own.

Alfin looked up from his phone, where he had been reading his messages. She knew his mind games: he was letting her stew before offering her the deal he mentioned. 'Find out why we have stopped,' he ordered.

The guard on the right opened the privacy screen and had a quick conversation with the driver. 'Lights are out at the intersection, sir. The traffic is backed up on all approaches.'

'So we have to wait?'

'I'm afraid so, sir.' The bodyguard settled back on his seat, surveying the cars either side of theirs for any threats. A white van was stopped on the left, two builders reading the newspaper in the front, ignoring everything but the football scores. On the right, a young woman driver was checking her texts with one hand, painted fingernails of the other drumming on the wheel. The north-running Lambeth Road on which they were stuck converged with three other highways at a massive road junction right at the foot of the MI6 building, but nothing was moving. Cars were filling the intersection, horns beeping, several road rage altercations sparking off as people tried to jump the jam. No one was going anywhere until the traffic police sorted it out.

Alfin must have come to the conclusion that, as the car was halted, he had time to start the game again. 'So, Kate—I can call you Kate?'

She shrugged. He could call her Donald Duck if he wanted: he was the one with the gun.

'We have to come to an agreement very rapidly as I am . . . ' he paused, searching for the right word, '*uncomfortable* to know that information is out there. I don't like being uncomfortable.' He shifted sideways so he could see her reactions. 'Do you understand?'

Kate nodded.

'Now you think you have been very clever negotiating with what you have, but you should understand you've always been destined to lose. What is going to happen today is this: you are going to tell me where that microchip is and then we either kill you or take you back to Indonesia to stand trial for our cousins' murders. That is the real choice, not your sentimental all-going-free demands. Understand?'

She dipped her chin, clenching her hands in her lap.

'Now the decision as to whether you live and go to prison or die today is yours. If you take us directly to the place you have put our information, then you live. If you remain silent, then you die. Simple, isn't it?'

Kate chewed on her lip, using the pain to keep her nerve. He wouldn't want her to die without telling them—about that he was bluffing. If he knew she had already sent the information to Kieran, she would not last five seconds.

'I can see you are still holding out for a miracle, so I think you need to stare the choice in the face.' He opened a side cabinet usually meant to hold drinks but instead took out a large jar. 'Remember these? Gani told us you were susceptible to a visual threat.' Six black scorpions scuttled over each other, trying to build a ladder of bodies to the lid, segmented abdomens gleaming like Darth Vader's armour. Alfin put the jar on her lap. Kate couldn't repress a flinch. 'So much quieter than a bullet and so much more nasty to contemplate. Fat-tailed scorpions, most deadly breed in the world. Like them?'

Cold sweat trickled down Kate's back. She shook her head. Even the guards turned from their survey of the street to give the scorpions a wary look. Yandi inched away from her.

Alfin smiled. 'I didn't think you would. My brother hates them, but I am rather fond of them.' He tapped the jar, causing the creatures to curl their tails and twitch. 'Gani used to look after them for me—one of the reasons why I was very sorry we had to kill him.'

Kate swallowed, telling herself that the jar was thick - that Alfin was not stupid enough to open it while in an enclosed space. It was just like being at the zoo—really it was.

'So Kate, think about this while we sit here: when we get to the hotel, we are going to lock you in the bathroom, handcuffed to the towel rail and then I am going to let my friends out for their evening hunt. If you haven't screamed out the information and still think to keep silent, then you will have quite a few minutes of excruciating pain and will beg us to put a bullet in you to end it. Alternatively,' Alfin tapped the glass, 'you can avoid all this drama, tell us what we want to know, and live. We fly out tonight—you could be on the plane.'

Kate licked her lips, trying to get some moisture back in her mouth. 'What guarantee do I have that you'll keep your word?'

'You don't, other than you know that we want you to take the blame for Gani and Agustina's deaths. You understand we only keep alive those who are useful to us?'

'What about my friends?'

'They were not useful.'

She'd known—of course she'd known. She had to trust that he had underestimated Nathan and Damien.

A bag lady pushing a shopping trolley and dressed in a saggy brown overcoat made her way down between the stationary vehicles, talking loudly to herself. The woman driver next to their car wound up her window. The tramp stopped to rearrange her precious cargo of plastic bags, leaning over so that her face was at the level of the window nearest Kate. She wouldn't be able to see in, but Kate could make out her features perfectly well.

Familiar sharp eyes scanned the vehicle. Kate had not seen Jan Hardy for a year but she recognized her old mentor in one of her favourite disguises: smelly tramp, everyone looked away. Kate's despair suddenly turned to desperate hope. The 'bag lady' let out a stream of foul language and shoved the trolley as if it had offended her. It bumped against the spotless paintwork of the limo, probably making a nice scratch down the side.

The driver leapt out. 'What are you playing at, you stupid cow! Get away from my car!'

She screeched insults, throwing tattered plastic bags at him as the builders roared with laughter in the front of their white van. The driver decided direct intervention was the only way. Grabbing her sleeve, he hurried the woman and her trolley off the road, shouting abuse at her, but there were too many witnesses to take a more violent approach. Jan pretended fear and scuttled away, her mission complete. The car had been identified and marked, the front door open briefly so someone watching from the high ground—the Cobra mentor, Taylor Flint most likely, he took that kind of mission—could spy how many occupants were in the back. Kate knew the YDA were coming for her.

'This country—unbelievable!' Alfin took out a cigarette case and lit up to pass the time. Sirens announced the police had finally arrived to sort out the traffic snarl—at least, that was what the Gatras would think. 'So, Kate, do you want to live?'

'Of course I want to live,' she said quietly.

'Then you'll take us to the data?'

She nodded.

'Once we are through this, where do I tell the driver to go—the address?'

Buy more time, Kate, she told herself. A house could be searched but not a whole park. 'I buried it under a tree in Greenwich Park—I'll have to take you there myself.'

'Then you have earned yourself a reprieve.' Alfin leaned back and blew a stream of smoke over her head, content that his threats were working.

Just then an unshaven bloke in a scruffy T-shirt and woolly hat approached their vehicle, his bare arms covered in tattoos. He had been making his way along the line of cars, squeezy bottle and sponge in hand, not getting a very warm welcome for his entrepreneurial spirit. Without asking for permission, he squirted the windscreen and smeared the glass so that the view was obscured. Excellent: they wouldn't see the police moving in.

'You moron!' howled the driver, winding down the side window. He was not having a good day. 'I didn't want my screen cleaned!'

'A quid for a polish with my chamois,' replied the man cheerfully ignoring the stream of abuse coming his way.

Oh my God, it was Sergeant Rivers! Kate had taken a moment or two to twig, as Rivers was always military neat, but he was here, just a few metres away—Nathan's adopted dad. She had to help. Seeing the operation from the YDA viewpoint, they had a limited window of opportunity to save her. The traffic jam wouldn't last for ever; they had identified her location but knew she was with armed hostiles; they had to think of a way of getting her out of the car but it was impossibly difficult without the Gatras realizing something was happening and using Kate as a hostage.

A motorcyclist carrying a passenger revved loudly as he edged up between the car and the white van. It was all happening so quickly. Kate recognized the helmeted passenger from the clothes Nathan had been wearing. The relief to know he was alive was immense. Quickly looking behind she saw two mopeds approaching, one ridden by a girl in a tan leather jacket, the other by a tall slim boy in a matching outfit. Then she spotted, through a tiny gap in between the cars, Damien on the pavement, standing with his face turned away. He was speaking into a walkie-talkie, coordinating the approach. They were definitely all in position. If she didn't act swiftly, the Gatras might guess something was afoot.

So the YDA had come for her—but it was her job to get out of the car. A sudden dash was difficult due to her wedged in position; she needed a distraction.

The cool weight of the jar on her lap gave her a dangerous idea. She surreptitiously unscrewed the lid.

261

'How long can this traffic jam last?' complained Alfin. 'Check the traffic news again.'

As the bodyguard on the right turned to speak to the driver, but he was still arguing with the windscreen cleaner. Kate said a quick prayer to whoever protected reckless fools, then said . . .

'Catch!'

She threw the jar to the guard on the left. Shocked, he let go of his gun and lurched to grab the vessel. The lid flew off. With a yell, he threw the jar away from him, down at Yandi's feet. The reaction was everything Kate had hoped. Panicked to be trapped with six fat-tailed scorpions, the occupants of the rear of the car opened the doors both sides and tumbled out. Kate followed Alfin, wanting to put as much distance between her and the freed scorpions as possible. Yandi yelled and danced on the far side of the car. He screamed in his language, from the little Indonesian she'd picked up it was something about being stung. Then he clutched his chest and fell like a tree with an axe to its root.

Kate didn't wait to see what Alfin did. She ran for Nathan, jumping on the bike behind him. The driver opened the throttle and roared away, banging wing mirrors of the stationary cars in his haste to escape. The mopeds followed, and behind them, more sirens and police converged on the car.

She had to warn the police about the scorpions. Kate batted Nathan urgently on the shoulder. He relayed the demand to stop to the driver. Pulling over when they reached the bridge by the MI6 building, Kate jumped off.

'Tell them quick!' she burst out. 'Scorpions in the car!'

'Thank God you're all right!' Nathan squeezed her in a tight hug, bemused by her panic. 'I know, love—they're being arrested.'

'Shut up—shut up! I mean it: real ones, not the gang. The police might get stung—they've got to be captured!'

The driver removed his helmet. Isaac—of course. Ripping free of Nathan, Kate grabbed Isaac's lapels and gave him a shake, forgetting he was her boss. 'Tell them, please! I let them out!'

'What's all this?' Isaac pushed her gently back into Nathan's arms. 'Calm down, Kate. It's over.'

Why did they both have to decide to be dense now of all times? Kate balled her fist and punched Nathan on the shoulder.

'It's not over! Fat-tailed scorpions—in the car. They were going to use them to kill me if I didn't talk, but I let them loose so everyone would jump out of the car.'

'I think she's serious, sir.' Nathan rubbed her fist trying to make her uncurl her fingers.

'Of course I'm serious! They had a jar of deadly scorpions—now they're running about the Lambeth Road.'

Isaac nodded and began speaking tersely on the walkie-talkie.

Finally free of the traffic, the two mopeds joined them. Raven jumped off her pale yellow one and swooped on Kate and Nathan. 'You're alive!'

Perching his black one on its stand, Kieran came over. 'Of course they are alive—they're responding to external stimuli, show every sign of breathing unaided, no indication of trauma.'

Raven executed a neat reverse move of her elbow to his solar plexus. 'I'll give you trauma—you know what I mean, Kieran Storm.'

He rubbed his stomach. 'Yeah I do—and good to see you both.'

'Kate, so pleased you got out safely.' Raven gave her a delighted embrace. Touched that the girl she had met only briefly had clearly cared about what happened to her, even if it was only for Nathan's sake, Kate squeezed Raven in thanks and then disentangled herself from the hug. There was no shifting Nathan though: he was not letting go of her waist.

This is a little awkward, thought Kate, looking up at the owlish Kieran. The last time she had met him she had been running from him, but he didn't appear to hold that against her from the smile he was directing at her. 'Um, hi, Kieran. What about the data: did you get it?'

He put an arm around Raven. 'It's in the lab at the YDA. The life-and-death emergency rather bumped it down the to-do list, but from my preliminary scan it reads like a comprehensive cache of information on every part of the Scorpion network until a year ago. That should give the international law enforcements agencies plenty of evidence to take them apart.'

Kate rubbed her eyes, finding it hard to believe that it was really over, that the danger had been neutralized. 'It's important that they do something for the victims—the people in the chain.'

Kieran gave a 'but-of-course' shrug. 'We can make that a condition of sharing the information if you like.'

'Will you?'

'Of course, we can. A perfectly logical request after all.'

Damien ran up, having pursued the mopeds on foot. 'Guys, it's a beautiful scene back there.' He leant straight-armed on Kieran's shoulder for a second, getting his breath back. 'All the bad guys are disarmed, lying on the road, screaming. Apparently, they didn't mind getting arrested, they just didn't want to risk lying down. Yandi Gatra is having some kind of seizure. Ambulance is on its way.'

Holding the walkie-talkie away from his mouth, Isaac tapped Kate's shoulder. 'How many scorpions exactly did you let loose?'

'Six.' She shuddered at the memory.

'They've isolated five in the vehicle. They suspect the sixth one might be what they found on the bottom of Yandi Gatra's shoe.'

'Did he get stung?'

'They don't think so. Taylor believes he's having a panic attack.'

'Shame,' muttered Nathan.

'Yeah, poor scorpion,' agreed Damien.

'I'll tell them they've got the lot then.' Isaac went back to his discussion.

Kate leant against Nathan, savouring his soothing rub of her arms as he filled his friends in on how he and Damien had escaped the warehouse. He made it sound easy but Kate had seen the height of that room; getting up to the roof had been an amazing feat.

Isaac ended his conversation and turned to his team. 'I think I'll be here some time to come sorting this out. Jan, Taylor, and Jim are staying with me, so you lot are free to go back to headquarters and report to Dr Waterburn. I'll tell her to expect you. Nathan, Damien, Kate—I want the agency's doctor to check you over. The police will be along later to take statements, and I'll also want to debrief you, so don't leave the building.'

Kate felt something curl up inside her in shame. 'But I can't go to HQ, Isaac. I could go back to Julian's, couldn't I?' She looked desperately to Damien.

'Kate Pearl, you are ordered back to HQ. You don't want to risk a black mark on your record now you've been fully reinstated, do you?' asked Isaac. 'You too, Nathan. Your suspension is rescinded and I'll make sure it is taken off your file.'

'Let's do as the boss says, Kate,' said Nathan. 'Don't you want to watch Kieran unravel the data?'

Put like that, she did, even though it was with huge reluctance. Arguing was only keeping everyone from their work. She could rely on the guys around her to stop any of the other students mistreating her. 'OK, I'll see you there later, Isaac.'

Raven returned to her moped. 'I can fit two passengers if you snuggle up—Nathan, Kate?'

'We can snuggle,' agreed Nathan with a grin.

Kieran waved Damien over to his moped. 'You get the short straw.'

'Damien, you've got a rip in your pants!' shouted Raven.

'Can this be any more embarrassing?' muttered Damien.

Smiling, Isaac started to head back to the knot of police surrounding the limo, then clicked his fingers. 'Kieran?'

'Yes, Isaac?'

'Lights?'

'Oh yeah. Forgot.' Kieran took out his phone and tapped in a number. Winking at Raven and Kate, he waved his phone at the nearest set of traffic controls, which had been flashing amber for the past hour, and pressed send. 'Lights, camera, and . . . action!'

The lights went green, returning to their normal sequence, letting vehicles onto Vauxhall Bridge. Over on the Lambeth Road, the tangle of vehicles began to sort itself out, working around the scorpion-infested limousine stranded in the centre of one carriageway in a ring of police.

Chapter 21

Nathan could feel the tension humming in Kate as she walked with him into the YDA headquarters. It took guts for her to enter because, no matter how many promises Isaac made, she still was expecting attack. He held her hand in his, brushing his thumb over the fragile bones of her fingers. Raven and Kieran had taken up places either side of them, Damien at their back. He hoped Kate had noticed the unspoken message of support that represented.

Mr Bates, the caretaker and, more importantly, Raven's grandfather, hurried out of his office on the ground floor as soon as he saw them enter. A small man who held himself as upright as his arthritis would allow, he supervised the cleaning staff and kept the students in check with his obvious decency and silent demand that they treat the building with the respect it deserved.

'Raven, are you all right?' He hugged her before she could get out her reply. 'Everyone all right? Boys?'

'Yes, Mr Bates,' Damien said.

'Well, in fact, no. Not Mrs MacDonald,' began Kieran, as usual following logic rather than sensitivity. Raven trod on his foot.

'Tamsin? What's this operation got to do with Tamsin? It's her day off,' said Mr Bates.

Nathan cleared his throat. The news would be out very

267

soon. 'I regret to say, Mr Bates, she was killed. Isaac will explain.'

Mr Bates was no fool. After a brief moment of shock, his face took on a harder expression. It appeared Raven had told him about their suspicions of a traitor in the organization. 'I see. I expect you all need to get on with things.' He waved to the upper regions of the YDA, the labs, classrooms, and briefing rooms. 'But Raven, Kieran, I expect to see you for lunch tomorrow as usual.'

He turned to go but Raven held him back. 'Granddad, this is Kate.' She brought Kate forward. 'Kate Pearl. She's one of us—been away, but back now.'

Mr Bates took in the hunched shoulders and wary look of the returnee. 'Kate?'

Nathan could sense that Kate made herself raise her chin. Her pride was still alive and well, even if her self-esteem had taken a kicking over the last year.

Mr Bates held out a hand for a shake, then thought again and converted the gesture to a grandfatherly pat on the shoulder. 'Lovely to meet you, my dear. Welcome home.'

Kate swallowed against a swell of emotion. 'Thank you.'

'Off you go, boys and girls.' Mr Bates went back to his office. 'I'm sure you've got a lot to do.'

'I like your granddad,' Kate murmured to Raven. 'He's a sweetie—like mine was.'

'Aw, thanks.' Raven smiled.

'He is—until you track mud across his clean floors,' teased Nathan, pleased that had gone so well.

Kieran had wandered over to the lift and pressed the call button. With a roll of her eyes at Kate, Raven snagged him by the back of his jacket. 'Where are you off to, sunshine?'

Kieran muttered something about lab and data analysis. But his exit was prevented because when the lift arrived it delivered a car-load of trouble. Nathan winced as his mother,

Uncle Julian, Dr Waterburn, and the YDA medic, Dr Hooper all descended on them. Dr Waterburn immediately caught Kieran and Raven, demanding an update on the events on Vauxhall Bridge; Julian cornered Damien for what looked like a thorough talking-to, and Nathan's mother—

'Nathan, thank goodness! We've been frantic about you— didn't even realize you were missing until this morning—I'm sorry, we should've checked, but I just thought you were out late with your friends.' His mother's outpouring of guilt was accompanied by hugs and pats to see he was in one piece. She soon found the bump to the head. 'Dr Hooper, please, is he going to be all right? Do we need to take him to hospital?' Nathan was herded into an empty office and pushed into a chair for an impromptu examination.

'I'm fine. Please, just let me . . . ' Nathan was desperate to return to Kate. He had lost sight of her thanks to the fuss being made over a slight knock.

'Double vision?' asked Dr Hooper, shining a pencil light in his eyes. A petite Afro-Caribbean woman with short black hair, she was used to dealing with reluctant teens so ignored his attempts to escape.

'What? No.'

'Memory loss?'

'No, no—I think I was out for a while, but I feel fine now.'

'Pupils are responding, but to be safe we should arrange a scan.' She now transferred her attention to his pulse.

'I haven't got time for a scan!' Where was Kate?

'Nathan Rivers Hunter: you will make time for your health,' snapped Maisie. 'I let your father enrol you in this place as long as it looked after you. It appears it hasn't been doing a great job of that over the last twenty-four hours.'

Dr Hooper let go of his wrist. 'I'll drive you to outpatients at Guy's Hospital. It shouldn't take long.'

'What about Kate—and Damien?' Nathan said desperately. 'Shouldn't they come too?'

'The nurse is going to check them—it's your head we're all worried about. Concussion is a nasty business.'

'I'm not going anywhere until I see that Kate is looked after.' Finally managing to shake off his mother and the doctor, he bolted from the room. Kate was sitting on a reception chair looking incredibly alone, as everyone else was swept up by family or friends. Nathan vowed that after today he would never see that expression on her face again. 'Kate, I'm being kidnapped.'

She looked up and gave him a wobbly smile. 'Again?'

'The doc wants to check my head.'

'Oh. OK. How long will that take?'

'I don't know. Guys, look after Kate?'

Raven immediately stepped in. 'Sure. Come on, Kate: let's watch Kieran unravel the data.'

'Thanks—I'd like that.' Kate brushed a quick kiss over his cheek and followed Raven to the lift.

His mother poked his ribs. 'Who's that?'

Nathan poked her back. 'That's the girl I'm bringing home to meet you as long as you aren't embarrassing.'

'I'll be on my best behaviour.'

Nathan knew that Maisie would—and she would mother Kate too if allowed, but really Kate needed her own family. 'Mum, can I borrow your phone?'

'Of course, darling.' She handed it over without a question.

If he was going to have to sit in hospital waiting for a scan, there were a couple of calls he wanted to make.

Watching the data unscramble across the screens in Kieran's lab, Kate curled up in an armchair pushed into a corner. Damien had fetched it from the common room so she could rest. Dr Waterburn and Kieran were very excited about what they were reading; she couldn't follow all they were saying but it appeared the information was very comprehensive. Amazing to think that she had been carrying all that just under her skin. She was feeling sleepy, exhaustion setting in after the events of a very full day. Nathan was still stuck at the hospital and fuming, according to the texts he was sending Kieran to relay to her. Damien and Raven were sitting beside her, quietly running over the details of the mission for their reports. From Raven she found out that they had Julian to thank for the speedy delivery of the data. Raven's phone had been out of service so Kate's text had never been read. Julian, however, had suspected something wasn't quite right when he watched her and Damien hurry off that morning, so he had poked his head into her room, just to see if anything obvious was out of place. He had found the envelope on the bed with its 'Urgent' note, and, being an inquisitive soul with a Damien-level respect for privacy, had read it. The contents had scared the silk socks off him, as he put it. Spurred into action, he had jumped in the car and brought the package to Kieran and Raven, thus setting off the necessary alarm bells that enabled the YDA to pull together a joint operation with the Metropolitan Police. Odd to think how, in the end, the success had hinged on something as impossible to predict as Uncle Julian's instincts.

'And what about Mrs MacDonald?' Raven was asking Damien. 'What was it she said about her reasons?'

'An investigation, that's what she mentioned, didn't she, Kate?'

Kate nodded, balancing her chin on her huddled knees. 'I didn't understand that part.'

'I was about to launch an enquiry into her son's conduct.' Isaac appeared at her shoulder, making all three of them start. He took a seat on the arm of Kate's chair. 'I didn't think she knew—I dropped it immediately he died so it didn't become common knowledge.'

'What kind of enquiry?' asked Raven.

'I was in Iraq as a captain in the military police. Our role is to investigate criminal behaviour in the ranks. A series of photos had come to light the morning we went out on patrol that seem to show Private MacDonald had abused prisoners being held for questioning. I thought I knew Joe—we were from the same area of Edinburgh and I'd known the family for years—I'd been a large part of the reason Joe had signed up for the red caps. I was going to talk to him afterwards, couldn't bring myself to believe it. Unfortunately, it looked as if he'd got in above his head, forgetting his training and basic decency.'

'So he was guilty?' asked Damien.

Isaac folded his arms. 'The matter was not pursued once he was dead as he could not answer charges, but I guess he was guilty. I don't know to this day if he just panicked at the idea of being questioned, or if he felt he was taking the easier way out, running into that bullet. He was very young—only nineteen. I thought that with a little more training and discipline, I could have saved him from making those mistakes—the original abuse and the suicidal cover up.'

'So he was why you set up the YDA? Because you wanted to help other young people who might be given similar responsibilities to Joe?' asked Kate.

Isaac nodded. 'And in his distress that morning, he must have left a message for his mother before we went out on the patrol, warning her about the investigation—perhaps asking for her help. That suggests that his decision to get killed that day was an impulse. I will always regret that I didn't act more quickly—that I didn't know that he knew he was about to be suspended from duty. One of his mates must have tipped him

272

off. We were following procedures, not paying attention to the feelings of the individual.'

'I'm sorry,' whispered Kate. She knew what it was like to live with the guilt of failing other people. As a good man, Isaac would always ask what he should have done to prevent the tragedy that had ended the lives of the son and now the mother.

'Thank you—particularly as you have been one of the ones to suffer as a result.' Isaac rested his hand briefly on her shoulder. 'Do you understand now why I say that there is a place at the YDA for you? I founded it on the principle that I had to learn from my mistakes. You'll be an even better student if you are brave enough to learn from yours.'

Nathan hurried back into the YDA three hours later, having been told that his scan showed no abnormalities.

'Except for a towering temper,' muttered his mother, signing the forms at the desk for his release. She reluctantly let him go, only after extorting the promise that he would bring Kate over to meet her and Jim the next day. She had promised Jim would be on his best behaviour.

He need not have worried that Kate was unhappy: she looked quite comfortable sitting in an armchair in Kieran's lab. Her head had dropped to one side and she was sleeping while everyone else worked around her.

Nathan brushed Raven's elbow to get her attention. 'Is she OK?'

'Yes, fine. Isaac talked to her about an hour ago and said some good stuff about how she can be an asset to the YDA. I think between us we are slowly reeling her back in.'

'Good. I'm not letting her run again.'

Raven grinned. 'None of us think that you would—unless you ran with her. Again.'

Kate woke up at the sound of his laugh and stretched. 'Nathan! What did the scan say?'

He knelt beside her. 'That my head is in one piece but could do with a kiss better.'

Chuckling, she kissed his ear. 'What's that noise?'

'That is my stomach rumbling,' he admitted.

'Time for dinner?'

'Well past.'

'Let's all go,' said Raven, pulling Kieran away from his computer. 'I'm starving.'

Nathan knew exactly what Raven was doing. It was fine for Kate to hide away in the lab with them all afternoon, but Raven sensed that Kate needed all her friends around her to brave the communal areas where the other YDA students would be gathered.

'Can't we grab something and bring it back here?' Kate suggested, still in hide mode.

He didn't want her to feel she had to carry on avoiding everyone. Better to face them while everyone was here to back her up. 'We could, but I really need a proper meal. My luxurious accommodation didn't include breakfast, and lunch got lost with escaping and getting the bad guys.'

'Oh, Nathan, I should've thought of that.' Deflected from her own worries, Kate was now focused on him. 'Yes, of course, we must go to the canteen.' She stroked his chest with the flat of her hand, checking for his heartbeat to reassure herself that he had emerged from a perilous situation unharmed. 'Right away.'

Over her head, Damien smirked. Nathan winked at his friend.

Kate was annoyed with herself for having missed the fact that Nathan hadn't had a chance to eat, having been sat in hospital all afternoon. He always thought of her first; she must start doing the same for him. If he wanted a hot meal then she would risk more than a few hostile students to make sure he had one.

The canteen was exactly as she remembered—on the ground floor with a terrace on the Thames, a favourite gathering spot for students out of class. Brickwork painted white, high arched windows, gleaming tables, it echoed with voices and laughter. As they walked into the dining room, the conversations died away as their presence registered with the groups gathered for dinner. Kate tensed. Nathan pressed her hand as he stared down the audience, daring them to say anything out of line. Kieran was watching the reaction with his usual puzzled interest, like a zoologist studying primate behaviour; Raven moved closer to Kate so that she and Nathan formed a kind of barrier against the scrutiny of so many eyes. Also true to form, Damien was ready to power through the awkwardness.

'I'll get some drinks to start with. What'll you have, Nathan? Coke? Juice? Water?'

'Whatever,' muttered Nathan.

'Kate?' Damien asked loudly.

'It is her!' hissed a girl on the nearest table. 'I thought so!'

Nathan pinned her with one of his looks.

'The same,' whispered Kate. She had to stick this out for Nathan.

'Right.' Damien rubbed his hands, enjoying the moment rather too much. 'Two whatevers coming right up. You find a table.'

'What's she doing here?' a boy asked his neighbour. 'Didn't she get in trouble somewhere?' The girl shrugged.

Then Kate spotted Miranda Yang striding purposefully towards them between the tables. She remembered Miranda from before—a formidable Wolf with a gift for straight talk. If anyone was going to demand she be thrown out on the street, Miranda was a likely candidate. Sure enough, long black hair fluttering, eyes narrowed, Miranda did not look happy. Nathan shuffled Kate further behind him—but, surprisingly, Kate wasn't her target. Miranda drew back her fist and punched Nathan in the chest, hard enough to bruise.

'You complete and utter tit, Nathan Hunter. You sent my team to flaming Lichfield on a wild goose chase!'

Kate made a move to step forward and defend him but Nathan held her back. 'Technically, Miranda,' he said placatingly, 'it was Isaac who . . . '

Miranda cut him off with a swipe of her hand. 'And now you have the cheek to bring her right here. You knew where she was all along, didn't you?'

'Her location was on a strict need-to-know basis.'

Miranda drilled a forefinger into his chest. 'But I thought we were friends. After all that's been between us, you could've at least given me a hint—sent a text or something to tip me off? You knew you could trust me.'

Kate felt as if the bottom had just fallen out of her world. She had once wondered if Nathan already had a girlfriend and here was the answer. Kate pulled her hand out of his. This was a disaster.

Damien tried to save the day for his two-timing rat of a friend. 'Miranda, don't give Nathan grief for something he couldn't help. He kept it from me too—I had to work it out for myself.'

'Is she even allowed in here?' Miranda asked, brow crinkling. She tried to look past the barrier of Nathan and Raven to spot her quarry. Kate didn't want to be seen right at that moment, not while she rethought her whole understanding of what she was to Nathan. 'Shouldn't we make sure she doesn't run again—lock her up or something till Isaac gets back?'

Kate tried to slid away but Damien was blocking a clear path to the exit.

'Don't be an idiot, Kate,' he whispered. 'Talk to Nat.'

Nathan quickly checked she was still behind him then turned back to Miranda. 'You're way out of touch with events. Kate is one of us—has been all along. She has just completed her year-long assignment to bring down the Scorpion gang.'

Miranda's mouth dropped open. 'She has?'

'Yeah, it was all very secret so none of us knew she was still on the mission. Isaac will explain. And if you don't mind, we're tired and hungry so we'll just get a few drinks and get on with the debrief.'

'Oh. Yes, of course.' Miranda moved back, then stopped. 'Kate, you really brought down the whole trafficking network?'

Kate didn't know what to say. It did seem like that, but somehow she couldn't believe it either.

'Cut off the head today—the body is dying even as we speak,' confirmed Nathan.

'Wow! That's amazing! Well done. I'll catch up with you later, Nathan.' With an elegant spin on her heels, Miranda stalked back to her team sitting over by the doors to the terrace, bursting to share the news.

Nathan swooped round just in time to capture Kate's wrist before she bolted. 'Let's sit down.'

'I'd rather not. Let's go straight to the lab.' She couldn't meet his eyes. They mustn't have this out here, not in front of so many watchers.

'We will when we've eaten, but let Damien get us something since he offered.'

Damien played along to lighten the mood. 'Yeah, I live to serve.'

Opting not to make a scene, she nodded and followed Nathan to a corner table on the terrace by the Thames. The area was fresher outside, a reminder of open spaces, beaches and old boots hanging on Sea Chapels. Raven and Kieran diplomatically went to join Damien at the counter.

Nathan didn't beat around the bush. 'Miranda isn't my girlfriend. She was once but now we're just friends—have been for a while.'

Kate rested her head on her hand. 'She doesn't sound as though she sees it that way.'

'That's because we left some fuzzy edges to our relationship—occasional kiss and teasing—that kind of thing.'

She drew a circle on the table with a fingertip. 'I don't mind, Nathan.'

Nathan clenched his jaw but Kate sensed his anger was *for* her, not caused *by* her. 'You should mind. I'd mind if you were still kissing a guy you'd been seeing.'

'That's not likely, as the only guy I dated recently is dead.' That was a stupid, tasteless thing to say.

Fortunately he ignored it. 'Kate, you should demand the best from me, tell me to clean up my act or you'll walk, not accept everything as if you are deserving of being treated like dirt.' He lowered his voice. 'Like Gani treated you.'

Her hazel eyes flicked briefly to his face then went back to her finger. Her self-esteem was still so fragile. It would take years to put her back together properly but she knew he was right—she had to start respecting herself. And that was, at heart, why she loved him: he made her feel worthy of his affection.

'All right then, you love rat, no more kissing other girls.'

He grinned. 'OK, you have my word.' Before she could say anything else, he took her hand in his. 'Kate Pearl, will you go out with me? I'm rather hoping you say yes because I bought two tickets for a Gifted gig next Friday at the O2 while I was waiting in the hospital. I promise that if you say yes, I will never kiss Miranda or anyone else, never embarrass you with another girl, never use you for my own ends, but be yours as long as you will have me.'

Could he be any more perfect for her? Her Saint George, helping her fight her dragons. 'I thought we were already going out,' she said softly.

'No,' his eyes twinkled with amusement, 'that's not how I would define it. That was more like running for our lives and falling in love. Now, back here where it all started, with no one trying to kill us, in a place where you are free to get up and never speak to me again, I want you to decide what you want. I know what I want. I want you. I always have, even as a puny guy who had a hopeless crush on the coolest girl in his year. But today I know that girl properly and I want you more than ever, and for much better reasons.'

Kate was flattered that he put it like that. She had known there was a fierce spark of attraction between them but it was important to know he saw beyond that. And if a nice guy like Nathan really loved her, perhaps she wasn't all bad?

'What about you?' he continued. 'Until now you've always had to be with me because I was your only lifeline; I don't want you because you're trapped with me, but because you chose me freely.'

Kate wanted to say so much—the words were queuing up, tripping over each other to get out. After a pause for thought, a small smile quirked her lips. 'You want me?'

'Desperately.' His eyes lit with a glimmer of hope.

She looked down at the rough wooden table, then up at him. 'As much as I want you?'

His gaze dropped to her lips. 'More.'

She shook her head. 'Not possible.'

'Does that mean . . . ? You'll go out with me?'

She nodded. 'And stay in with you.'

With a whoop of delight, he got up, came round to her side of the table and lifted her onto his lap. 'That sounds even better.'

She rested her head on his chest on the spot where Miranda had thumped him. 'And if you break your word, I'll warn you, I've got a better punch than Miranda and I'd go for a lower target.'

'I remember. That's where we started, wasn't it: you kneeing me in the . . . um . . . essentials? I won't break my word.'

'I know you won't. You are the best person I know. Thank you for . . . ' her voice died away. Instead, she drew a heart on his T-shirt.

'For loving you? It is entirely my pleasure.'

His expression of absolute joy made her feeling like shouting to the passing seagulls but she restrained herself. With difficulty. She settled for confession. 'I love you too.'

'Here, two whatevers and I picked lasagna for you both.' Damien dropped the tray on the table. 'Everything back on track?'

'Yes.' Kate reached for a mineral water and took off the lid. She passed it to Nathan. 'I think it is.'

'Great, you guys are so cute!' exclaimed Raven, as she and Kieran joined them with their trays.

A phone buzzed in Nathan's pocket. He pulled it out, glanced at the caller, then smiled. 'I'd better take this.' Easing Kate off his lap, he walked away so he could talk privately.

'Him and Miranda—it wasn't serious,' Damien explained, digging in to his meal.

'Don't worry, Damien. We cleared that up. Thank you for always being there to back him up.'

Nathan came back to the table and held out the phone. 'Kate, there's someone who wants to speak to you.'

She put down her fork. 'Who?'

'Your mother.'

'What!'

'I got the number from the file and rang her from the hospital. She's coming to London with her husband and Sally.'

'Why?'

'To see you, of course. She wants to arrange a time and place.'

Kate took the phone from him and put it to her ear. 'Mum?'

'Katie, is that you?'

The familiar voice filled Kate with such a maelstrom of conflicting emotions. 'Mum?'

'Oh Katie, I'm sorry. No, no, I'm not sorry—well, I am sorry, but what I meant to say was, I'm so happy to hear you're all right. You can't imagine what it's been like. I lost you but you've come back—it's a miracle. I'm not going to waste it. Forgive me for being so . . . so immature four years ago? We both hurt each other with the things we said but I should've been old enough to mend the damage so much sooner. You'll see me, won't you, please?'

'I . . . ' Kate looked to Nathan, who was smiling broadly at her. It would be silly to squander a second chance. 'Yes, any time. Just call when you arrive. I'd like that.'

'Right, that's settled then. Early tomorrow we'll be there. Sally's over the moon to meet her big sister—she won't stop talking about you.'

Kate chatted for a little while longer, letting her food get cold, catching up on her mother's life and telling Maya a carefully edited portion of her news. When she ended the call, she handed the phone back to Nathan.

'I've got a family again.'

'Yes.'

'You did that.'

'Your mother would have got in contact as soon as Isaac told her you where you were.'

'But you did it first.'

'I suppose I did.'

'That deserves a kiss.'

'Yes, it does. Maybe more than one?' he added hopefully.

'As many as you like.' She tugged him towards her. 'Come here, gorgeous.'

Damien mock groaned. 'Here they go again: Hunter diving after his Pearl. Avert your eyes, people.'

To the cheers and whistles of the other students, Kate made sure Nathan felt very appreciated.

'This hunter has found his pearl and isn't letting go,' Nathan whispered as he came up for air, nuzzling her ear.

She laughed. 'That's a deal, Mr Wolf. And this time, you won't even need handcuffs to keep me.'

BOOKS BY
Joss Stirling

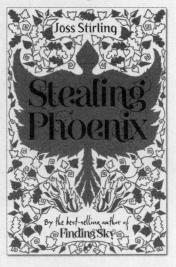

Joss Stirling lives in Oxford and is the author of the
bestselling **Finding Sky** trilogy. She was inspired to write
Stung by the heroes of British crime fiction
and by years of watching cop dramas.

You can visit her website at **www.jossstirling.com**.